Volume 1 of the Holy Spirit Series

The

H.S.

Anne Church O'Planick

Carpenter's Son Publishing

The H.S.: Volume 1 of the Holy Spirit Series

©2022 by Anne Oplanick

Published by Carpenter's Son Publishing, Franklin, Tennessee

Published in association with Larry Carpenter of Christian Book Services, LLC
www.christianbookservices.com

Cover Art by Anne Oplanick

Cover and Interior Design by Suzanne Lawing

Edited by Ann Tatlock

Printed in the United States of America

978-1-954437-53-1

Contents

Foreword

Ten years ago, I was riding with my husband on Interstate 77 heading north through the Wytheville, Virginia, area. A voice suddenly spoke saying, "This is where your story begins." Gazing out the window, I caught sight of a scene transpiring on a hot and dusty hill just above the highway. A police officer was animatedly talking to two young men who were leaning against the hood of an older model car. What? What story? Though the directions were a mystery, by then I knew such a clear directive came from the Holy Spirit.

It took me seven more years to gather my thoughts and be willing to be available to the Holy Spirit to author His story in novel form. He provided the story line, characters, and connection. I provided the hand to hold the pen. The last three years have been starts and stutters of editing as we dealt with health issues and moves.

I have always had head faith, but that kind of religious expression does not satisfy. Trying to please God does not either. In my frustration of pleading for more of God, I took the leap of submitting myself totally to His will, and immediately, the Holy Spirit showed up—really showed up! He had shown Himself to me prior to this event in bits and pieces, but now He was real and front and center in my life. I had the privilege of experiencing the realness of God.

This book is written primarily for Christian believers to encourage your search for fullness of faith in the Holy Spirit. Doing so can bring a completion of self and a revelation of the Godhead. For those who are not believers, my hope is that through these words, the Spirit will bring God into focus, making both Father and Son real and remarkable. It is my desire that every follower of Jesus Christ as well as those seeking God, come to know the Holy Spirit in the first person and recognize His role in revealing the Son of God. That was God's plan from the beginning.

Immerse yourself in the life of the H.S! May you find that He "… lives with you and will be in you" (John 14:17b) all the days of your life.

Special thanks to my four children for their encouragement, thoughts, prayers and editing: Carrie, Colleen (contributed the name), Michael and John. My appreciation goes to those who reviewed the content and assisted with edits: my sisters Carol and Ellen; friends Connie, Janet, Debbie, Sally, Ann, and Denise. Special thanks to Jean Hannan for her grammatical expertise.

My deep-felt thanks to my husband Richard who has supported me through this faith walk in the life in the Spirit. He motivates me to always seek the Lord in all things.

Thank you, Holy Spirit, for showing me your Presence so that I can share your work with those who seek your face.

Blessings,
Annie

Chapter 1

Ricardo Medina

June 2036

"I keep asking that the God of our Lord Jesus Christ, the glorious Father, may give you that Spirit of wisdom and revelation, so that you may know him better. I pray that the eyes of your heart may be enlightened..." Ephesians 1:17-18a

The world was a smeared pallet of gray—ash gray, charcoal, and Payne's gray. Ricardo mused about the recent events in his life as dirty droplets of rain spattered the windows of the old bus. Love was gray. Patriotism was gray. Family was gray and now he was being thrust into a work world of the bleakest gray. His mind swirled into the dullness of his thoughts until he drifted to sleep through the thump, thump, thump of the revolving bus tires. With the rough downshift of the rickety bus, Ricardo jerked wide awake. He rubbed a layer of pasty dirt off the window and peered at the shabby town at the bottom of the hill.

After the dusty and stuffy journey on a bus filled with the riffraff of forgotten society, it was a relief to step down onto what once was a well-paved highway. The edges had chipped off with each successive rainstorm and the yellow line delineating the center of the road was left to the imagination. His gaze took him to the pencil-thin plumes of smoke rising from the simple houses below. With an inner smirk, he laughed at the smoky streams originating from coal or wood fires. They were illegal and dirty; carbon horrors that had once been soundly enforced by the EPA.

The government now decided to distance itself from the plight of these Middlers as pirated news clips from underground journalists filmed the result of their elitist class experiment. This underclass population, far removed from the watchful eye of those in power, had been victims of the carbon footprint fuel restrictions. During the past winter, locals were videotaped lying dead in their beds. The empty, glazed stares of frozen children wrapped in layers of homemade rags made the viewers squeamish and changed the public discourse enough to allow a reprieve for the moment. Though illegal, there would be no enforcement. Like most government experiments, if it did not work, it was better to just talk louder about its benefits to society and dismiss the reality of its consequences. The alternative was to nod in agreement that something would be done, then move on to more comfortable dialogue. And so, the fires for the moment were temporarily ignored, and the government chose to turn its gaze to more important matters and people.

Ricardo knew that life was not going to be easy here. It was not easy anywhere. But this was a backward hellhole. He did not like having this assignment. Action was a rush for him. This place would put him in a deep depression. He had been here before. But it was the only option at the moment. He would have to figure out a strategy for completing his assignment here ASAP and get back to the enticing life of the city. Perhaps the metropolitan life was not any better, but it was more successful in numbing his mind. He grabbed his worn military duffle bag stamped with the name Medina by the side carrying straps and slung it over his shoulder.

"Going somewhere, soldier? Family around here?" asked the bus driver.

"No," said Ricardo, miffed. "Just movin' on." He hated people who were fake friendly. Better to just live in your own cocoon.

His was a mission that he was not fond of accepting. His mind vacillated between all-out support for this objective to the pendulum swing supporting the opposition. He questioned whether the intended outcome would make any difference in the grand scheme of things. While it had the chance of bringing him either notoriety or an increase in rank, probably it was just a wild goose chase, taking him into an environment out of his comfort zone—the Middle Region—full of backward, gun-toting, ignorant people who were not willing to move into the twenty-first century. He had no desire to figure them out. It was his intent to chase out the remaining vestiges of the Blues Resistance, a military-based resistance opposed to the current government. This was one of the regions which held the Blues Resistance in high esteem, backing and supporting their objectives. Ricardo, who had no faith in mankind whatsoever, could not understand why these foreigners swore such fealty to the revolutionaries. What could they gain now in the game? Well, he would do what he could to smoke them out and eliminate them for the last time. It would make his world a bit simpler and tidier. And it certainly would bring its benefits.

Somewhere down there in this sleepy town of Whitsville's environs, the renegades were still causing havoc with military transports, security zones, and technology transfers. The Blues were mainly composed of young men and women recently returned from combat in the Middle East. Many were horrified at what had happened to their families, their towns … even their country while they were gone. Small towns that were once thriving centers of regular Americans had been shuttered by the government, redirecting the necessary resources of electricity, tech communication, food, and shelter to larger designated metropolitan centers. Schools and hospitals were closed. The last four years had been a time of unrivaled social upheaval unheard of in the history of the United States. *Well,* thought Ricardo, *what was left of the States.*

Ricardo had been updated during the last several weeks in Washington D.C. on the current knowledge of the Blues operations. They had a loose chain of command that made it difficult to track down their plans. They were experts at stealth combat, surpassing the professional instructors who had taught them during their military training. Every day, the Blues practiced their skills of invisibility and disruption to the chagrin of the government chain of command in Washington. In this they were aided by the most advanced stealth technology the Army had available. How they got these supplies, who was behind their organization, how they could be infiltrated ... that was the mission of Ricardo Medina.

He sauntered out of the musty bus stop. The snack-dispensing machine advertising long-since extinct drinks like Coke and Mountain Dew with sun-bleached advertisements had been emptied years ago. He had a strong urge to guzzle a big, cold bottle of soda. *Those were the good ol' days,* he mused. *No more drinks now can be consumed which are deemed unhealthy by the Department of Health and Wellness. The pricks!* He would have to wait to find something else to quench his thirst. He headed down the small incline into town. All but a few of the storefronts were boarded up. Three old men sat outside what was once a thriving hardware store. The faded sign above them said in okra yellow, "Smyth's Hardware - Established 1908." The men stopped talking as he stepped by, and he knew they were all thinking the same thing, *Why was he stopping here?* Their eyes held suspicion of any newcomer.

"You fellas know where I can get a room for the night?" he asked a grizzled man who was leaning back in his chair.

The crusty man replied, "You Army?"

"Yeah," responded Ricardo. "Glad to be back in the States … or what's left of them."

"You from around here?" asked another man who was almost indistinguishable from the first. Although he was only in his fifties, he looked seventy, his grizzled beard mostly white.

"Baltimore, a while back. Just movin' on. Lookin' for work."

"Ha," the second man guffawed. "Ain't we all! Around here, we just make our own work. Work to eat, work to sleep, work 'til you die." He paused a bit, taking in the situation. "You can go down the hill there and turn onto Second Street where the church sits on the corner. Just up the street you'll see a small white house with a screened porch on the side. Belongs to Pastor Singleton. He takes in strays on a regular basis. Don't know if he has any room or not."

The term "Pastor" was strange to Ricardo. He could only think how antiquated this population was compared to his life in the city. The formal church structure in the neighborhoods he had lived in had all but disappeared in the last ten years. His mother had been heartbroken to see the decline of her beloved faith tradition. She had remained faithful to the end. About all she had at that point was her rosary beads, and they certainly did not do her any good. He could have cared less. Religion was boring. Even worse, it was for the weak. He had no use for such tripe.

"What's his first name?" asked Ricardo. He was not about to call him Pastor.

"That's what everyone around here calls him," said the first lazy fellow with a bit of suspicion toward Ricardo. "We still respect people in the faith, even if we don't go no more. You better get going before the patrol comes along."

Where the heck is this place? thought Ricardo. He was beginning to become depressed with the thought of having to live for months in such a forsaken spot. Yet he knew at this point he was a prisoner of the choice he had made. Upon returning from the war, he could not find work. In desperation, he contacted a person of influence within the Army hierarchy. Now he swore to accept this mission at the behest of General Sturgis Lu. There was no room for failure.

General Lu operated from the mindset that the Blues were public enemy number one, and they were to be eliminated one by one. The general was resolute in crushing this band of renegades, and he did not care who or what got in the way. What he hated most was the treason displayed by these former soldiers. For him, they were the most dangerous of enemies. They had betrayed their country and worse, were a bad reflection on his leadership. He hated their daring, their heroism, but mostly their selflessness. They were not like him. And so far, they had outsmarted him. He would have no more of it. He would not allow this to continue.

At the bottom of the hill was a rusty street sign on a leaning pole that said Second Street in faded black letters. The building on the corner—which he surmised by the front door was the church—was padlocked. Constructed of white clapboard, it was not so much in disrepair as only tired looking. A cement pad was in the front yard with two wooden posts sticking up out of the clipped grass. Any sign that had once been attached had been removed and the orphan posts were like solitary sentinels looking for their lost companion.

While Ricardo's mother had taken him faithfully to church as a child, he was thrilled when the government in 2034 voted to make any form of faith a private venture. Public gatherings were no longer tolerated and public structures used for this purpose were either razed or padlocked. Ricardo thought for a fleeting moment of his priest and his last words to him in the presence of his mother. "Ricardo, life for you has been difficult. While you did not know your earthly father, your Father in heaven loves you and wants the best for you. Serve Him." Ricardo well remembered the priest's graying moustache and the cold hands that took Ricardo's hands in his. "Find truth, dear boy," he said. Ricardo found the priest's faith distasteful. His mother cried as she nodded assent to these words. Eliana Medina died three months later in a senior ward for terminal patients. He never saw the priest again. "There is no such thing as truth," muttered Ricardo under his breath.

A cobblestone path of limestone rocks led to the manicured but smallish framed house up the street from the church. The grass around the rocks was hand trimmed and swept clean. As he knocked on the rippled screen door frame, he noticed movement on the porch. He did not know who was startled more, him or the young woman settled in an overstuffed chair of sun-worn paisley. Her book dropped to the floor as she slowly came to the door and asked what he wanted. For a moment Ricardo struggled with his bearings. He was stunned by the violet-blue eyes that held his gaze. Her natural brown hair was pulled back around her neck in a simple flipped bun and the dress she wore could have come out of a WWII movie. Dress! When was the last time he had seen a woman in a dress? It was longish … below her knees, and plainly cut in a shirt-waist style made of white fabric with thin blue stripes. He caught his breath.

"I came to talk to … " he hesitated, "Mr. Singleton. I am looking for a room to rent on my way through. The men at the hardware store said he might have something I could use."

Mercedes looked intently at him, but her gaze revealed little. "I'll get him. He's in his study."

Ricardo perked up a little. *Maybe this venture won't be as boring as I thought. Where did this woman come from? She surely doesn't belong stashed away in some podunk town like this.* Out of the corner of his eye, he detected movement coming from around the corner of the house. Ricardo knew someone was watching him. He stared in that direction until the form materialized and glided out from behind a hedge of clipped yews.

"Howdy," came a voice stronger than expected. The figure that followed the voice was a younger man, probably in his thirties, who moved with a noticeable limp from his left leg. A silly grin seemed to be pasted on his face. "You're new in town. Welcome to Whitsville."

"Who are you?" quizzed Ricardo, forgetting his training to be distant but hospitable. He chastised himself for making this job more difficult than it had to be.

"I'm Walt. I take care of this here house for Pastor Singleton. Been doing it for about ten years." Walt looked proud of the longevity.

"Nice," said Ricardo, looking at the beginnings of peeling paint and the unimpressive structure. "Who's that person who just came to the door?"

"That's Miss Mercedes. She's the pastor's daughter. All he has left here." And then his face changed. "She keeps this house and this town going. We all love her and watch out for her. Nobody tries nothing with our Mercedes or me and the boys will make sure they're taken care of. You know what I mean?"

Somehow Ricardo felt that there was validity to this veiled threat. Walt seemed to be intellectually handicapped, but Ricardo was sure that there were other men who would not mind giving some stranger a deserved beating or worse. There was no formal law structure in place anymore in these regions, and problems were remediated by vigilantes, or as they termed it, the local militia. He was going to have to watch his actions and be careful not to stir up any suspicion. So far, he was doing a miserable job of it.

Ricardo heard a noise at the door and swung around to see a tall, slender older man with close-cropped white hair and a slight stoop.

He had a youthful look for his age. An ancient brown sweater clung to his shoulders but hung loosely from his bony frame.

"May I help you?" he asked in a friendly voice.

"My name is Ricardo Medina and I'm looking for a job and a place to live for a while."

"What brings you to these parts?" asked the pastor.

"Just movin' on since the war. My family's gone and I can't seem to find my bearings."

"Well," said the pastor, "seems like there is someone like you stopping by here almost every week. I do not take in strangers frequently anymore as we have had problems with an occasional drifter. We did not have the best of luck with the last two guests we invited to stay. Yet sometimes, I just feel I should be willing to give someone a second chance. Do you know anything about engines and generators from your time in the service?"

There was a pause in the conversation. Pastor Singleton continued, "Please be honest."

What a coincidence, thought Ricardo. He could not have had a better segue into being a welcome part of this town. Aloud he quickly rambled on with a reply. "It just so happens that my first detail in the war was running the IT system for the Army Rangers unit I was in. I know that has nothing to do with generators, but it led to me landing there. You see, they were having so much trouble with the cooling system for the building in the desert that I began to monkey with the generators so that we could keep the computers operating, and before I knew it, I was reassigned to the mechanical division. Not bad work. Kept me moving and wasn't as boring. It moved me up a class, but the pay was still lousy."

"Well, we need some generator repair for the school and hospital, so you can start tomorrow at seven a.m. How about a one-week trial? I will come by and walk you over. Oh, about a place to stay. Follow me."

Virgil Singleton called to Mercedes to bring a pitcher of water and snacks for their guest. He walked down the steps, letting the screen door slam, and up a small sidewalk to a haphazardly built shed in the backyard. Walt stared at them both. Virgil opened the tattered shed door. "Make yourself at home. No electricity of course, but there is an oil lamp on the table and the privy is out back. Heads up that occasionally we get a black bear wondering around here in the dark, so keep your eyes open when you go outside. He is just looking for garbage. You know what a bear looks like don't you?" Virgil could not resist keeping the smile from showing on his face.

Where the heck is this place? mused Ricardo. *The sticks – privies and bears!* He had seen much worse in the Middle East: death, destruction, starvation of locals, kids begging for a morsel to eat, chemical killing. But this was the USA! Why did these people insist on living like they were in the nineteenth century instead of moving as mandated by the government to one of the designated metropolitan centers?

He thought of his residence in Baltimore. He had found it a suitable place to live, an older bungalow that had not been updated in a quarter century. Life had become structured by the government; the requirement to have two families reside in an apartment or house, public transport or car with a minimum of four passengers, electricity and heat most days … some entertainment. But he could not shake the thought that something here in Whitsville might be an improvement as he opened the door to the shed and found a bed covered with a bright but well-used quilt in yellow and orange squares, a small metal table with two mismatched chairs and a comfortable sitting chair of a warm brownish velvety fabric. A wash bowl sat on the table with a precious bit of soap, a hot commodity in these parts. Somehow the place smelled clean.

"Here's a bite to eat, Mr. Medina," said Mercedes walking up behind him. "It's just a bit of cornbread and some butter made by Walt. He's a good cook compared to some of us in this house." She carefully placed the water on the rickety table, making a mental note to tell Walt to straighten the legs when he had a chance. "How long do you think you will be staying here? Do you have plans for some future employment?"

Ricardo could take the hint that she was hoping he would be a rolling stone sort of wanderer. It was a good guess that she endured most of the work required for the strangers that the pastor took in. And he could tell she was tired.

"I really don't have any plans," he said mildly. "It's been tough coming back to the States after the war. Just tryin' to get my head screwed on straight."

She did not show any compassion for him. She could tell his type—shifty and lazy. She turned with a look of disappointment on her face and walked back to the tired house.

Ricardo watched every slow step, and she knew he was doing so. As she went into the house, she glanced up at his staring face in the shed door frame. He did not look away. Neither did she. But her face was not a happy one. And something in Ricardo told him that she was much sharper than he gave most women credit for. He had better be aware of what he said and did around Mercedes.

***

The year 2036 was one most people hoped to just survive. The Middle East conflict of almost a decade was finally over for the time being with an unsteady peace. The world was still reeling from the massive explosion in the volcanic region around Yellowstone in 2027 that slowed the world economy, affected the climate of millions of people, and prompted massive migrations of people searching for food, clean air, and employment. In America, it buried the Dakotas and Minnesota, and practically shut down Chicago and its neighboring states. Then, perhaps because of such turmoil in the climate, a predatory disease assumed to have begun in India, spread around the world with such alacrity that there was no way to hinder its progress. Named the Drakee virus, it was an airborne viral disease which caused death like consumption in the 1890s. It had many of the same characteristics as SARS and the Covid-19 virus but was much more devastating to both the elderly and infant populations. It first broke out in five different provinces in China simultaneously and spread with lightning speed, too quickly for the Chinese to even attempt to control. The general populace held to a conspiracy theory that India, in its quest to deter population growth, had been experimenting on a biological agent that could take out wide swaths of population. China surmised that India had purposely spread the seeds of this pandemic to hinder its encroachment on India's neighbors. They had gone through an intensive investigation as to the origins and discovered that a group of Indian business leaders had been in the first outbreak areas. It made sense, but the World Health Organization was on the hunt looking for the actual culprit. Whatever they discovered would certainly be detrimental to their enemies and positive to their benefactors. Most were afraid of the truth and the ramifications of biological warfare between these two giants.

What was different from other world virus pandemics for the past two decades was the fact that highly qualified independent research centers had provided empirical evidence that this virus was not natural but fabricated. New anti-viral vaccines were sought by pharmaceutical companies hoping to cash in on a world that was paralyzed with fear and ineffectiveness yet again.

They were helpless in slowing the progression of the disease. When a partially effective anti-viral drug was released by the government of Communist China, there was no means for American pharmaceutical companies to get in line. We had long ago cut our ties for drugs and medical supplies from a nation that manipulated the market. It was a bitter pill to swallow. The virus killed indiscriminately—government leaders, blue collar workers, and newborns. And Drakee virus had the ability to mutate at amazing speed. The lungs were the major focus as the alveoli at the end of the bronchial tubes lost their ability to exchange carbon dioxide and oxygen. Death came by suffocation.

The Chinese accused India of intentionally releasing this fabricated agent into the world to destroy their economy. There was a rapid buildup of troops on the Chinese border with Pakistan. Yet these troops suffered as well through the pandemic, and the world seemed to be holding its breath to see what would develop. The world prepared for a nuclear conflict.

Millions died from the virus between 2028 and 2035, particularly in Africa and the Middle East. There, resistance was particularly low due to less access to the curative inoculations of previous pandemic respiratory infections. Government systems were decimated. There was no relief or aid available. The pandemic spread with alarming speed and terrorized the world as though a mass murderer was stalking one in a locked house with no point of exit.

As governments crashed, warlords took over divvying out food in return for loyalty. They were ruthless and power hungry. While the death toll from Drakee virus was catastrophic, the death toll from these civil conflicts matched their number. This part of the world for a time gave up on the code of civilization and the blood ran deep. Most countries pulled back within their borders and tried to survive with the resources at hand. Around the world, struggling nations faced doom. There was no country that would heed their cries.

America, after trying to come to the rescue of a citizenry facing annihilation in a wide swath of Africa and the Middle East, found they did not have the stomach to lose the lives of more soldiers. After five years of intrigue and attempted rebuilding of nations and with the death of over 100,000 men and women in the armed services, the United States withdrew with a signed peace plan. It meant that nothing would change. The treaty was an imposter for peace. Nor did it save face for those who returned from the disaster.

Soldiers returned to an economy that had crashed and a populace that partially blamed them for atrocities perpetrated against the enemy and recorded by news agents. War always had a dark underbelly. They found their homes were either forcibly moved or reassigned to multiple family groups, squeezing families into a single bedroom or at the best two. Apartments became tenements overnight. There was no source of employment, other than the black market, or occasionally a government assignment in a dead-end position. They felt like failures and were blamed by many of the country's citizens for being part of an effort to impose our national identity on others.

It was at this point that the president, Santaya Woodring, running for a second term, promised a more vibrant economy and help for our own. Her rise to the top was spectacular three years before. Her campaign promised "Peace through Prosperity" and the crowds loved it. In a way, she brought hope and light into a world of fear and darkness. Her predecessor had been elected to bring stability to a flagging economy and skyrocketing inflation from the overspending opiate which comes with power. Yet, his weakness was in his inability to hear and feel the pain of his people. President Pardis promoted the Middle East War to bring peace to the region and move the USA back to its strength position regaining the upper hand in the world economic platform. It had not panned out. People were ready for a change from the old standard politicians, and they gave Ms. Woodring a chance.

During her first year in office, her vice president had lost his life in a car "accident." An angry minority blamed it on the president, but most of her supporters felt sympathy for her losing her loyal confidant. As a government outsider, she had few friends left and anonymous enemies, but the people trusted her honest appraisal of events and her candor in crisis. She did not make excuses and let the buck stop with her.

Her first campaign had promised remedies to the current crises through government programs, but with the extreme slowdown of international trade and agricultural exports and threats of full-scale war looming in Asia, her executive promises were an impossibility. She was required to renege on the expansion of programs and agencies which most hoped would finally repair the brokenness of the country. While the majority of Americans supported her vision, the reality of the actual situation kept most of the populace in a state of despair.

Their chance for a better New Deal now was not to be. The House and Senate had left their offices in Washington to move to the new capital of Atlanta. It was warmer and sunnier. There was the perpetual assumption of importance for those who revolved around the sphere of government influence. It never went away, no matter who was elected. Although they were not solving any problems, they felt that somehow, they were the ones who truly made the difference to the well-being of their fellow citizens. Just give them time and more money. The Pentagon stayed in Washington D.C. There were plenty of players vying for power there as well.

Ricardo smiled when he looked up on the shelf and saw a campaign flyer of Woodring's tucked in the panels of the wall. Her campaign slogan from her first term blazed in bright yellow, "Peace Through Prosperity." Not much tied the country together anymore. While the factions jockeyed for power, the problems just got worse. He knew America was in a tailspin and only a miracle could pull it out. Santaya could make any promise she wanted. Pretty soon it would be a tale for survival of the fittest. He thought he would be one of the winners.

Chapter 2

Mercedes Singleton

July 2036

"Ask and it will be given to you; seek and you will find; knock and the door will be opened to you. For everyone who asks, receives; the one who seeks, finds; and to the one who knocks, the door will be opened."
Luke 11:9-10

When Ricardo and the pastor arrived at the hospital at seven a.m., Mercedes was already working in the small, cramped cafeteria preparing a simple breakfast for the thinly clad school children who chanced to come to school that day in the old west wing of the schoolhouse. She also prepared trays for those in the east wing which served as the hospital ward caring for the sick and indigent who could not stay home any longer. Chances of getting better in the "hospital" were slim, but most people in this area still clung to their independence and a private view of life accepting whatever came their way with a quiet dignity.

"Hey, Sue Ann, would you carry this tray to Miss Meribeth in Room 14? She will be sleeping, so just leave it on the table next to her bed. I'll get down later and feed her when she wakes up." Mercedes thought about how the elderly were abandoned by their families when they had moved on to the city centers. Miss Meribeth was one. She had refused to follow the dream. She knew it would only end up being a perpetual nightmare. She was aware her life on this earth was coming to its conclusion.

Mercedes was again dressed in a simple shift, but this time with tights and a warm sweater, as a cool breeze was relentless, sending in a touch of frost on this July morning. She looked up to smile at her father but lost her pleasant countenance when she gazed at Ricardo. For her, it was another mouth to feed for a lost soul just moving on. Probably like the others, he was waiting to get his belly full before pulling out in the middle of the night.

When would her father stop dragging in these lost soldiers and wanderers? They usually fleeced them of the little reservoirs of food and clothes they had accumulated through arduous work. Couldn't her dad realize that they were just as hard off as these sojourners? Did he think of all those "users" when he and Mercedes were scrounging through the clothing donations dumped once a year at their church? The clothes were not much better than rags sent from the metro areas. Well, most likely this one would soon move on to another town and another unsuspecting soul would appear to ask for another free handout. He did not seem like the type who hung around long enough to make a house a home. She was thankful for that. His stares were enough to make her uncomfortable.

She was exhausted. Mercedes had been called to the "hospital" in the middle of the night by old Doc Hyde.

The knock on the door about midnight had startled Mercedes. For a moment, her mind rushed back to the camp and the guards, but then she came to her senses as she smelled the familiarity of her bedroom and the dried lavender placed in an antique vase belonging to her grandmother. She stumbled to the door and there stood old Mr. Thomas who helped around the hospital at night.

"Miss Mercedes," he mumbled politely. "Doc needs you right away. He has an emergency surgery to do and asked for you to hurry down."

"I'm coming once I get dressed. Anyone I know?" she asked hurriedly.

"A young kid, Danny Howmeiser. He was raised by his aunt and uncle, but when they both passed last year, he was taken in by a couple of relatives who have been rough on the kid. Needs an emergency appendectomy according to Doc. Amazing they even bothered to get him in here."

While stumbling through town with Mr. Thomas trying to keep up, Mercedes wondered how they would do this simple surgery with the lack of equipment. How were they going to be able to sedate the fourteen-year-old boy?

"Hey, Doc," smiled Mercedes. "Looks like you can't get a decent night's sleep around here. Your wife is going to get suspicious that we are meeting like this again."

Doc smiled but his face quickly took on a worried expression. "We got to get busy on this kid. Think that appendix is about ready to go if it hasn't already. Hopefully he is adequately sedated with this tank of carbon dioxide and sleeping pills. I have already given those to him. He looks like a baby sleeping there."

"Does he know what's going on?"

"Yeah. I talked to his relatives after the exam, but they did not want to stay. Made an excuse to get the heck out of here as quick as they could. I think they do not want anything to do with this kid. He seems like a nice enough young man to me. He's got a decent head on his shoulders. He's had it tough with his aunt and uncle passing with the fever."

The operation went quickly and smoothly. Doc was a trooper. He was as professional as the surgery docs at Baltimore National Hospital. Once he was gone it would be impossible to run this institution anymore. He made no salary.

After the surgery, Mercedes decided to just nap in the chair beside Danny's bed, as she would need to be back here in a couple of hours anyway. She slept fitfully and had nightmares of substituting herself as the patient in a filthy, blackened operating room. The past flashed back.

Now the cafeteria was bustling with dirty children accompanied by parents, siblings, hospital volunteers, teachers, and plain hungry walk-ins. Everyone pitched in making the toast with plum jam, cornmeal muffins, and a sprinkling of dried cherries from last year's crop. No coffee or tea. Just water, cold and amazingly refreshing. The old artesian spring in the spring house near the center of town was still producing drinkable water after one hundred years. It was integral in keeping the town alive and healthy.

Ricardo was quickly introduced to the hospital and school staff, all volunteers, most who politely ignored another drifter moving through. He grabbed a bite to eat and was then led down to the boiler room of the old school by Virgil. Ricardo was shocked by the disrepair and age of the neglected heating system and what was called the back-up generator. "Let me know what you need," said Virgil. "Just go up to the hardware store for any replacement parts. They will give you what they have. Free of charge." And then he left.

Virgil glanced back once he left the basement. He surmised that there was only a slim chance that this was going to work out. But it could not hurt to try. "Things are getting to the point that even we won't be able to stay here much longer," he whispered to himself.

Leaning on the door frame, Ricardo's mind sized up the situation just in time to see Mercedes pushing a teen boy down the hall on an outdated gurney. He had a shy smile on his heavily freckled face as he talked quietly to her, but the paleness on his face spoke of the internal pain he was experiencing. Ricardo recognized that look. He had seen it often in the war when the wounded returned to camp. Occasionally, he had visited a buddy in the rehab center on base. At least there they had decent medical facilities. Here there was no one except that nurse and a doctor who learned his craft from reading a book. *No*, he thought, *they don't read down here.*

Mercedes could not help worrying about Danny. Already he was showing signs of a fever and infection. They had absolutely no antibiotics on hand, although she had weekly made an urgent request through the shoddy communication system to the Department of Health and Wellness in Atlanta. Events were proving critical, and she knew that Kingston Central Hospital, as they were named, was on the bottom of the requisition list. Any hospital or public facility that decided to stay active in an independent zone separate from the centralized Federated Government, was invisible and considered traitorous. Communities that had chosen this course of independence and refused government mandates were left to survive on their own. They had paid heavily for their lack of fealty to the federal system, and they knew all too well how difficult it was to claim the title of a "Freedom First" community.

Back in 2029, she had thought that southern Virginia was stupid and ignorant for withdrawing from the Federated Reorganization Plan. Her small community and the county officials were a bunch of ignorant hotheads who thought they could survive just fine without the intervention of the federal government. When the Baltimore/Atlanta/Denver government branches had redistricted the states and local communities into new governing areas, it was chaos … sometimes controlled; often not. Communities that opted out of the plan were to be denied support for education, health care, utilities, shelter, food, transportation, and safety. Most individuals and families saw the handwriting on the wall. It would be impossible to survive without their help. There would be no future for their children: no jobs and no contact with the outer world if they chose to stand their ground and claim independence.

Despite the negative side of the decision, a small swath of the Virginias, the Central States and the Mountain States had voted to go it alone. It was a disaster. Within the first year, ninety percent of this area had petitioned to rejoin the Federated States. Now there were just pockets of holdouts remaining and the population in those areas dwindled by the day.

When the first vote was taken, Mercedes was in college in Maryland. She had a full-ride scholarship at The Public School of Nursing - Baltimore, formerly St. Mary's, and was working to complete her residency as a surgical specialist. She spoke to her parents every few evenings, asking them to use their wisdom and influence to support the move to join the Federated States. Yes, it would mean leaving Whitsville and moving to one of the governmental designated population centers. But this was the only wise choice for themselves and others in their town. Independence was simply a death knell for those who thought they could survive on their own. She remembered watching the vote counts for the move to Federation on that frigid January night. The whole western part of the Virginias balked at the idea. The vote was decidedly lopsided. The locals in Whitsville were celebrating with firecrackers and gunshots when Mercedes managed to reach her parents. She was crying in despair. "What have you done?" she yelled at her father. "How can you be so ignorant of the facts? How do the people down there think they can live without a government system that provides about everything we need to exist? Can't you see this is suicide?"

Her father tried to calm her down. "Now, Mercedes, don't worry about us. I tried my best to convince our friends and our congregation of the need to support this plan. You are right. It is the only way we can survive with a semblance of the life we have lived in the past. But these folks are an independent sort. They do not like being told what to do. And they are old fashioned. The laws that were passed last year restricting gun ownership and religious freedom sure didn't help remove their suspicion of the Federated Government and their promise to be accommodating to everyone."

Mercedes' mother Abigail got on the phone. "Dear girl, this isn't about us. We have our church community to think about and serve as we promised when we came here. There is more at stake than having a roof over our heads and a doctor to visit."

"I know that," said Mercedes with shortness in her tone. "You are wonderful examples of people who actually care for the least and the lost. But you do not have to suffer for them. Nobody else does. Stop trying to be martyrs."

"We have to be faithful to God. When we came to Whitsville, we made a covenant with Him and dedicated ourselves to His people here. They are a hurting bunch. We need to honor that promise."

Mercedes interrupted, "God wouldn't want anyone to live such an uncivilized life. You have no requirement to complete your tenure at that church. Those people are going to cut and run anyway once they see how dreadful things are going to get. You cannot be so naïve, Mother! You won't be able to survive!"

"Well, we've survived so far. I do not think your upbringing was that bad here in Whitsville. You used to love this community. Don't you still think of it as your hometown? You must have a love for the people here. They still love you."

"Oh, stop it, Mother. Come up here to Baltimore. I am being offered a job at the Baltimore National Hospital as an Emergency Room

Nurse Practitioner, and you can live with me. It would be a perfect set-up for our family since I am going to soon need a family to live with so I can meet the government protocol for multi-family housing."

"We've heard from God. He has said that though we suffer for our choices, He will never leave us or forsake us. I believe He wants us to stay. I clearly heard Him speak to me today and say that He wants us to minister to the people who are left behind. They are to be our new mission field to spread God's love. We can't abandon them now."

"Mother, you are so ignorant. God did not tell you anything. You are just as stubborn as those damn people in Whitsville." She slammed her cell phone on the kitchen counter. *It won't be long 'til they come to their senses,* she thought.

But they did not. Each year the Middle Region became more isolated from society and the norm. Each year more people matriculated to the Federated States and blended into the ebb and flow of society. Each year along with the devastating isolation, the government saw to it that these regions felt the full effects of their separatist ways. Rare food shipments were allowed. Government assistance to individuals ceased, and utilities were rerouted as much as possible to bypass the Middle Region. The only connection with the outside world after six years of separation was a healthy black market of transporting forbidden goods, an occasional stealthy tapping into outlawed utilities when the opportunity permitted, and a deplorable transportation system that continued to ply the highways, most often taking the former protesters in their sorry and defeated states back to civilization.

***

As the day dragged on, Ricardo disassembled the nineties-era generator which looked like a disfigured dinosaur. He would occasionally see Mercedes in her duties hurrying from charge to charge in the musty hospital. Though she was not aware of it, a look of sincere concern hung over her face like a dark veil. Late in the morning she stopped by the boiler room and asked Ricardo if he could spare a half hour to go to the bus station to see if a shipment of medications had arrived from Baltimore National Hospital. She had still been able to network with a handful of employees from her former health care network who were willing to take a chance on sending illegal substances to the Middle Region. One of her fellow emergency room nurses, Gwen, had been able to slip in Sertraline in the last shipment disguised among a pile of government pamphlets encouraging the public to conserve electricity. She smiled at the thought that someone in customs had failed to reason that there was no electricity in the Middle Region and had allowed the package to be forwarded. The medicine could help with anxiety, but they needed staples of antibiotics and real pain killers.

"Sure. I'll be glad to help." Ricardo stood up and wiped the sweat off his forehead. The airless boiler room was a moist swamp compared to the airy rooms above. Occasionally he had to come up for a respite from the heat.

"Thanks," said Mercedes. "I'll see if I can find something cold for you to drink. Sorry we do not have electricity to run a box fan down here. It would help."

When Ricardo returned twenty minutes later, he found a very cool glass of water on the table with his tools. Chugging it down, he went in search of Mercedes with the depressing news. "Sorry, Mercedes. Nothing for the hospital or you at the bus station. I'll be glad to do errands for you anytime," he said with a slight flourish of the hand. It bothered her.

"Please call me Ms. Singleton when we are at the hospital. It is more professional."

Ricardo thought inwardly about the title she had chosen. It seemed odd in an era where titles were frowned upon as being elitist and divisive. But he was not about to jeopardize his mission over a little sur-name. Anyway, he really did not care what she wanted to be called. He was thinking of other possible names that might fit as well.

"Fine," he said coolly.

Mercedes went to check on Danny. The veil came over her face again as his temperature registered 104 degrees.

The Beginning

Chapter 3

Mack Gersham

Fall 2024
12 Years Earlier

"Hope does not put us to shame, because God's love has been poured
out into our hearts by the Holy Spirit, who has been given to us."
Romans 5:5

Mack and his twin brother Walt sat on the hood of Aunt Lilly's 2005 Ford Mustang GT. It was now a dusty screaming yellow from the wild run they had taken down Highway 460. This was not the first time they had stolen her car and gone joy riding. But it was the first time they had reached a speed of 110 mph and were elated with the accomplishment, even though they had almost rolled it twice. Mack loved speed and thrills and his brother Walt reveled in the excitement his brother got from such escapades. Walt just loved doing anything with his twin brother because it made him feel normal, like one of the guys. He idolized Mack.

When they were born, something was wrong with Walt. He had barely survived the birth. There were issues with a deformed left leg, and before long, it became obvious that he would have mental challenges as well. His face was drawn up on the left side which gave him a silly lopsided grin, but it fit Walt's personality well. However, when the occasion called for somberness, Walt would be all covered with a smile. This was such a time. Here he and his brother sat handcuffed on the hood of Aunt Lilly's car and all Walt could do was grin.

Sheriff Waldron was upset, to say the least.

"This is the third time I've gotten a call from Aunt Lilly saying that you took her car out without permission. What were you thinking?"

"Well, Sheriff," shared Mack, "she gave us the keys to fill up the tank out on their old farm outside of town. Now that her husband is gone, she needs help putting in the gas and keeping the car ready in case she needs to go somewhere. Funny that she always has that car prepped for a trip and then never goes any place except town. She could walk there as fast as driving. Her husband sure did her a favor in keeping that underground gas tank full before he passed."

"Aunt Lilly never told you guys to drive off in her car. She has you there to do her chores. She's your momma's cousin, and she feels sorry that you boys had to grow up without your mother. Is this the way to treat her?"

"Well, she is good to us," Walt replied. "She always sends us packing with some dinner and treats from her stove. Have you had her peanut butter fudge?"

That car was such an enticement for Mack. "Hop in," he had called to Walt, and before anyone could think of the ramifications, they were tearing down the road. This time however, Aunt Lilly was furious. Gas was hard to come by and expensive in these tough times, and she didn't want it wasted on any joy riding. She was afraid her nephews would kill themselves. It was time those Gersham boys were taught a lesson.

Sheriff Waldron spit out a wad of chewing tobacco and yelled at Mack. "You boys are rotten. You are goin' to turn out just like your daddy; wasted and drunk half the day. I am going to put you both in jail for a week with no chance of parole and parade you around town doing chores in an orange jumpsuit. And you are going to apologize to Miss Lilly and do chores free for her for a month."

Walt giggled. But Mack got serious. "Sheriff, I can't go to jail. Not this week. The big Division III game is tomorrow night. We might have a chance at the State Championship. I gotta be there. We have our last practice tonight down at the school field and leave tomorrow afternoon for Blacksburg."

The sheriff came back to reality. How could he have forgotten that Mack was the star quarterback for this team? It was about the only good thing happening in these parts in 2024, and if he arrested Mack, his chances for re-election would be zero. People around here never forgot anything. He also knew his oldest boy would soon be trying out for the high school team in a year, and he did not want to complicate matters there either.

Mack Gersham was a natural-born leader. He had led a rag tag bunch of coal country kids to a state championship game with the help of a couple talented running backs. He was scrambling for a good excuse for a release for both of them just like he did when he was pressured on the grid iron. "And Walt needs to be there too. He's our manager."

"He's not necessary," spit the sheriff. "He stays in jail. That way I can make sure you will come and do your time later." Walt's face blanched as he heard his sentence.

"Mack, don't let me go to jail. Help me, Mack. I'm scared." He reached his fingers across to the hand that was cuffed with his and stroked his brother's hand.

Mack suddenly became serious. With amazing alacrity, a thought crossed his mind that his careless antics were jeopardizing his brother. It was one thing to put himself in danger driving 110 mph down Route 460, but doing it with Walt and then getting Walt arrested for his bad judgment jolted into the reality of consequences. Walt would never be able to stay in a locked cage. He would go crazy. He had done it before. While usually Walt was mild mannered and grinning, there were instances when a switch would flip, and he would become defiant and destructive. Usually, it was with his old man at their house. If it happened here, they would both be in jail, game or no game. He felt guilty that he had dragged his brother into this mess.

"Listen, Sheriff Waldron. It is all my fault. You know Walt had nothing to do with this. I promise you we will never do it again. Let me talk to Miss Lilly and apologize and smooth this over. You are right. If I don't straighten up, I am goin' to end up just like my dad. And by God, that is the last thing I want to happen. Plus, he will bust our butts if he finds out we've been joy riding or, worse, locked up. I don't know why I didn't think of that when I convinced Walt to go for a ride."

Sheriff Waldron ruminated on Mack's seemingly honest remarks. Knowing that the townsfolk would not tolerate the lock-up of their star quarterback for a little joy riding when the big game was on their doorstep was just not smart. But these Gersham brothers were getting out of hand.

"All right. I will put it in as a misdemeanor with six months suspended sentence. Another incident and you are both toast. Get that car back to Miss Lilly and don't let me catch you again or I'll put both of your carcasses in jail and throw away the key." He unlocked the cuffs and the boys slid off the hood and breezed onto the front seat.

Mack started up the engine and gave the gas a bit of revving but pulled back onto the highway with a dignified turn of the steering wheel. When he was out of sight, he floored the gas for one last time. "I gotta be more careful what I do with you around," he said, glancing affectionately at Walt. "I'm done being stupid." He slowed the car down to the speed limit and moseyed back to town. Walt stared straight ahead and smiled and waved at anyone they drove past.

"I love you, Mack. I'm so sad it is your senior year and you'll be leavin' home soon like you said. Do you think I can go with you? I don't know how I will get along with just Dad and me. You know he brings out the worst in me. Sometimes he is just not right in the head."

Mack smiled at the observation by his brother Walt.

"Don't worry so much, Walt. We'll figure something out. Maybe once I get settled in the armed forces or at college, I'll make enough money that I can send you some and you can move out on your own."

"Yeah, but who will take care of Dad?"

"I don't give a shit. He's the meanest son of a bitch I know. He can go to hell for all I care."

"But he's our dad."

"Well, maybe. But when has he acted like it? I don't know why Mom married him. She must have been out of her mind. She was a saint. I think living with him ate her up inside."

"Naw, I think life has been eating up Dad from the inside for a long time. He really doesn't hate us. He hates himself."

"Man, little brother. You have smart observations. Now let's get back to Miss Lilly's and put this car back where it belongs and sound like we are really sorry for what we did. We can promise we will never do it again. Pinkie promise. Now wipe that grin off your face and be serious."

"Sure, Mack, anything you say."

Chapter 4

Titus Singleton

Summer 2024

"For our God is a consuming fire." Hebrews 12:29

When the football team at Whitsville High School came to their first practice in the summer of 2024, no one had any thought that anything would be different from the last five seasons. These mostly tallied in the loss column. For coal country boys, defeat was a ready commodity. They did not mind it. It was a diversion from a lackluster life.

But this year, Mack Gersham showed up for try-outs. His dad had been extra drunk by the time he got home as a coal chute operator for the coal trains. They still occasionally scuttled down the valley toward old electric plants but more often headed for the docks in Virginia Beach to be shipped to factories in China and India. While America had all but negated the use of coal for power and industrial energy, the other parts of the industrialized world that depended on it were more than willing to invest in this cheap energy source. They pointed to the fact that the markers for carbon monoxide pollution were decreasing worldwide, so they were not seriously impacting the environment. Of course, the decrease came from the States and Europe. Their hiatus on coal usage and their clamping down on emissions of the gas-powered cars and trucks that plied the road had changed transportation availability.

Mack knew it was a good opportunity to slip off without being detected for the rest of the afternoon. He told Walt to tell his dad he was doing chores down in town if he asked. He was a natural athlete and he wanted to get something on his resume that would stand out if he decided to go to college or into the military. The coach could see that he was skilled and substituted him as quarterback at the first practice. Mack was smart, savvy, and had an uncanny ability to smell trouble and escape. After practice, the coach gave Mack a ride home. He knew the family well enough to know that he would have to sweet talk Mack's dad.

"Hey, Mick, nice seeing you today. I brought your boy home 'cause he needed a ride, and I was coming your way."

Mick just stared at the two through the car driver's window. "What's my boy doin' in your car, Coach?"

Coach Gadley and Mack got out of the car simultaneously. They both knew that this conversation could go off the rails very easily. "Well, Mack was in town doing some chores when I spotted him as I was drivin' to practice. I asked him if he could join us for a few hours and he agreed since he was done with his work.

"Your boy is a stand-out football player, Mick. Just like you when we were on the team twenty years ago. He has the same kind of quickness and savvy that you had. Thought he was you for a minute. Anyway, I want to know if he can come to practice and help us out this year. You know the team has had a mediocre record for the past several years. We need a shot in the arm and Mack can help us."

Mick just stood there chewing on his wad of tobacco. "What do we get out of it? I don't want Mack tired every day where he has chores to do around here."

Coach Gadley took Mick by the elbow and walked him up to the rickety front porch. They sat down and chatted for ten minutes, and the boys saw the coach slip their dad a bill or two.

Coach told Mack's father that he should be proud his son was working to make something of himself. He had him sign the permission papers, which was not so hard once the bills were passed between them ... enough money to buy a fifth, really three fifths. As far as the other expenses, Coach would either pick them up or have the school give Mack a scholarship. Mack also had volunteered to help clean up the cafeteria during study hall so he could earn cash. Now those funds would be going for his team costs. He did not like handouts. There was never any extra money in the Gersham household. Mack's mom had died when he was six. Life was hard.

In practice that fall, Mack was befriended by the favorite team member of everyone–Titus Singleton. He was also a senior and he played left linebacker. Titus had a stealthy strength. He looked wiry rather than muscular until someone tried to push him around. Most often the opponent was taken by surprise. Something deep drove that young man to give his all on every down. His teammates were in awe of his work ethic and tried to emulate him. Mack had the same drive, but it was more obvious. When the first-string quarterback broke his leg during the first home game, Mack stepped in and kept his spot. One day after practice mid-season, Titus asked Mack if he would like to come over for dinner and then stay for a revival that was being held at his dad's church.

"Sure," said Mack, thinking only of a home-cooked meal. "I'll let Walt know where I am."

"You can bring him too. Mom is used to having extra mouths to feed. She actually likes having company."

The meal that night would long be remembered by Mack, Walt, and Mercedes.

"Mercedes, will you set two more plates for supper?"

"Sure, Mom." Mercedes thought nothing of it. Likely, she surmised, guest speakers for the revival later that night. But when Mack and Walt walked in after knocking at the door, scrubbed cleaner than they had been in weeks, Mercedes could not help but blush. Here was the star quarterback in her house, cleaned up with the nicest shirt he could find and manners that remembered to compliment Mrs. Singleton for her excellent cooking. Mack thought the food was a feast. So did Walt who thanked them profusely each time something was offered for seconds. Mack even complimented Mercedes on her serving skills. He knew she was a freshman, but her youth did not faze him. He had never seen anyone quite like her. She moved with the grace of a dancer, and he was taken by her shy, honest smile. That was as far as he ever allowed himself to think about her. He knew he was the son of a loser and there was no way he would ever think of pulling someone like Mercedes into a family relationship that was so chaotic and dysfunctional.

Mack and Walt shook hands with Mrs. Singleton as they were leaving a house still smelling of pot roast and browned potatoes.

"Thank you, Mrs. Singleton. I don't know when I last had a meal as tasty as that. Walt is not such a good cook, you know. But he is getting better."

"Well, I don't have much to work with," countered Walt. "But I'm trying. Anyway, it was a pleasure to be here, Mr. and Mrs. Singleton. I'm always glad when I can do things with Mack."

Mack glanced towards Mercedes and was surprised to see that she was looking at him with a quizzical expression on her face. She recovered quickly and said, "I hear that you are going to the revival tonight with Titus. I hope you enjoy it. Please excuse me but I must leave now to play the piano for the gathering music at the beginning of the service. It was nice to have you come and enjoy our family dinner." She seemed naturally cool and composed.

Mack felt his hand getting hot as he shook her hand. "Thanks for the hospitality. Your mom sure does know how to cook." He pulled his hand away quickly. It was a meal he would never forget. He allowed himself to gaze into her face for just a moment, but she had already turned her head, withdrawing her hand just as quickly. Mack could not describe what he was feeling, but it took him by surprise. He brushed it off and followed Titus out the door and down to the church with Walt in tow behind them.

When they arrived at the church revival, Mercedes was playing favorite, familiar hymns to get the older folks to settle in. Then a praise band appeared on stage and played their set of songs to a rowdier crowd who clapped, swayed, and shouted "Amen." The music got the assembly powered up with expectation. Mack saw recognizable faces from school and noticed that they were singing along with familiar words on the screen. Some waved their hands. He was fascinated and a bit scared. What was up with this? He thought about ducking out early with an excuse about his dad. He sure did not need any more noise in his life. Solitude, for him, was good medicine.

But before he could gracefully exit, the band strolled off the stage and a fiery man, named Billy Cramer, ran up on the stage and everyone cheered and clapped for him. He had a mesmerizing hold on the audience as they watched his every move. This was the last of Billy's three nights of revival talks and the crowd had appreciated the prior evening services. When people heard he would be coming to town, they made the effort to show up whether they "had religion" or not. He just had the ability to make them think about God and the possibility that they could live a better life with Him than without. When he left, the town always was a more contented and kinder place for a while. Somehow it did not last, though.

Mack could not help but be pulled in by the story of the Prodigal Son. The evangelist made that lost son come alive. And he made the father in the story even more real. When the two reunited, after their long and sordid separation, Mack was moved almost to tears. The revivalist yelled, "My son was lost but now he is found!"

Mack hurt inside, relating to the story of a dysfunctional relationship between father and son. When the preaching was over, Brother Cramer spoke in a quieter, more reserved tone.

"Now bow your heads. I want to ask if any of you would like to have a new relationship with your father whether it is on earth or in heaven. Just raise your hand," called the preacher. "Take what the Lord gives you. No one's watching but Him. You see, the Father, our Father God is always looking out for us. He is attentive and waiting for us. The son had to want to come home, though. Do you want a restored relationship with your earthly father or someone else you are battling with? Do you want peace? Your Heavenly Father is waiting for you. Just raise your hand and show you want this relationship. No one is watching but the Father."

Mack raised his hand halfway. He could bet that Walt had raised his hand too. He was most likely the first one to do so. There was an emptiness in Mack, and he wanted what that preacher was talking about. Later that evening he opened the door to his dilapidated house and sauntered in with Walt. He felt good about himself and strangely light; God's presence like the preacher said?

His dad swung a whisky bottle at him which Mack did not have time to adjust to. It hit him sharply across the cheek. "You dumb shit. Where's my dinner? I'm starved and no one was here to get me something to eat after slaving all day in the coal yard. Get cookin'! Where you boys been?"

Mack slammed the door to his bedroom while Walt fired up the stove and cooked the rest of the slab of bacon that had been hanging in the kitchen and fried potatoes to go with it. *So much for the good Father*, he mused with a sarcastic grimace. *Fairy tales.*

Chapter 5

Mercedes Singleton

Summer 2036
12 Years Later

"In the same way, the Spirit helps us in our weakness. We do not know what we ought to pray for, but the Spirit himself intercedes for us through wordless groans. And he who searches our hearts knows the mind of the Spirit, because the Spirit intercedes for God's people in accordance with the will of God." Romans 8:26-27

Danny was struggling. Getting an old compress from the portable cooler that had been sitting in the artesian spring, Mercedes could see from the pallor of his skin that the infection was spreading.

Dear Jesus, she said to herself. *Come and give this boy a chance. He does not deserve to die this way. He didn't have any choice about living in this forsaken zone of hotheads and liberty zombies.* And then she refocused her words. *He needs your help, Jesus. By your blood heal him. And your authority. By your power and your compassion. I call on all of these in your mighty and precious name, the Author of mankind, the Lord Jesus Christ of Nazareth who came in the flesh. He is just a kid. Help him. Thank you.* Mercedes smiled. She thought of her friend Olivia who had taught her to be strong in the power and authority given to her by Jesus. It was not an easy behavior to replicate. But she knew that a life depended on it—Danny's. There was nothing else she could do. She knew that the Spirit was at this very moment lifting up this prayer to Jesus. That was a relief for her troubled and tired mind.

She sat next to him and mused about what his chances for survival would be if he were in the Federated States. At least he would have been provided antibiotics to fight the fever. And a decent surgical room. She squeezed his hand as his eyes fluttered open.

"Miss Mercedes, am I dying?" Danny asked matter of factly.

Hesitation made his eyes open wide.

"I don't know. Your infection is getting worse, and your temperature is elevated. We are waiting for antibiotics to come from Baltimore. Hang in there, young man. Be a fighter. I'm sure everything will be better tomorrow." She hesitated and then said, "I'm praying for you."

Danny spoke again in the faintest of whispers. "I'm not really afraid to die. I gave my heart to Jesus years ago at that revival with Mr. Cramer at your dad's church. My mom took me. She loved those revivals. They made her hard life a little bit easier. Remember that one, Mercedes? I was a little kid, but I remember giving my life to Jesus. But I don't know what death will be like. Will I see my good Aunt Mary again in her right mind? How about my mom and dad? Will it be boring? Will I be able to see God or Jesus? I think it will be beautiful like the valley behind Uncle John's house in the spring when the pink and white blossoms cover the old apple trees."

Mercedes held her breath. She wanted to be honest and yet comforting. She decided to share part of her story.

"Danny, I have been close to death once before. I was extremely sick with an infection from surgery just like you, and I had no one to properly care for me. The proper medicines were not available as well. I believe I was dying. Anyway, that night in the hospital I fell asleep and was taken on a journey far away. It was totally dark. Just no light whatsoever. I was suspended high up in the darkness above some sort of activity below. When I looked down, there was a long row of people, dressed in nondescript brownish clothes and quietly talking to each other. They were in a line, waiting and anticipating their destination where the Presence would greet them. I could not see who that was, but in my mind, I knew it was Jesus. Anyway, while everything around me was dark and void, behind those people were the most fascinating strands of lights. They were twirling and shimmering and swirling in three distinct colors of blue, red, and yellow. Strand after strand, repeating themselves over and over, all turning and spinning at the same time like multi-faceted crystal jewels moving in a celebration dance. I think they were the gate to heaven. Oh, what a supernatural sight! I surmised there was going to be an amazing blast of color once they were parted for entry. Then I woke up. Heaven is going to be even more beautiful and colorful than we can imagine. It will be full of space and warmth and places that we remember with love. What do you think of that?"

Danny had a faint smile on his face and squeezed Mercedes hand. Somehow, he seemed almost happy.

"I'll be back on my rounds in an hour."

Mercedes got up with a sigh. She was exhausted. The exhaustion reminded her of her residency as an Emergency Room Nurse Practitioner after graduating from The Public School of Nursing -Baltimore.

Part of your initiation into the business was to work twenty-four-hour stints with twelve hours off for weeks. No breaks. They wanted to see who would crumble under the pressure. Mercedes was determined to make it through the program with flying colors. She did.

It had been a good place to work in a variety of ways. Her skills were honed for emergency situations, and she became quite adept at controlling her emotions in emergencies while she worked there. The good news as the years passed was that there were less and less gunshot wounds and vehicular accidents. Not surprising with the turn-in program for firearms, the confiscation of weapons from those deemed mentally unfit, and the tightening of permits to own cars. Society was progressing to a kinder and gentler place; or so it appeared. The news was pared down to mediocre stories of special interest or political gain. Stories questioning the political climate or human crises were either ignored or buried. They just riled up a portion of the citizenry who were still reeling from all their individual losses of the last few years. While revolution had been derailed for the time being, there was such an undercurrent of unrest, that no one dared be frank about their feelings.

Hard to ignore were the frequently increasing cases of neglect. She was disgusted that children failed to take care of their parents, often seeing them emaciated, withered and unresponsive by the time they got to the hospital. Bed sores racked their buttocks, and their breath was putrid with rotting teeth. They were barely kept alive by their kids for their government check. Yet the worst were the forgotten, vulnerable children. She was shocked at the number of babies who were dropped off at the hospital dying of starvation or failing to thrive because of lack of touch.

Her mind traveled back to a situation she had dealt with in her stint in Baltimore.

She had had to deal with a mother one morning as she was entering the emergency room entrance to begin her shift.

"Hey, lady, do you work here?" asked a slight, becoming lady in a green coat. "I want to drop off this kid."

She held out a small toddler, about one and a half years old. "He's just too much for me. I got a new job, and it costs too much to put him in the government daycare. I don't want to pay those bills anymore. I need to get myself back in shape, and I got a boyfriend who doesn't want the noise. He wants nothing of kids hangin' around. He is a good kid. I love him, but life is short. You know what I mean?"

She pushed him into Mercedes' arms.

"What's his name?"

The mother turned around and called back, "He's got a note in his pocket. Goodbye, Stevie. I'll miss you."

She left with no kiss, hug, or anything. Mercedes was trying to withhold her tears. *How could she?* she mused. *What kind of a world do we live in where this happens every day? It's such a broken, dismal, disgusting way of looking at life.*

Mercedes took Stevie into the hospital and called the Children's Welfare Agency. They took him, but not gladly. This was the fourth run they had made to the hospital that week.

"Geez," said the agency social worker. "What's with all these kids getting dropped off?"

Mercedes shrugged her shoulders. "I don't get it."

Thinking of these children from the past brought her back to the reality of the present. Mercedes checked in on the four remaining patients, took vital signs, and then walked to the first floor to see if Ricardo had made any progress with the ancient generator. She felt an unsubstantiated unease around him as though something was just not right. Looking into the darkened boiler room, she saw a myriad of machinery pieces all over the floor.

"Do you know where these go when you're ready to put this back together?"

Ricardo just looked at her. He did not bother to answer. Her tone was judgmental, but he did not care. He knew this placement at the hospital was a godsend. He could innocently gather information from the people who lived around here if he played his cards right. There would be a steady flow of locals at the hospital, the cafeteria, the school, and he was coming to the rescue with generator repairs. The longer he was a fixture in the boiler room, the more he would be seen as one of them. If he could get this old generator to work, the hospital and the school might have electricity part of the day. *Heck*, he thought, *I could be the town hero!* He laughed to himself. *Maybe they'll put me at the front of the parade on the 4th of July.*

Mercedes saw the strange, twisted smile on his face. "Hope you found lunch satisfactory. Will you finish this tomorrow?"

Ricardo made no reply.

She stopped by Danny's room and saw him sleeping peacefully—too peacefully. She checked her breath and walked over to his bed. "Jesus," she said with force. "He's so young. Give him a chance." Then she laid her hands on his heart, got down on her knees, and prayed for a miracle.

Chapter 6

Ricardo Medina

2008-2028

*"Those who live according to the flesh have their minds set
on what the flesh desires; but those who live in accordance
with the Spirit have their minds set on what the Spirit desires.
The mind governed by the flesh is death, but the mind governed
by the Spirit is life and peace." Romans 8:5-6*

His first recollections were of sitting on the cold, chipped cement step at the Washington D.C. row house. He remembered the loneliness. His mother had grabbed his wiggly body.

"Ricardo, put on your coat and hat and don't forget your mittens. I want you to wait outside for me on the steps and do not wander away in the neighborhood. It isn't safe."

Ricardo had cried. "Mommy, it's so cold out there. My butt freezes on the cement. Can't I stay in here with you? Why do I always need to go out when that man comes here? Is he bad?"

"Just sit on a piece of cardboard to keep warmer. This man is giving us a roof over our heads, so be more accepting of his visits. He just does not want kids around while he is visiting. I'll tell you what. I will take you to the neighborhood park as soon as our guest leaves."

Ricardo had little interest in who the guest was. He just knew how cold it got outside in the wild winds of late autumn. The constant visitor had a fancy car, so he must be important. He always left a treat for his mother–extra cash. He never left anything for Ricardo.

Whoever he was, Ricardo did not like him. His mother always seemed so sad when he left. The stoic man never acknowledged Ricardo's presence. He just brushed past him as he left, jumped in the car, and accelerated too quickly, impatient to move on as he drove over the rustling trash that took flight as the car sped past.

Ricardo's mother had met him when she came to the United States during the early part of 2006. It was a time which secretly welcomed immigrants who would take the menial jobs no one else wanted. The government put on a show that they were not welcome, but like everyone else, they knew that companies pulled the strings and cheap labor improved the bottom line. She had walked from Honduras and was terribly thin when she arrived in Washington D.C. to stay with her cousin. She applied for a humanitarian visa which came after a year's delay. Her cousin ran a cleaning business for two government buildings, D and H, and had gotten this minority contract because, frankly, she had turned in the most detailed application.

Eliana was a diligent worker. Her shift started at six p.m. and finished at six a.m. Cleaning was not that hard and there were few distractions. She was thankful for the work but missed her home, the warmth, and the familiarity. She enjoyed looking at the freshly waxed floors and the government desks neatly in rows, ordered and clean when she was done. It made it seem like there was a place, a refuge where normalcy existed.

Over the weeks, she began to share pleasantries with a couple of employees who chose to stay late. One of them was Lieutenant Colonel

Sturgis Lu. He rarely smiled but he thanked her when she dumped out the trash and retreated without imposing on his work. He was tallish in stature, with black straight hair and steel gray eyes. Lt. Col. Lu was ambitious and angry. He worked late to advance his career and compensate for the shortcomings on his resume. He was known to be ruthless in discarding or stepping on fellow officers if it benefitted him in his career. And he was careful to always appear as an officer should in public. Yet he had weaknesses. His pent-up fears needed appeased, and he had ways of unwinding. One of them was with women.

One night when Eliana was quietly cleaning the room, he asked her where she lived. She was fearful to respond, but knowing her paperwork was in order, she told him she lived in a flat with five other workers on the crew. As the weeks went by Lt. Col. Lu continued short conversations with her. One evening about a year after they met, he moved into a different line of conversation.

"Eliana, you look so much healthier now that you've been in the States for a while. I noticed how shiny your hair has become. I am glad you are growing it long. I like long hair on women."

Eliana was embarrassed by the private observation. She flushed.

"Would you like to have a flat or townhouse of your own?"

Eliana was confused but not ignorant of his intentions.

"I don't know. I'll think about it," she responded, her eyes still not making contact with the lieutenant colonel. The next few weeks were unbearable as her fellow workers started to pester her about the new boyfriend she had at the Pentagon. One of the men who boarded with her also tried his best to seduce her, and she found it was almost impossible to use the shower in privacy. Despite her reservations, she said yes.

That night, Lt. Col. Lu drove her four blocks from her current home to a small apartment in a ramshackle brownstone. The furniture was falling apart, but this place was all hers. It was close enough to walk to work and fairly safe with the double padlock and bars over the windows. As she sat down on the dusty couch, she looked over at the lieutenant colonel. "Undress," he said in a nondescript voice. She reluctantly followed his orders.

He said little for the rest of the night. But he did pull her to him after their heated sexual encounter, and Eliana somehow felt appreciated and loved by a man she hardly knew. In the early hours of the morning, Sturgis slapped lukewarm water on his face, got dressed, and headed home to his wife and his two sons.

Before he left, he gave her instructions. "Now you need to keep this private. You do not share with anyone the fact that I see you occasionally. Do you understand? None of your friends from the other side. You got that? You know I can get you sent back any time, right?"

Eliana nodded. "I understand."

"I'll order some modern furniture. This place is a dump."

Although Eliana would see him most nights at work, he would usually show up on Friday evenings once or twice a month. He was smart enough to realize detection of an affair would not look good for an aspiring officer, and his wealthy wife would terminate their marriage. His favorite pastime with her was not the sex but role-playing scenarios as to how he was planning to get ahead at the Pentagon, even if he had to step on every bastard in the building to earn an additional rank.

"I hate those prissy show ponies who went to those elite military schools," he would share with Eliana. "They never had to work for anything; served up their rank on a silver platter while I was busting my ass."

Eliana found herself mesmerized by his strength, grit, and his extremely forceful personality. He did not seem to think much about her welfare. She did not seem to mind. While she found him captivating, she also found herself pregnant.

Sturgis demanded that she have an abortion and Eliana balked.

"I can't do that, Sturgis. I was raised a Roman Catholic, and I believe all babies are sent from God. And besides, I want this baby. He is mine."

"If you do not have an abortion, I'll shut this apartment up tomorrow and leave you on the streets. You will never get a job with the government again. No gutter Central American bitch is going to ruin my life. I will make the appointment. Be ready at seven a.m. tomorrow morning to be picked up. Don't disappoint me."

Eliana was in turmoil over the love she had for both the baby and the lieutenant colonel. She cried out for help in her predicament. She was so unsure of what to do that she called her cousin and took a taxi to visit her. She also packed her most treasured possessions in case she decided to leave. It was a short visit. Her cousin Marissa told her she could move into her old flat and that she would find her another job for a while. There really was no choice. The child had a right to exist. It was her love child.

Sturgis was furious when he arrived the next morning to find a cold apartment and no tenant. He let it go. He knew she was smart enough to keep his name out of the conversation if parenthood came up, and most women these days slept with so many men, there was not even any question as to who the father might be. When she was eight months pregnant, he happened to see her walking to her new job at the Human Services Division and pulled his car over to the curb. He put down the window. "Get in," he ordered. She did. He drove her out to a hotel on the outskirts of town and checked in.

"Please," she said. "The baby."

"Who cares? I am just thrilled to see you again. I missed you."

They spent the morning together, and then he gathered up his things. He took her glossy black hair in his hands and pulled her head up to his sharply. She let out a small cry. "I'm sorry. You can move back into the flat. Keep the kid. Just keep him out of my way."

She did. She kept her promise to him.

Lt. Col. Sturgis Lu rose in rank twice in the Army during the Afghanistan War and was sent abroad in 2025 to the Middle East when trouble started to brew. For his expertise, he would be chosen to lead the Army several years later when they were tasked with defending America's only ally left in the region, Israel, and to restore peace in the Middle East. He was rarely in Washington anymore, but when he was, he would pay a visit to Eliana, and Ricardo would wander over to the playground to play basketball with the other lonely kids in the neighborhood. If the weather was nasty, he took his cell phone and sat on the steps leading down to the neighbor's flat. Sturgis hardly ever brought treats or money anymore to his mother, but she seemed not to mind. His uniform was covered with medals and now stars on the shoulders. She hung on his every word and treated him with the deference of a king. Ricardo was no dummy. He knew exactly what his mother was to this decorated general. He had given her enough money so that she could pay off the mortgage to her flat.

"I hate his guts," Ricardo whispered aloud as he sat on the apartment's filthy steps.

Then one day he came home from school to find his mother sobbing in her bedroom. He was eighteen. She had been told her cleaning job at Human Services had been terminated. The cleaning crew now was mostly automated. There were required cutbacks from an economy weakened by the volcanic eruption and the unfolding war.

Lu had been promoted again to a two-star general, then three, then a four star and finally chief of staff. During that time, he sent Eliana a brief note explaining his need to stay focused on the call to his country. He never returned. Ricardo's mother became listless, lethargic, and withdrawn. She seemed to age overnight. Her hair grayed and posture stooped. When she was diagnosed with breast cancer a year later, she practically gave up without a fight. Although she was only forty, she was given a minimal regimen of chemo treatments and sent to a warehouse-type health facility set up for those who could not afford a more detailed and hope-filled cancer protocol. Though the country touted equal medical care for all, it was obvious to the regular citizen that a select group of people had preferential treatment. Lower income patients like Eliana lacked adequate staff and rarely had their basic needs met. Most sat in soiled diapers. The stench was overwhelming. The sick moaned from their extreme pain. The care was so substandard that patients died long before their treatments were over.

Ricardo was the only person who came to see his mother, other than her cousin. He made himself visit her out of duty. The conditions of the ward were appalling, but he knew his mother was a victim of a health care system that had overextended its promises. Most often she stared at the peeling wall while he shared what was happening at night school, but one day she handed him a note addressed to the general. When he read it, Ricardo was sick to his stomach. He hated his mother for reaching out to a man who had discarded her like a worn-out pair of shoes.

After repeated phone calls had been placed by Ricardo to General Lu, the general finally responded, asking Ricardo to deliver the note from his mother personally. He knew if there was any hint of a disturbance, he would be able to manage it privately. There was no way he wanted any incriminating evidence floating around to jeopardize his career.

On a cold and glazy day in March, Ricardo walked into the Pentagon, passed through security checkpoints, and was escorted by an overly zealous officer to General Lu's office. It had been years since they had seen each other face to face. The office of the general spoke military. It was clean, bright, organized, and devoid of anything that had no practical use. Ricardo glanced around at the award plaques on the wall. He could think of plaques he would like to replace them with. The corner of his mouth could not hide the smile these thoughts generated. He did not recognize it yet, but deep down, his greatest desire was to get revenge on this man who cared for only himself. Someday those thoughts would manifest in a concrete way, but for now he tamped them down with a heavy-duty clamp.

The general's face was emotionless as he read the letter. When he was finished, he looked coldly at Ricardo and said, "Your mother wants me to get you a position in the military when you graduate. That I can do for her. But only because she is an old friend. Do you know what I was to her?" he asked with some derision.

Ricardo did not want the general to know that his mother worshipped the ground he walked on. But he knew. He had known it from the first day and that was why she was a safe bet. "You were a … good friend," he said through clenched teeth.

"That is so," chuckled the general. "The best of friends."

"Can you get her into Walter Reed or the Cancer Clinical Center? She is dying of breast cancer, and she is just being warehoused like a discarded stray animal at the Liberty Treatment Center. They have her locked in a dormitory for people with memory loss, and it is nothing more than a prison filled with stench and the endless shrieks of the insane."

The general did not react. "I'll see what I can do," he mumbled. "Sorry to hear that she is so sick." He picked up a blank pad of paper and jotted down some scratched out lines, folded it, and sealed it in a plain envelope. He did not bother to put a name on the outside. Staring at Ricardo, he stated matter of factly, "I don't want any more contact with a bastard son. I have enough trouble with the two sons I have at home. Their mother has made them into sissies. If you want an assignment from me like your mother asked for, contact me when you are out of school. I will see what I can do … for your mom's sake. I've written a brief note to your mother letting her know I am thinking about her in her time of difficulty."

Ricardo left the Pentagon office seething inside. He gathered up his phone and returned the temporary ID they had given him at the security checkpoint. A hatred he had never felt before welled up in his soul. He hoped the bastard would be eaten by worms … slowly. He hated the fact that his mother had always loved the general more than him. In a twisted way, he had made Eliana feel special. As he walked along the cracked sidewalk, he tore tiny bits off the envelope he was supposed to deliver to his mother, letting them flutter to the ground. They fell like the leaves that had clung stubbornly to the trees through the winter, but in the stiff spring breeze, had finally released themselves, knowing this was their eventual fate. They represented the end of Eliana's sad investment in General Lu.

That was the last time he ever hoped to see or hear of the general. He might not be out of his DNA, but he would hopefully be out of his life. At that moment, Ricardo had fallen under the sway of an immensely powerful force. It marinated him in bitterness and rejection. The more he hated the general, the better. The general long ago had decided that a false identity of rank and power were the epitome of success. He had worked incessantly to climb to the top, and he was on the brink of living his life-long dream. Both men teetered in a world of deception. They seemed content there.

Ricardo's mother fell into a coma the following week and never recovered. She died two weeks later. She was cremated as a pauper the next day. The old graying priest who had ministered to him long ago repeatedly called Ricardo, but he never bothered to answer his calls.

Ricardo heard that he had come to the crematorium to say the last rites for his mother.

"Waste of time, old man," he laughed.

Chapter 7

Mercedes Singleton

2030-2033

"I pray that the eyes of your heart may be enlightened in order that you may know the hope to which he has called you, the riches of his glorious inheritance in his holy people and his incomparably great power for us who believe." Ephesians 1:18-19a

Soon after graduating as a Nurse Practitioner Emergency Room Specialist, Mercedes was assigned to the surgery ward in the Baltimore National Hospital. It was an enormous facility comprised of a bank of interwoven buildings each housing its own specialty. Baltimore National seemed like a city unto itself.

Her work was enjoyable once she got past the insane internship requirements. While assisting with surgical procedures, she also cared for the patients postoperatively. It made good sense to collaborate this way with patient care. However, often her work was discouraging. A large part of her patient load consisted of young men and women returning from the front in the Middle East conflict. Chemical warfare had left so many with massive burns. Others had lost limbs or were missing faces. Mercedes knew that there would be little chance for them to reenter the workforce other than as manual laborers, if they were capable physically of doing the work. The usual scenario was that they would end up in a veteran's home or rehab center for the rest of their lives. Those would be short.

In her second year at Baltimore National, she met a quiet young surgeon who would occasionally be the lead doctor in her surgical rotation. Dr. David Kim was sort of an enigma; reserved and aloof, he often answered questions with just a yes or a no. Most people thought he had too high an opinion of himself to speak to them. Others decided he was just overly analytical and could not connect with them on a personal basis. Mercedes, however, discovered the human side of him. He was enamored with politics and his two dogs, both things that she had a proclivity to enjoy. When he tore his Achilles tendon in a tennis match, Mercedes asked if she could walk his two golden retrievers in the morning before work and in the evening after she left the hospital.

"It really isn't an issue for me," she replied. "I exercise every day before and after work, so this will just be a variation to what I already do. Anyway, I miss my dog back home and this would be enjoyable for me. Do you want me to start this evening?"

"Sure. Try it out and see if it works. See you at six?"

When Mercedes arrived at Dr. Kim's house, she was stunned at the immensity of his home and the up-to-date accessories that graced every room. In these trying times, most everyone led such mundane lives and barely scratched by.

"Your home is absolutely a sight for sore eyes," she said demurely. "I haven't seen anything this magnificent since I was in Paris."

"Now what were you doing there?"

"Oh, I was a foreign exchange student through the Rotary Club the year after I graduated from high school. My host family lived on the edge of the city in the most amazing apartment. They were enthralled by my simple ways. Well, not enthralled, as they immediately set up a plan for me to get a bit more 'culture' in my life. It was a whirlwind year."

Mercedes blushed. She was thinking of the guided tours through the Louvre, Musee de l'Orangerie, and others with the uncle of her host family. He was a divorced gentleman in his early fifties who was swept off his feet by her simple American charm. His intensions were not chivalrous, but in the beginning, Mercedes could not have known.

"Did you study while you were there?"

"Yes, but mostly it was art history and the mercantile trade. I still love fashion when it is not too gaudy and has practicality about it. And my favorite hobby will always be an appreciation for the era of the Impressionists. I could stare at their paintings for hours on end and let my imagination run wild."

David seemed impressed by her surprising talents.

"Come into my bedroom and let me show you what I have been saving to impress the young ladies who stop in."

For a moment, Mercedes hesitated.

David laughed. "Trust me. It is just a painting. I don't move that fast."

Mercedes followed him into a lush retreat. A petite painting was sitting on a gilded stand next to the bed and held what she surmised was a Van Gogh copy. Despite the elegance of the room, this painting held her gaze as though she were hypnotized.

"My father gave this to me a year ago. Do you like the placement? I was not sure whether to put it over the bed or here next to it. I like to look at it when I get into bed after a weary day in the hospital."

Mercedes was spellbound and could not say anything for a moment.

"You mean this is an original? How could you afford it?"

With a chuckle, David shared that his father had been in the art auction business for decades and had purchased this painting when it came out of hiding. It was placed on the market by a private source. Through this means, he was able to afford the asking price. Mercedes assumed that a private dealer meant that someone had been in an unsavory business and had gotten caught. More than likely, it would be drugs or the sex trade or munitions or recycled military hardware.

But she could not keep her eyes off the painting. "It is amazing."

"Come on into the kitchen and let's have a drink. You must be as exhausted as I am after the day we had. What would you like? I've got martinis, wine coolers, and I make a really smashing margarita."

"That sounds perfect," said Mercedes, knowing that she rarely drank. She would sip it slowly. If anything, she preferred a glass of chablis but she wanted to impress Dr. David.

Thus began a long and involved relationship which sometimes was healthy and sometimes destructive. David had no interest in old-fashioned marriage. He himself had lived with parents who eventually got a divorce. In that process, his angry parents would draw him into their verbal battles which eventually morphed into a custody battle. He was always caught in the middle. Now that he was independent, he would have nothing to do with either of them other than an occasional phone call or an offer for peace and reconciliation, as the Van Gogh painting had been.

Once his tendon had completely healed, Mercedes continued to visit the house regularly under the guise of seeing the dogs she had grown attached to. Dating became a frequent activity for them, mostly just seeing a movie or going out to dinner. Occasionally they attended a reception at one of the art institutes in the area. One evening, they discussed the possibility of her moving in with him.

"Come on, Mercedes," coaxed David. "There's nothing wrong with moving in with me. I must take someone in soon to meet the two-family requirement for housing. Might as well be someone I like."

The problem for Mercedes was that she was not sure she loved him. In the back of her mind was a voice, probably her mother's, which said that this was not right. She pushed it as far down into her subconscious as she could.

In a variety of ways, being around him was a thrilling experience. He was daring in a quiet way and loved to push boundaries. Late at night, he would climb into his two-seater sports car and race through the streets of the city, ignoring the traffic signals if he had the chance. His love and support of the arts and the theater kept them in the center of gala events in Baltimore as well as in what seemed like a never-ending merry-go-round of patron receptions. Mercedes was thrown into a whole new life revolving around the ambiance of wealth and notoriety. She had never been in such an environment in which she interacted with the rich and the famous. It was attractive, and she felt that somehow, this increased her self-worth. Often at these events, she would think of her parents and her brother and their lives as simple people, withdrawn from civilized society. If they would only join her, she could show them a life that most envied.

The conversation at most parties centered on the arts or politics, and she found herself quite versed at both. David loved her as a decoration at his side. She was simply a natural beauty, even in the simple gowns she wore. Her time spent in Paris taught her how to accentuate the positive features of her figure. She also had a knack for picking out clothing that simply turned heads when she entered the room. Her svelte figure and long auburn tresses were also a magnet, but it was her smile that attracted others to their conversations, and it was the ice breaker David needed to gain attention and feel comfortable in the competitive circles.

He loved the comradery of these parties and being an expert in an elite field. Yet, his introvert personality kept him from being open to friendly conversation until he had had two or three drinks. In the interim, Mercedes could provide the back-and-forth repartee until his brain relaxed with the alcohol. Unfortunately, he often drank too much.

"So, who is this lovely lady?" asked Congressman Roker one evening.

"Oh, I found her in an operating room," chuckled David. "She needed some refining, but she is one top-notch nurse practitioner. Her family goes back to the hills of the Virginias. I still find her amusing when she falls back into her simple way of life. Check out her legs to make sure they are the same length from walking those hills."

The congressman gave her a good look from top to bottom, pausing a bit too long to admire her shapely figure. Mercedes made no move to discourage him and tried to smile.

"I'm not simple, David," she said, smiling coyly. "I always will treasure the life lessons I learned growing up. But I am past the shallowness and slowness of that type of existence. My family has no desire to move into the reality of the present. After staying in Paris, I realized I could never go back to that emptiness."

She turned back to the senator. "You know, I'm still trying to convince my family to move up here. There is so much opportunity in the city despite the crowds, and life is not as hard. I feel sorry for my parents. They are suffering and they don't need to be."

"Why in God's name would they stay in that godforsaken place?" asked the senator. "Well, I'm glad you made the smart move!" The emphasis of the last sentence caused a stream of spit to trail toward Mercedes. She just smiled as he looked her over. "I can tell you are quite intelligent despite your upbringing. Let me know if you want to move up from your regular job. We are always looking for additional medical personnel to be part of the Federated Health Task Force."

"I can imagine how difficult that would be. I see on the news that they are currently working to decide on the regulations for determining the viability of end-of-life care. How do you get guidance for something that distressing?" asked Mercedes with some compassion in her voice.

The senator could see that she was genuinely concerned. It was always helpful to have these types of people around in the office to deal with the public. He was working right now on an introduction to the public of his new program that would be compassionate and yet realistic. That was a good formula for escaping the wrath of the always crusading progressive warriors.

"Oh, it's not that difficult. We are moving to a one-size-fits-all system that uses age and a health assessment as a fixed checklist for care. It is simple and fair. But do not grow old on us. Seventy is the end of help." He laughed. "I'm sixty-five but thank God I work for the government. We have better choices." He laughed again. "Now don't forget to visit me sometime. I could use intelligent ladies to make my office a brighter place. If David moves on or if you do, I'll be available."

Mercedes turned a bit pink. "I appreciate the offer, Senator. Would it mean I would have to move to Atlanta?"

"Oh, don't worry about that. We have branch offices here in Washington and Baltimore, and much of the work we do is by tele-communication. What I really need is direction in how to roll out these plans so that they have a touch of compassion in them. The public thinks we are just sticking it to them. They do not get the fact that this is what they asked for in the last election. Everyone gets the same treatment. That's equity." He pulled a business card out of his pocket and handed it to her. He held her hand just a bit too long and then moved in and placed a slobbery kiss on her mouth. She gave no hint of the revulsion she felt.

Mercedes was taken aback. She knew the senator was married. Was this the lay of the land around here? She just could not decipher what was up in these Washington conversations. This reminded her of her host family's uncle back in Paris. She was just not good at figuring out what people were up to and what they genuinely thought. She had always been too trusting. It had already burned her several times. She hated herself for those mistakes.

"Don't think I'll let her go anytime soon," David chimed in. "She is valuable to me." He pulled Mercedes closer to his side. He was surprised that Mercedes was bothered by the overreaching friendliness of the senator. He moved on to the next group of friends with a wave.

"You are so old-fashioned, Mercedes. I hardly know anyone who lives in a single committed relationship anymore. Get with the program. Live a little. Do not get boring on me. I am in love with all life has to offer, and I do not want anyone dragging me down. Cheer up. You will never be boring. I know you have fire inside of you."

During the two years she was with David, Mercedes became involved in the Compassionate Church movement. David had no interest in a church group. He kidded her about the childishness of believing in a God, but she still had a desire to please the God she had known growing up in her father's church. This church had begun two decades earlier in Baltimore, gaining traction with social justice issues, particularly with minority populations and women. The movement was both active and abrasive at times. She marched for removing all restrictions on abortion, quotas for women in leadership positions, and an overhaul of the first amendment. Mercedes' mother often chided her in their phone conversations about her affiliation with the group.

Mercedes was always searching for the truth, and weekly participated in the back-and-forth chat room with the lead pastor. He liked her being there as she lent an air of sophistication and acceptance. Pastor Kidd had shared that they would be discussing the Holy Spirit and her role in the movement of their social justice campaign.

"So, you see," said Pastor Kidd, "that the Holy Spirit lends her credence and her power to what we are trying to accomplish in our society. She provides you with talents and gifts to change the world for the better. She is the one who has informed us of the evils of our society. Yet she does not leave us orphans. She moves through your gifts to change the world. That is really what we are all about. Isn't it great that this part of God can be in our camp?"

Behind Mercedes, a young man cleared his throat and asked a question. "I thought that we were to be concentrating on making disciples for Jesus as our primary focus as Christians. Why are we always trying to change the world, when we do not even seem to bring Him into the conversation? And if the Holy Spirit wants us to do something, won't He be the one who will inform us?"

Mercedes turned to look intently at the young man when he emphasized the gender of the Holy Spirit.

The pastor gave a condescending glace at the spirited man. "Why would we need to have people become Jesus' followers and just leave it at that? That would accomplish nothing. We need to concentrate on getting things done … on doing what He wants us to do. Don't worry about that evangelism stuff. If we can just go out and be a good neighbor and care, that is enough."

Mercedes thought about this response. "Then, do we need to know Jesus or just do Jesus works?" she posed.

"You are so old fashioned. I can see how you were brought up and that your faith focus was on knowing Jesus and being promised salvation. That does not get the job done. He is not going to change the world. We must do that. We've got this figured out and the Holy Spirit is just the girl to carry us in the right direction. Right, gang?"

"So, can everyone just do good works and fix this unjust society and that's enough?" asked the kid who was getting more perturbed by this line of theology.

"Yeah, I guess that is enough, as long as we accomplish something," said Pastor Kidd. "We've got to concentrate on injustice, not the tired fruitless subjects of holiness or salvation or even relationship. They have no connection with the young people of today. We want to change the world. We will do it."

Everyone clapped and the pastor smiled. He waved for the young man to come up for a little more private conversation, but he declined. She could hear him muttering about the Holy Spirit's gender and what the Bible stated. Something in Mercedes' mind felt troubled, but she could not put her finger on it. *What is wrong with me?* she mused. *He's right. We need to change the world.*

That night, she called her parents. Her mom picked up the phone and Mercedes shared the church activities with which she was involved.

"Mercedes, you are right to care for women and the distressed. But can't you see that many of your stands tend to separate us into groups rather than blend us together? How can you not defend those little babies? They are God's most precious gift to the world."

"Yeah, Mom, I see the way parents treat those 'precious' babies. They come into the hospital with burns, starved, ragged, used as sex toys. They would be better off dead."

"Well then, what good are you doing in that group or church fellowship? How are you helping besides screaming for various laws to be changed? Are you personally getting involved in any of the lives of people you are trying to better? Or is this more ideological?"

Mercedes usually got angry over her mother's accusatory tone. "I really am trying to help in my own way, Mama. I feel for these poor women who get trapped in a situation where there is no way out."

Mercedes knew from her medical work and her participation in surgical abortions provided by the government that the products she saw during surgery were human. She saw the movement, the kicking of legs and the flailing of arms before death came. What gave her nightmares were the movements of the fetuses, completely aware that something was gravely amiss, trying to save themselves as she extract-ed them from the uterus. She was trying to concentrate on making sure that they were harvested with all body parts intact so that they could be purchased for medical consumption. At least they were using the skin for the war's burn victims. Often a voice would be speaking to her, "Mercedes, how can you harm my children?"

She tried to drown it out, calling it a guilty conscience from her conversations with her mother. This made her even angrier. So, if the subject was broached in their weekly calls, she would cut it off and move onto more pleasant topics.

After two years with David, something changed. She did not know what it was, but she felt totally unsettled. Her mother was extremely ill with the same Drakee virus that was decimating much of the world population. It had finally found its way into the back country and was claiming victims but at a slower pace. She had not been able to obtain either the partially effective vaccine developed in the States or even enough antibiotic to help her fight the possibility of a bacterial in-fection. Mercedes felt helpless for the first time in her life. She took a two-week leave of absence to help assess her mother's health and do what she could to help her regain her strength.

"David, I need to leave for a few weeks to check on my mother. She is not doing very well with the Drakee virus and of course medications and medical care are nonexistent in that part of the country. I have already decided to apply for a leave of absence. Is that all right with you?"

"Well, you think your parents would come to their senses. Choosing to stay in the Middle Region is like suicide. They are plain stupid. I do not know how they got a daughter like you—smart and progressive. I just cannot understand why you think it is your responsibility to take care of her. Your brother can step in. Isn't it about time for them to move on anyway? Old people clog up the system."

Mercedes was stunned by his candor and lack of compassion.

"But she's my mother."

"I just don't care. I only care about you. Go if you must. I have plenty to keep me occupied while you are gone. Remember the big Baltimore Charity Art Auction is next week. We are hosting a table, remember? I am displaying my Van Gogh. Everyone is talking about it."

"You can do it without me. I'm sure you can find a co-host among your circle of friends." She had in mind the daughter of Senator Roker who liked to attach herself to David and cover him with compliments. He liked it.

***

Now she was back in the Virginias. The transition was stifling.

Sitting by her old poster bed each day, Abigail would ask Mercedes to read her favorite passages from the Bible. It was easy to pick them out. They were underlined in assorted color pens each time she chose to give them emphasis. The cover was brown leather, cracked and worn. Mercedes remembered that book from her childhood when her mother would faithfully carry it to church each Sunday morning. She could remember as a little girl pretending to read from it while her father was preaching.

Those two weeks turned into a month, then three months. In that time, there were continual conversations of a personal nature. It seemed strange to be sharing her inner thoughts with her mother, but in a way, it was also comforting. Her mother was a good listener. When Mercedes had finished with one diatribe or another, Abigail would calmly ask her daughter questions about her relationship with David, her involvement in the Compassionate Church or her stand on social issues. These questions made Mercedes think of why she felt as she did. They also made her substantiate her personal convictions which up to now had more than likely followed the popular narratives of culture.

At night after administering her mother's evening dose of the sleep medication she had managed to "lift" from the hospital storeroom before leaving Baltimore, her mother would be relieved for a moment from the crippling contractions of her lungs. Mercedes would often lie on her bed contemplating the scriptures or the discussions. She was finally giving herself time to think. Although she could have been depressed with the confusion that ran rampant in her mind, she felt a weight being lifted from her soul. It was as though she was finally seeing and hearing something she had been searching for her whole life–truth!

Could there actually be a God being like the Bible suggested? A God that informed a person with truth and righteousness? A Savior raised from the dead? She had been raised in the church. Often it was monotonous and tradition bound. Sometimes she was stunned at the meanness and pettiness of the congregation and how they often blamed her father for things that were problems of their own.

The church loved with a peripheral love but was never willing to get down to the dirty part of life. That was the preacher's job. The congregation talked a lot. They signed initiatives and started programs. But they never really got committed by facing the glaring needs of the world. They were too comfortable with themselves. This was the promise of the Compassionate Church, but somehow, they did not like to get down and dirty either. They were hypocrites like everyone else. They just did it with more flash and pizazz.

While she was at her parents, they received a phone call from her brother. Titus had been out in the Western States, dividing his time between rock climbing instruction and social work inner city ministry. He worked for a government agency called Next Day. It encouraged teens to change their destructive relationships with gangs or drugs in their communities and move to a new day where they could find alternatives. Often, he would bring bands of youth out to the wilds of the wilderness country and teach them the beginning elements of rock climbing, something that seemed insurmountable. He was good at it and the intended consequences of team building, focusing on goals and the deeper discussions of who really was in control of the world. Titus was a missionary in his own right.

But his progress was not celebrated by everyone in his office. He had twice been reprimanded and written up by his superiors.

"Titus, you know the rules. You cannot be teaching that there is a higher being called God with these kids. They are impressionable. You need to stay on script. You are going to destroy your career if you do not watch yourself. And really, I have little sympathy for people who let their religion dominate their lives. This is a final warning. Knock it off or you will be let go."

The next day, Titus gathered with the small clan in the Denver area that was his church family. "My dearest brothers and sisters, I want to share something personal with you. Sadly, I have been called away from this place and this ministry. I am going to miss this gathering of the faithful. For the last few weeks, Jesus has been showing up at night and asking me to tend to his sheep in Nepal. They are being terrorized and eliminated. He wants to use my mountain climbing skills to help our brothers and sisters in Christ escape the ravages of persecution in China. I am going to be part of a team that spirits those lucky enough to escape over the mountains and off to freedom."

The Gathering did not say anything. As a group, they knelt around Titus. "We are called to anoint you in your mission for our Lord," said one of the women in attendance. "You know the cost. You know that He has called you according to His perfect plan. In His Mighty Name we anoint you with the oil of His grace to do the work set before you.

May the Lord exhibit His Mighty Power and provide you with His providential protection. May His light shine over you on the steep mountain trails. May you be guided over every step of your journey by the wisdom of the Holy Spirit and may you hear His voice loud and clear."

The following hour of praise and worship covered Titus in a supernatural aura of His Presence. They all sensed it. He was called. The Lord would be by him as a shepherd guards his sheep. Titus was the most excited of those gathered. He was off to do his life's work.

He called his parents the next day. "Mom and Dad, I am quitting my day job to answer a call to ministry. The long and the short of it is that I have been called to Nepal to help the persecuted Christians in China. God is giving me this opportunity to help His children on the Chinese border escape into Nepal and then to be escorted to a safe independent country. I am excited, feeling this calling as my purpose in life."

In the discussion he was matter of fact. He had to go. Jesus Himself had appeared in a dream and told him he was needed in these mountains of Nepal. The people there were calling his name. He planned to come home for a two-month visit, pack his bags and head east ... far east.

"Son," said Virgil, "you must answer the Lord's call. There is no turning back. He will honor your submission and your sacrifice. We will start lifting you up for wisdom and protection. May God have mercy on you now and in the days to come. Your mother and I love you, Titus."

Abigail added with trembling lips, "Titus, we love you. As parents, we want you to stay safe in our little world. But you are a man who is wise beyond your years. God has a plan for you, and we will not interfere, despite the worry and the danger. We know that Jesus has you in His hands no matter what happens. Dear son, we are proud that you have been called to do this special mission work. What a privilege to give your life and your dreams to God. May He always stay in your sights. We will see you soon. Can't wait to hug you, you gentle giant."

Both Mercedes and her parents knew that this venture was going to put his life in danger. They knew it was their job to pray for protection and to encourage him in his weakness.

Chapter 8

Titus Singleton

Spring 2034

"And I will ask the Father, and he will give you another advocate to help you and be with you forever – the Spirit of truth. The world cannot accept him, because it neither sees him nor knows him. But you know him, for he lives with you and will be in you." John 14:16-17

Titus' return for a two-month visit with his mother Abigail was a turning point in Mercedes' life.

Each night when their father, Virgil, had nodded off in his easy chair in one of his very ancient tweed sweaters, Titus and his mother would sit in the corner nearest the wood stove in two comfortable corduroy chairs. Titus first made sure the stove was drawing well and that all the smoke escaped up the pipe so that his mother's breathing was a bit relieved. Then he lovingly read favorite passages from Abigail's Bible. Most often a faint smile appeared in the corners of her mouth despite the obvious pain she was enduring. Mercedes would sit opposite them, busying herself with a hand-held project, repairing a hem in her father's pants, writing letters, or reading. She could not send David daily emails or cell phone calls due to the lack of reliable electricity. He could not understand.

Walt always hung out on the edge of these family times, not sure where he fit in. He volunteered to clean up after dinner and then sat quietly in the corner. Now that Titus was home, Walt moved temporarily back into the shed. He did not mind at all.

But Titus and Abigail, son and mother, had a special bond which made their conversations a small glimpse into heaven. They would talk for hours, Titus contributing a large part of the sharing. Often, he repeated the story of his journey to a place where he knew Jesus was real in his life.

For all his growing up years, he could recall something special about Jesus, but now he was sold out to living a life directed by someone who had taken on Presence. And that Presence had set him on fire.

He shared with his mother conversations or directions he had received from the Holy Spirit and visions he had had on rock-climbing expeditions. "Do you know, Mom, that once a group of angels stopped me on a mountainside cliff and warned me about the rocks that were just about to break off over my head. I never climbed down so fast. Just as I reached the bottom, down came a thundering boulder the size of a car. I could do nothing but get down on my knees and shake like a leaf, thanking the Holy Spirit and the angels for saving my life."

Titus spoke so tenderly of the presence of the Holy Spirit that Mercedes thought he was in love. Well, in a way he was, because his life was now caught up in walking in the footsteps of another.

Mercedes' mom occasionally asked questions, but she usually just listened to Titus' amazing journey into the Spirit world. She did not seem at all surprised when Titus gave more details into the Nepalese call that he had received. "In the dream, a Christian of Nepal ... how I knew he was a Christian I do not know, I just knew it. Well, anyway, this man seemed desperate. He kept waving at me to come, motioning me toward him insistently. Then he pointed to the rocky crags of the Himalayas behind him and made the sign of the cross.

"That dream was so real that when I woke up, I knew I had a clear message from the Spirit. He was calling me specifically. I did just a tad bit of research and was able to find a link to a Nepalese Christian Church that is part of the international outreach to the persecuted church from the faith home I attend, True Identity Fellowship. A phone call or two and arm twisting with government officials took me to the Nepalese contact and guess what? When I patched in a video call with him, it was the man I saw in my dream! He told me that on the night I had my dream, he also dreamed that I was coming, and he knew that I would be contacting them soon, for he knew God answered prayers. In fact, he had so much faith, that he told the other believers that God was already preparing me for my journey, and I would arrive at the appointed time in His time schedule. What faith! How can I desert these people?"

"Do you know how dangerous that part of the world is right now?" asked Mercedes, cutting in on the private conversation. "And it's not like you can blend in with the locals. Look at you. Extremely tall, white skin, light brown hair, and blue eyes. You will stick out like a sore thumb! And," she continued, "the Chinese government is cracking down on any Christian trying to escape their country. With their most recent purge of the faithful, they shoot first, as you know, and ask questions later. They have Nepal in their sights and really control their puppet government. There is even a Chinese flag flying over the capitol. Why do you think you won't get caught and what help can you be to them anyway?"

Mercedes was angry with the fact that her normally down-to- earth brother was considering a mission that would be precarious at best but would probably cost him his life.

"These Nepalese Christians risk their lives, leading believers daring to escape China, over the rugged terrain. I cannot share any details, but there is an underground system that gets those who do escape to a neutral country. My mountain-climbing expertise is being used by none other than the Holy Spirit. You know, Mercedes, that He will be with me. Don't fear what might happen. He does provide a hedge of protection."

"You'll never come back," she said, her voice rising.

Abigail had tears in her eyes, but she opened them wearily and spoke to Mercedes. "There comes a time in our lives when we must put away our childish ways and follow the Lord. He does not typically call us to the easy journey but to His service. He has come to your brother in the presence of the Holy Spirit, and He has called him for His kingdom. That is what life with Him is all about. Your brother is ready and willing, and the Spirit knew he would not have to do a great deal of coaxing. You realize that we stayed in Whitsville for the same reason. The Holy Spirit said to me, 'So many lambs are hungry. Feed them at home.' We could not leave our flock. It is our duty and our calling." Then she closed her eyes in exhaustion.

Titus pulled the afghan up over his mother, gently picked her up and carried her to the bedroom. She was lighter than a feather and he noticed how slight she had become in her illness. When he returned, he said, "Mercedes, don't fear for my safety. God will take care of me. He is sending me to our brothers and sisters in Christ who are trying to escape with their lives from the Chinese Army. Someone with the right set of skills and connections needs to help them. God needs people to step in and be His hands and feet and His heart. I am happy, even thrilled to have heard Him speak my name. Now I need to follow no matter the consequence." He said in his more normal jovial tone, "We all know where we're going to end up anyway, so your map and my map lead to the same destination. I might just get there earlier than you." He touched her softly on the arm.

"Sis, can you patch my jeans over there on the chair? I'm going to the ten-year reunion of the 2024 State Champion Football Team at Whitsville High School tomorrow night," he said with overemphasized puffed-up gestures. "I want to look presentable."

"Well, you won't look presentable with those old pants. You will look like a tattered mountain climber. Get those new Dockside pants out of the closet that mom bought you two years ago. She would be so happy to see you finally wearing something she thought you would look good in. They should fit. She wasn't happy when she saw you had left them behind after another slim year of Christmas gifts."

"I hate getting dressed up. It's not me."

"Make Mom happy … and me. It really is not so bad. You might find that you look so good that an exquisite female will saunter over and say, 'Who's that really handsome fella on the team?'"

He looked at her with brotherly affection.

"You know, I used to get dressed up in gowns and fancy clothes almost every week. I was even considered the belle of the ball at times according to some of the compliments I received."

Titus appeared shocked. His sister, a society girl?

"Yes, you know my live-in boyfriend, David. Well, he is connected to the Baltimore/Washington society crowd through his support of the arts. He is just enthralled about art exhibits, the Impressionists and New Age drawing. So, we often find ourselves hobnobbing with the jet setters. It's been eye opening for me."

"Do you like that sort of thing?"

"Well, to be honest, at first I loved it. We were having conversations with people you see on the news. And it was a chance for me to feel like a princess, dressing up and being with my own Prince Charming. David is shy, but he is so enthusiastic about art and politics that he attracts people to him like a magnet. He always liked me to be the ice breaker and charmer in the group. Once things were warmed up, he could continue with the best of them; especially if he had a couple of drinks to loosen his inhibitions. He really is not a bad person. I do love him in some ways."

"I don't think he's good for you. His life sounds kind of empty."

"Oh, don't judge him too harshly. He saves lives every week in the Emergency Room through his medical prowess. He is an amazing surgeon, especially with facial reconstruction. He has a gift."

"Does he know anything about God? Does he have any faith background?"

"Well, no. And he does not care to. He thinks I am feebleminded when I go to church. He just does not get the fact that there can be something else out there that he doesn't understand. Frankly, it has put a distance between us. He thinks it makes me too sober minded to be thinking of religion, God, purpose, and death. But somehow, I cannot escape thinking on these things. I've tried."

"God has His grip on you, Mercedes. Like me, you have your own miraculous call. Trust me."

"You are funny, Titus. Go your way to Nepal. Do not expect me to come rescue you. You know I'll give you a lecture when I do." She laughed a merry laugh and gave him her best sisterly squeeze. "Now I'm serious. Don't take unnecessary chances. Promise me?"

"Okay, Sis. Pinkie promise." It was their way of saving precious promises from childhood. They both giggled.

Mercedes proceeded to tell him about the rest of her life in Baltimore with her live-in boyfriend David, her church, and even her emptiness. It felt good to share this time of excitement and despair with someone who genuinely cared about her and not about appearances. Well, sort of on the appearances. It had been so long since she had made an honest appraisal of her life, what she had been doing and where she was going, that the conversation was like a troublesome weight lifted off her soul. Titus made it so easy to be honest. He listened for the most part and asked questions of Mercedes that she was forced to answer for herself.

Two days later when Titus and Mercedes were washing the dishes, he said, "Guess who asked about you at the football reunion?"

Mercedes tried not to blush. She got control of her thoughts. "Who? No idea."

"Come on. He's had his eye on you for ten years, since you were a freshman passing him some browned potatoes."

Mercedes knew who he was talking about. Mack Gersham. "What's he up to?" she murmured.

"Who?" joked Titus.

"Mack Gersham, I suppose." Mercedes smiled in return.

"Yep, lucky guess. He is working in Washington now at the Pentagon for General Marcus Hamilton. Been there for a year working on communications and what he calls 'top secret intelligence.' Well, he didn't say the second part, but he always changed the subject whenever someone asked for more details as to what he actually did, so I guessed it was something that the public was not privy to."

"What about his private life?" Mercedes was curious but tried to ask very casually.

"Don't know. He mentioned an ex, so I guess he must have been married at one time. When you mention 'ex' most people like to move on from that subject too. But I did hear from the other guys that he had met her in the Army, but she had been killed in the Middle East war after they had divorced. It was a short marriage. Guess it's hard when you both are in the military and caught up in armed combat. That doesn't make for a quiet home life where you chat about the weather and the dog."

"Did anyone ask you why you're not married?" joked Mercedes. *Really,* she thought, *Titus is about the best catch a girl could want … smart, athletic, caring, and full of exciting adventures and the best storyteller I've ever heard.*

"Mack was asking the same question … about you! I told him you had a doctor friend you were close to for a while, but that the relationship was most likely ending."

Mercedes seemed embarrassed and Titus wisely changed the subject.

"What do you think about Mom, Mercedes? You have better medical expertise than I do about her prognosis."

"Well, her time is short," she said matter of factly. "Probably less than a month. Should we say something to Dad? I just cannot think of him being by himself. How is he going to survive on his own? Mom really kept everything in order around here."

"I don't know what to do with Dad." Titus frowned. It was so unnatural. He was struggling with his call to Nepal. Should he postpone that for a while and help the folks? He knew this was something he would have to include in his evening prayers for tonight.

"Do you think Walt can fill in for me?"

Chapter 9

Mack Gersham

2025
9 Years Earlier

"I will not leave you as orphans; I will come to you." John 14:18

When he turned eighteen in his senior year, Mack walked into the Army recruitment center and signed up on the spot. He did not need his dad's approval. He wanted to get as far away from Whitsville and booze bottles and dirty dishes and sympathetic stares as fast as he could. His only concern was his twin brother. How could Walt survive? Mack had always protected Walt from his father's wrath, which was usually directed at Mack. With his departure for the Army at the end of the school year, he was concerned. He had a plan. He just could not bring himself to carry it out.

Four weeks after he graduated, he was notified of the date when he would be required to show up for boot camp. He called three of his buddies, and they went out to celebrate as any eighteen-year-old would do in such a situation. They reveled in an evening of raucous behavior as they went from bar to bar getting intoxicated. When he came home from joy riding with his friends, he was drunk. He was angry at himself for starting to act like his father, angry when Walt sauntered in and asked him why he was weaving around so much while trying to get ready for bed.

"Shut up," said Mack. "Stop trying to take care of me. You need to take care of yourself now. I'm leaving."

"Yeah, I know," murmured Walt. "I'm not stupid. There's just something I need to talk to you about."

"Tomorrow," said Mack sleepily. "I got to get my wits about me. I feel like hell."

Walt had smelled the booze on him too. It scared him to think that his brother might turn out like his dad. "Do you think I could join the Army and go with you?"

Mack heard him but did not reply. *Can't break the kid's heart,* he thought. *That would be a hot day in hell when I would do that.*

When Mack crawled out of bed the next morning, he knew he needed something to eat. Hopefully Walt had something ready on the stove, which was standard fare at their house. He saw Walt carrying water from the pump outside, but something was wrong. Walt's face was all swollen on the left side and his eye was purple and half closed. It was not Walt's normal left-side lopsidedness. He now looked like a monster kids would run from as he looked up with the distorted face and the crooked gait.

"What the hell happened to you?"

"Oh, nothing." He couldn't keep a secret; never could. "Dad just lost his temper when you weren't here to drive him to Adam's Bar, so he took it out on me last night. I told him you were all grown up and could do whatever you wanted. He told me to find you. I wouldn't, so he took a swing at me. Guess you didn't notice when you came in last night. You were soused. Dad finally fell asleep in his chair after drinking the bottle and cursing me out for like an hour. I left him there. He's still out and it's best we leave him that way, the old bastard."

Mack turned around and looked over the front room with a look on his face that frightened Walt. "He'll never do that again. Come on. Let's go to town for breakfast at the new diner. I need something in my stomach. Get cleaned up. I'll drive. And I'll treat."

In ten minutes, they were climbing into Mack's beat-up Impala. It still had a fine engine and ran almost as well as when it was new. He babied that car. "Just a minute. I got to get my wallet," yelled Mack as he headed back into the house. He was gone about ten minutes. Walt hummed an old country western tune from the radio he had heard that morning. As he looked up in the rearview mirror, he saw that Mack was carrying a full Army knapsack. "You are leaving already? Is this our goodbye meal?"

"Not quite yet. Just decided I had better start packing as boot camp is next week and I don't want Pa throwing away the stuff I need before I leave. I'll finish packing my stuff tomorrow." He stepped on the gas and dust flew into the windows. Walt loved speed as much as Mack. His face was filled with pure joy.

"Look, I'm flying," said Walt as he flapped his arm out the car window.

Both boys howled in delight. Mack threw his arm out the left window and provided the other wing. *I'm free,* he thought.

While they were eating breakfast, the sheriff's car pulled up to the diner. "You boys come with me," he ordered.

"We ain't stole no car," smiled Walt. But he thought about how fast they had been speeding into town.

The sheriff motioned with his thumb for the two boys to get into the squad car. They both silently climbed into the back seat, and then the sheriff raced up the hill with two ambulances and a fire truck on their tail. "What's goin' on, Sheriff?" asked Mack matter of factly.

"Your place is on fire."

"No, Dad!" cried Walt.

They climbed out amid the tangle of rescue vehicles spraying water on what little was left of their once dilapidated farmhouse. Walt was wailing and Mack was holding him back from trying to race into the house.

"Any idea how this started?" quizzed the sheriff.

"I was going to cook some eggs and bacon for me and Mack and Dad this morning," said Walt. "I might have turned on the burner for the stove. I don't remember. He was smoking' and drinkin' and yellin' almost the whole night. He was at his finest. I didn't notice any lit cigarettes when I was in the kitchen, but he could have been smokin' before he dozed off. The house always smells like cigarettes."

"Where did you get that shiner?" asked the sheriff.

Walt dropped his gaze to the table.

Mack cut in. "I thought it would be nice to treat Walt to a breakfast at the diner this morning since I'm leaving soon, and he looked like he could use some time away from Dad. I should have been home last night to make sure Walt was okay, but instead I was off with my friends. I just thought he could use some cheering up and I needed to apologize for not taking better care of him."

The sheriff got the gist of the conversation. He looked disgusted. "Your dad probably fell asleep with a lit cigarette. It must have either dropped to the floor or into his chair. I will investigate when the fire's out. Sorry, boys."

He walked over to talk to the firefighters. They had made a preliminary foray into the front of the house to see what had happened. Talking to the sheriff, they said, "Looks like he didn't even know a fire had started. He is still sitting in his chair ... what's left of him. Probably stone drunk as usual. There are a couple of empty bottles near his chair on the floor."

The sheriff came back to the place where Walt was crying softly, and Mack was staring stone-faced at the smoldering ruins. "You boys need a place to spend the night? I will check in with the pastor to see if you can stay in his shed where he puts up company. I think it's empty right now."

The boys got into the sheriff's car, picked up Mack's car, and headed back up the hill to the pastor's house. Walt ended up staying there as the caretaker for the house and the church. He was a godsend.

As Mack was preparing to leave for boot camp, the Singletons came out to say goodbye.

Pastor Singleton gave Mack a firm handshake. "Son, I'll be keeping you and your brother here in my prayers. It has been a mighty tough couple of weeks for you, losing your dad, your house, and so many memories. It's a real tragedy, and I hope you know that God has known what's been going on in your hearts and is there to bind up the brokenness."

Mack had to bite his lips so as not to straight-out laugh. His memories were bitter and hopefully soon forgotten.

"But good comes out of the ashes," continued Pastor Singleton. "Having Walt come to help us out is a miracle from God. He can now do the physical work that Titus has been responsible for, since Titus will be leaving for college shortly. And I am sure Walt will find a welcoming home here. We will treat him like family."

Yeah, thought Mack sarcastically, *some miracle.* He had wished that Mercedes would be around to see him off to boot camp, but she was not around the house that morning, as she had gone shopping in Roanoke with friends. *Just as well,* he thought.

Chapter 10

Mack Gersham

2025-2034

*"When the Advocate comes, whom I will send to you
from the Father - the Spirit of truth who goes out
from the Father- he will testify about me." John 15:26*

The U.S. Army wanted a few good men, and they got one with Mack Gersham. He found basic training that year, 2025, physically challenging, but he was quite prepared. His football conditioning helped as well as his ability to compartmentalize and access whatever came his way as his formula for surviving. Some of his peers were not so lucky.

Mack ended up in technology training as he had an aptitude for computers and programming. By the time he was sent overseas, the war that had started as a local conflict in '24 was already engulfing the Middle East region in chaos and bloodshed. He was second in command in the Bureau of Cyber Security at his current assignment within the Army's deployed unit. Their camp in the desert was secure, but no soldier ever slept soundly. Quite often during the night, Mack was awakened by the sounds of explosions or gunfire, or to man the communication lines if top-secret messages needed to be transmitted. These were communications between the top generals and the chief of staff in Washington. Often, after the calls or face time/real time communications were complete, the staff would work far into the night, repositioning their battle plans or reworking their strategic plans to figure out what was next in a war that could not be won.

It amazed him that the fighting men and women from the opposing forces known as the United Arab Alliance showed no care for their personal safety. They were determined to drive out the Western interlopers for the last time. The casualties from their suicide bombings kept rising. For every one of them, they could usually take out at least ten or twenty Coalition soldiers. Often these enemy soldiers had embedded themselves in the Coalition troops as friendly or neutral players, trying to just get ahead in the world. No one dared to trust anyone anymore. It was kill or be killed. This was deadly for morale. It proved doubly difficult for local security forces who were dedicated to the allied forces to be trusted. Yet, the general insisted that they remain in their midst, as they were their most valuable asset in scoping out the plans of the enemy. He had no other choice.

Mack often wondered about working with Shamir Wells, General Hamilton's chief of staff. Yet Shamir seemed completely trustworthy and a bit enamored by the notoriety of his position. One thing was sure. He was totally dedicated to the general in all aspects of his life. When the general breathed, he breathed.

It was during these late-night events that Mack began to build a relationship with General Hamilton who had worked hard to gain his four stars. He had risen to his position purely through pluck and intelligence. He was adept at wielding power when needed but was also willing to listen to those who disagreed with his plans. At times, Hamilton would be completely at odds with General Lu in

Washington, but in the end, he was always aware that Lu outranked him, and that the final decision would rest with Lu.

Lu trusted Hamilton to make him look good, portray strength through appearance, and not cause too much stir in the world. Hamilton on the other hand had a deep desire to finish the job of eradicating the Arab Alliance and its desire to eliminate Israel and its allies from existence. He also knew that those local spies who had taken a chance on befriending the Western Alliance would be unprotected once the troops returned home.

"Listen, General Lu. I can't just discard these assets who have given us their allegiance," Hamilton had argued. "They have been serving as our translators and intelligence gatherers for years. We would all be dead if they hadn't let us know what was happening within the Arab Alliance. We just can't leave them to certain death when we pull out. Not only will they be mercilessly killed, but so will their families. We owe them something."

"I don't care about those people," Lu countered. "They did what they wanted to do. We must protect our soldiers first. Leave them behind. It is always risky to save people like that. They cannot be trusted. It's better that we give them up rather than risk our own." He was willing to sell out their loyalty for appearances. "Now get our people home," he said. "That is your top priority while we sort out this sham of a peace process. Peace, bullshit!"

The preliminary peace treaty was signed. It was a bitter pill for Hamilton to acknowledge. They were selling out the few friends they had protected. It made him sick, so he worked diligently behind the scenes to provide safe transit for the network of spies and translators and their families to bring them to the States and settle them in as new citizens. He was not going to leave any man behind. They could be valuable assets in the future if things kept unraveling at the Pentagon.

Within six months of their retreat in late 2033, the Arab Alliance overran half of Israel. The land was reclaimed by The Palestinian Union as their new homeland. Jews were forced to flee for their lives to what remained of their tiny nation. Jerusalem again became a walled city, separating Jewish and Palestinian territories. Many of the displaced Jews returned to their homes of origin, but others determined that their homeland in Israel would be the place to take their last stand. A small peace-keeping force stayed behind, maintaining stability in what remained of Israel.

Mack Gersham returned to the States with the last division of American Allied troops along with General Hamilton and Shamir Wells. Although they were fired upon as they left Israeli air space, the recently installed anti-missile jamming devices did their job and their military transport returned home safely. The missile fell into the sea. Mack realized how critical this innovative technology would be in the days ahead to keep the world at peace. With the support of General Hamilton, he reenlisted in the Army and became an employee within the Homeland Security division which General Hamilton now chaired.

One evening late in May 2034, when he warily stumbled home to the residence he shared with another military family, there was a soft knock on the door. His video camera picked out the face of General Hamilton and Mack opened the door in surprise. Without saying a word, the general slipped in and closed the door himself. Then he put his finger to his lips, motioned to the back door, and grabbing Mack's coat along the way, coaxed him out the back door into a dark sedan parked inconspicuously behind the garage.

It was the beginning of Mack's work as an undercover spy within the department of Homeland Security and the American Government.

Chapter 11

Mercedes Singleton

April 2034

"It is for your good that I am going away. Unless I go,
the Advocate will not come to you; but if I go, I will send him to you.
When he comes, he will prove the world to be wrong about sin
and righteousness and judgment." John 16:7-8

The darkness was beginning to invade her soul. It felt like the old tents they used to make out of blankets as kids. Everything was one shade of slate when she returned to Baltimore after her mother's death. Mercedes was plagued with thoughts about the meaning of life, God, Spirit, religion, faith, and re-birth. She had nailed all of these as she left home, at least with theological assumptions. She decided to try her best to be a good and honest person and knew she was in a profession known for its kindness, sacrifice, and compassion. Were these enough to be acceptable to God? She had been convinced that she had a ticket to heaven, knowing she was good.

But after the weeks of conversation with her mother and brother Titus, she was no longer sure. There was no way she was even remotely on the same page. Brownie points for heaven were of no interest to either of them. Rather, their conversations focused on who you are or whose you are as objects of what matters in faith. From those foundational truths, the relationship and the revelation of a new life would flow. Titus got it. Mercedes was troubled. Had she deceived herself into thinking all was well with her soul?

These next eighteen months were going to be the most trying year and a half of her life. She had terminated her live-in arrangement with David while she was still back in Whitsville. It was not hard. He understood that she was distancing herself.

"David, I just don't think we are made for each other. I have had a lot to think about since my mother died, and I need some space to get myself oriented again."

"Well, Mercedes, I wish I could help you, but as you know, I am headed out to California to take that head surgeon job at San Francisco International Health Center. It is a once in a lifetime opportunity that I just cannot pass up. They're providing lots of perks for me to move too."

"I wish you the best. Are you going to have a connection to the arts community there as well?"

Mercedes wondered if there were groups of supporters continuing to sponsor the arts still around in these economically depressed times.

"Of course. They have already invited me to their first grand gala of the year. But I will miss you, my sweet. You always made those soirees so enjoyable. You are so lovely. And so easy to get to know. What am I going to do without my little ice breaker?" David chuckled quickly and uncomfortably.

Mercedes did not say that she had heard through their friends that the senator's daughter was also taking a position in the same medical facility. She knew he had already lined up the next lovely to grace his side. It made her sad and a bit envious for a moment. She was willingly allowing that life of luxury and excess to slip away. But it did not take her long to regain her thoughts.

"What are you going to do with the dogs? I have missed them so much."

"I've given them to a friend in Baltimore. I will not have time for them. Finding exercise facilities for myself in San Francisco will be tough for me, much less for Isabella and Ferdinand. Listen, I will give you a call when I get settled in. You can have your friends come by this week for your things from the house before the moving van arrives. Hope you find everything you want out of life. Do not take it all so seriously, Mercedes. Love you."

And he was gone—for good. He never called and Mercedes did not miss his charm or his connections.

The state of the country was anything but stable. These were nicknamed the Chaos Years for good reason. Before anyone could realize what was happening, the National Guard had been called in by the president to enforce additional laws of the Emergency Relocation Doctrine crafted by President Santaya Woodring and her cabinet. It was touted as the "compassionate and patriotic" way to house the tens of thousands, soon to be millions, who were rapidly moving to the sanctioned metropolitan centers. Militants all over the country protested with shows of force or patriotic gatherings. The country narrowly missed entering a civil war and most likely would have found itself in conflict had it not been for the catastrophic effects of the volcanic explosion that sapped the energy from their riotous assemblies. People were too busy trying to survive to fight for what they once had. It was the perfect opportunity for the government to seize complete power over the lives of American citizens in the name of a national emergency.

All people moving to these centers were required to register, given a government identification chip in either the hand or chin, and assigned work. Mercedes' hospital became a troubled war zone as employees, scores of them uneducated and at times unmotivated, were dumped into the medical complex. Often, they mixed up medications, questioned the decisions of medical personnel, and disrupted rather than assisted in the patients' care. Mercedes herself was frustrated with the time she had to spend each day training new employees who seemed little interested in providing medical assistance for the sick. She was blessed however to be on day shift where the climate was more concentrated on providing medical care rather than the turmoil of job training and personnel issues, or worse yet, the night shift.

She was totally exhausted each evening as she relaxed her aching body after a fourteen-hour shift. Her tired legs screamed for mercy when she finally settled into her one soft easy chair. It was the only luxury she had in her cramped bedroom. The view out the window never changed. A tiny bungalow sat across the street with overgrown shrubs and a peeling black door barely hanging onto its hinges. It looked like how she felt. She hardly knew her housemates, a newly married couple. No one wanted to get close to anyone else, for distrust was the foundation for all personal interactions. An awkward kitchen occasionally brought them together hastily preparing a dinner meal. Usually, they could smell each other's cooking and chose to wait until the other party was finished. Mercedes was thankful that their home was unnaturally quiet in the evening. Her brain could mellow out.

There were hospital employees with whom she felt a connection in an inexplicable way. One was Olivia Polysoing, who worked as a prep nurse in the surgery center. Although shy, she had initiated the first conversation between the two of them, and after their first surgery together, she invited Mercedes to join her for lunch in the cafeteria.

The more Mercedes got to know Olivia, the more curious she became as to Olivia's background and her ability to put a positive spin on the world rolling out of control around them. There seemed to be no means of making independent decisions anymore. Olivia's sunny disposition seemed to take it all in stride.

"I was born in Cambodia twenty-four years ago. Things there were unbelievably turbulent. The Communist government kept us under their control and regularly came and stole from my father's business. He usually did not say anything, because he knew that he would be putting our family at risk. One day, after our first harvest of the year, the local governor sent his men to my father's small factory in Phnom Penh. He packaged and shipped rice to international localities through ports in Singapore. The governor demanded that half the profit made from the sales be sent to his office immediately. My father agreed but said that the profits from his spring sale would not be realized until the products reached their shipping destination. It was agreed that my father would have a month to access the funds. But the world turmoil slowed down the shipping markets, and the rice still sat in the harbor warehouse.

"My father tried to explain the situation to the thugs who came to his factory, but they dragged him away and called him a traitor. We never saw him again, and we were put under observation since they thought we would eventually get the money coming to us. My mother knew how extremely dangerous our situation was, so she made plans for us to individually find safe places to hide. She also took the threats of the governor seriously when his soldiers threatened to sell me into the sex market trade to China as partial payment for the money he never received. She took me to the International Rescue Mission in the city where they assisted in rescuing girls from the sex trade. She made sure that I was given a false identity to keep me safe. She also left them with the little money she had hidden for emergencies as a payment for my first month's care. There were no questions asked.

"I was only ten, and at the time she promised that she would see me on a regular basis, but it soon became apparent that my mother had left me for good. I realized that by being anonymous, I would have a chance of being saved when the government agents arrived and demanded fees for keeping the orphanage up and running.

"I was shown love and care at the orphanage, but I also was lonely. And I wondered what happened to my mother and my brother. I truly felt like an orphan. I spent a lot of time praying that my brother would not join the insurgent militia like so many of his peers. They were wicked and heartless. But where did young men who had no place else to go find acceptance?

"At the mission house, I was taught self-esteem, grooming, hygiene, and cooking. It was a special day when we would have visiting mission teachers who would stay with us periodically to teach the Bible, English, and math. One of those teachers, Beverly Stapanski, took a liking to me and my interest in math. I remember the first day she taught our class. She was tall and striking and had blonde hair. I felt like she was an angel, and I did not hear a word she said. We spent extra class time together learning the basics of mathematics and when she left for a sabbatical to the States, she asked if she could adopt me and take me with her. The directors gave their approval, but they all knew it hinged on receiving clearance for adopting a Cambodian child. The government would expect a hefty kickback for processing.

"In some ways I was extremely excited about this gesture. I could go to the United States and not have to live a life of fear. But I was also unhappy. I wanted to know what had happened to my mother and brother. I did not want to leave them behind. It did not seem fair that I should be saved when there was no way to know of their welfare. I became angry at the God who was taught to me at the Mission House. They said He cared for me, but He could not even give me my family back. I really did not have any choice. I finally got cleared by the government to go with Miss Bev when they received their payment for adoption.

"Am I boring you?" asked Olivia, looking at Mercedes through soft black lashes tinged with moisture.

"Oh goodness, no," Mercedes responded. "I realize that your life and mine have both taken quite different paths. How did you survive?"

"It was not easy. The first couple of months at Miss Bev's home were exceedingly difficult. I had decided that I would never love anyone again. I was broken by my birth mother's abandonment, and so I decided that I would cut her off emotionally. In my mind there was the probability that Miss Bev would someday leave me at some mission house when things became difficult for her as well.

"It was in the home church of Miss Bev's that I first felt the influence of the presence of Jesus. I wanted to feel nothing, and I often was standoffish with people whose intentions were good, but still attempted to invade my space. I loathed myself when I experienced emotion. I willed myself to feel nothing.

"Somehow time began to heal my soul. I began to trust Miss Bev and the teachers at Overland Community Church here in Baltimore. One evening in a conference for renewal, a guest speaker from Vietnam came and spoke on healing and reconciliation. A victim of street gangs and violence, she had been left to die on a dirty, deserted street after a particularly bloody weekend between rival drug gangs. She had been knifed several times in the abdomen and almost bled to death. Like me, she pulled back from the world and mentally put herself in a cocoon to protect what little identity she had left. As she healed in a substandard hospital, she was ministered to by a nurse who had become a Christian. This nurse had also withstood danger, persecution, and trauma, yet she was different.

"Then the speaker shared how she was given the opportunity to finally feel real love from someone who was a stranger. Her attending nurse not only healed her physical wounds but spoke of a means of healing the emotional running sores which festered in her mind.

"I was in tears. My heart was reeling, pounding so that the blood was banging on my eardrums. When the guest speaker led the group into a series of prayers to forgive those who had hurt us, I did not want to forgive, but I saw her face. She was free and I wanted to remove the straightjacket that I had put around myself. I let my guard down long enough to ask the Lord to heal my sobbing heart. He did so on the spot.

"I couldn't believe how free I felt immediately. It was like I had had a life sentence commuted and the prison doors had opened wide for me to escape. I cried such deep sobs and with each gulp of air, a piece of anger, disillusionment, and desertion left me. I went someplace that I had never been before. It was a place of healing, and a presence came over me that I could only describe as pure light and acceptance. There was absolute beauty in this light, and it touched me and changed who I thought I was into who I really was. Finally, when I opened my eyes, I realized that I had been on the carpeted floor up near the altar.

"I reached up to be lifted off the floor and rejoiced with my new mom and our speaker. I was still crying from the freedom I knew the Holy Spirit had poured over me like a healing ointment.

"Can you tell, Mercedes, that I am a changed person? The darkness that was in me was driven away and defeated. I am born again. I feel so alive! Every day I give thanks for this chance at a second opportunity to live."

She met Mercedes' sincere stare with soft words. "The Holy Spirit can meet us at the deepest parts of our hurts if we just let Him. He wants nothing more than to see us healed the way Jesus healed while He walked this earth. We just need to fight the enemy, so we are released from the bondage he has over us.

"I probably should stop. But I have just a bit more."

"Good grief! Keep talking," Mercedes said. "This is lifting my spirits. You have such a story of a life revived and saved."

"Well, then my new mom took me in her arms. I knew I would belong to her forever. She was a spiritual counterpart to me.

"'Dear daughter,' she told me, 'I pray that you will always see yourself as Jesus sees you, perfect and kind and full of love. You were fearfully and wonderfully made, and I am going to try to protect you from the destructive darkness the world tries to throw at you. You are so precious. I love you with all my heart.' She would not let me go!

"For the first time since I was with Miss Bev, I said, 'I love you too, Mom.' And I broke into tears again. My healing was a welcome relief.

"After this event, I gradually gained strength and resolve to serve a new Master. I cared about life again and asked my mother if I could go to a nurse training program being held at the former St. Mary's Hospital. I wanted to be like the nurse in Vietnam who brought life out of the ashes of despair. I graduated two years later."

Mercedes could surmise that she was one of the top academic students in the class after seeing her professional skills in the operating room. Involuntarily, she reached out her hand over the cafeteria table and rested it on Olivia's petite hand. "Thank you so much, Olivia, for being bold enough to share your story with me. You are one tough lady, and I love your heart for the hurting. The light shines through you. I can see it. You make my heart warm and give me hope in this dreary world. I must get back to my next shift in the ER. I will never forget your bravery in sharing something so personal with me. It will stay close to my heart. Thank you." Mercedes gave Olivia's hand a squeeze and, without another word, she rose and dumped her lunch trash into coordinated receptacles for recycling and reuse. Then she brusquely walked down the main hall.

***

The years 2033-2035 brought a series of earth-shattering events to the States. They were known as the Years of Chaos. How the country escaped a civil war was beyond understanding. Everywhere there was turmoil, dissention, death, and division. There were consequences to the chaos. As people continued to move to the sanctioned metro centers after the volcano, the virus outbreak and the war, commodities were rationed by the government, private companies were required to sell their assets to governmental enterprises and basic constitutional rights were slowly eroded under the guise of solidarity, fairness, justice, and compassion.

The legislative branch of government was locked in a constant battle pitting half the country against the other. Those in power were insistent in their strong-arm moves to continue the erosion of individual rights for the sake of the whole. Those who represented the minority clamored for transparency and common-sense adherence to Constitutional Rights. Deep down, most citizens knew that the path they were on was dangerous. Rights came at a price. Giving them up in stages made it easier to justify, but the result left most Americans angry with their losses and nothing to show for it.

There were years of protests, assassinations, prison internments of radicals and regular citizens caught up in the chilling breakdown of their country. No one trusted anyone else. Even in family units the darkness of this sterilized, distrusting atmosphere was reflected in the faces of the people. Hate and discord were everywhere. Violent riots and clashes between police and protesters were reported daily on the internet and government-controlled television networks. Pockets of hothead fanatics and just ordinary citizens were still challenging the overreach of the government. These strange coalitions were comprised often of former enemies; far-left progressives and equally solid right-wing shills who both realized that their only hope for the republic to survive was to regain its lost footing in the individual rights battle.

They tried to fight with little support or resources and usually were quashed by a government that held all the cards with internet and media exploitation and control. Individualism and capitalism had died. No one was allowed to offend others, and individuals were monitored and judged by the people they surrounded themselves with. Trust and compassion took a big hit. It was easier and safer to withdraw into your modified world of governmental control and let another sucker sort out the way to effectively protest.

One of the rights that took the hardest hit was the freedom of religion. At first it was defended by representatives within the system as the country's foundation for justice and peace. Yet at times the insurgent groups resorted to physical violence calling themselves religious people supported by Almighty God. When violence and rhetoric reached the breaking point, the National Guard was called in to show these zealots who was really in charge. They were violent themselves. Protesters were maimed and killed. Large swaths of religious folk were rounded up and branded as revolutionaries. They were punished severely, at times more so than the regular murderer or drug lord. Religions had to be dealt with. The party line was that they were divisive and dangerous. It was easy for the public to see that the moniker was accurate in the crafted clips they saw through social media and the screen. Perhaps the reporters were correct in targeting the faithful as a major cause of the division and breakdown of common decency.

Part of the penalty for lack of fealty to the system required houses of worship to remove what they saw as controversial and offensive signage that would disturb the sensibilities of those who knew themselves to be wiser in their secularism. Religious expression was deemed allowable if it was done in the confines of a private setting. Any act of public worship was curtailed and labeled seditious, citing the havoc of the protests and the assassinations of public figures. Many churches and worship centers closed their doors or were fined out of existence. Some went into hiding.

That did not stop the faithful. Overnight, underground churches sprung up by the thousands. Christians and those of other faiths dared the government to interfere. There was a new boldness and willingness to suffer for something they cherished more than life itself. Society in general could not understand the draw to faith. Not much thought was wasted on those who were foolish enough to still think there was a God and that somehow, He cared and was in control of events.

Olivia had joined such a gathering in her neighborhood. It was a lifeline for her when her adopted mother, Miss Bev, suddenly died of the Drakee virus. Although she was alone in the world, she felt the presence of the Holy Spirit who had not deserted her in the dark world as she negotiated her way through it.

Chapter 12

General Hamilton

2035

"I will give you a new heart and put a new spirit in you;
I will remove from you your heart of stone and give you a heart of
flesh. And I will put my Spirit in you..." Ezekiel 36:26-27a

Lt. Col. Shamir Wells drove the dark sedan slowly through the streets of Washington D.C. and continued a predetermined drive into Baltimore near the harbor. Traveling carefully through a dilapidated warehouse district, he slowed. Then he quickly flicked a garage open-er control on the dashboard and slipped the car unobtrusively into a warehouse through its rusty corrugated metal door. The door silently closed behind him.

The drive from Washington to Baltimore had been an eventful one. General Hamilton had slid into the back seat next to Mack and had done the talking on the journey. Mack knew that what he was hearing was top secret, and he also knew he would not leave here alive if he decided that this venture was not for him. These men were taking no chances. The general had fully explained the crux of the problem on their trip.

"So," Mack said, "the president is complicit in passing our military secrets to the World Nations Alliance because she is determined that it is best for us to completely relinquish our national identity?"

"She's not the kingpin in this treason," scoffed the general. "She's just a weak-minded pawn who has always lived in the progressive bubble. She comes from a background of government indoctrination that believes man can fairly govern with equal justice for all. If she had bothered to step onto our battleground in the Middle East for the past few years, she would have seen how mankind cares for each other. Somehow, she believes that people can change their innate inner nature. She does not see or at least chooses not to see the hypocrisy of those who espouse the same doctrine yelling that we are all the same and that we must live for each other's benefit. Have you noticed that the politicians who espouse this garbage are the ones who still have cars, still have private homes, and still get upgraded medical care? History takes a back seat to facts with these people, son."

"Well, who else could control the release of military secrets then?" Mack gazed at General Hamilton with a bit of suspicion. Lt. Col. Wells looked at the general in the rear-view mirror. Would he be frank with Gersham?

Hamilton continued. "It's General Lu. He has negotiated a secret pact with the WNA to turn over all our military technical schematics, codes, and top-secret navigation documents in exchange for being appointed second in command of the WNA. Knowing his record, he will not dally too long in being appointed chairperson, if you catch my drift. It just takes one little accident or a cozy coup to achieve his desired end game. He has already sweetened the pot by passing off part of the research on our satellite protection program. Scumbag!"

The look on Mack's face said it all. Although little emotion showed, his eyes spoke of the shock in realizing the chief of staff of the United States had sold out his country for his own self-aggrandizement. Mack did not have difficulty swallowing this assessment of Lu. He had seen the signs of his dictatorial personality in the battlefield decisions of the war. It was his way or the highway.

"What does he think?" asked Mack. "Does he really believe that he can initiate a perfect peace in the world? Or does he just want to take over?"

"He's enamored with Roman civilization," shared the general. "He pictures himself as a new breed of Caesar. Peace through strength, but his peace would mean that the military would not have checks and balances. It is the way dictators eventually come to power. They destroy the branches of government that prohibit their sole claim to governing."

"What's your proof of this?" asked Mack and then thought better of the question. He knew of no other man who was more loyal and honorable than General Hamilton. Before the general could respond, Mack said, "I'm in. What do you need me to do?"

Mack could see the shoulders of Lt. Col. Wells relax and his hand lift something in the front seat.

They got out of the car and onto an assembly floor. Wells spoke. "We have been putting together a small and secretive resistance inside the military under the command of General Hamilton. And our work continues to solidify as quickly as possible a power base structure within the Pentagon. It is tough because we must be absolutely sure that those we approach, will see that the work we are doing is reflective of the integrity of the country we pledged our allegiance to when we joined the military. We've been able to form a loose group of trained units on the outside and have provided them with hardware and software for retaliation and disruption when the opportune time comes."

Wells glared at Mack as though he was suspicious. It was just his manner. Mack had become used to that stare when they were on duty back in the desert. He was just a serious character, no time for frivolity. "We've got a steep road to climb to achieve success. Each of us knows that the odds are slim," stated Wells. Mack stood there wondering what they would end up with if they were successful. How were they going to untangle the nightmare of a mess that the country had become?

"Mack," said General Hamilton, "your job will be to generate orders for the military supplies that will provide the backbone for these outside independent units. We have a new computer system that has not even been rolled out for public use in the Pentagon. It will cloak the actual orders, making them appear to come from other supply requisition sites linked to military facilities around the country. The orders appear legit and are filled. While the orders would originally specify a military base destination, the computer program will change the location of the delivery site for the delivery team. Orders that you manipulate will go to our specialized delivery teams who are part of the system. When the order is logged as completed, the program will switch the arrival destination back to the original military site. The orders themselves will be impossible to track for the time being because multiple computers will be generating the requisitions."

Mack was amazed at the technological progress in masking computer activity. "Never thought we would be fighting one of our own," he mumbled stiffly.

"You are going to remain in your same facility in Washington, but when you get to work on Monday, you'll find you were promoted to an enclosed office. Your co-workers will be told that you are now doing personnel work and need the privacy for employment matters. They will understand and probably won't ask many questions. And I will get you tapped into our other military resources so you can keep an eye on anything else that seems suspicious on their end. We cannot trust anyone at this point. You will need to set up a private coding system for use with your work. No one is to have access to it except the general and me. Oh, and our three contacts at the Pentagon. Theirs are to be sent out separately in another order. They each have code names and ways to contact them that you will have to learn about. This high-tech world has produced a method we have found extremely helpful in masking information from the system. One of our people is a genius."

The general chimed in. "I'll be the one to let you know if you need to download any information, like access codes, for any reason. For now, we will just have to trust you with all the information. It is better we do not have it at this juncture anyway. Someone eventually is going to get suspicious. Lu is a weasel who is great at sniffing things out. We have shipments headed out right now to bases in the Virginias and Kentuckee. Those old states, Kentucky and Tennessee, are my old stomping grounds. I see you are from the town of Whitsville. Are you familiar with Kramer's Station?"

"Sure, it's down by the old railroad tracks connecting to Hepton," said Mack, surprised at his knowledge of this remote village.

"There's an old depot building we've been using there to store ammo, rocket launchers, and uniforms. Seemed like an area where we would eventually find support from the locals. It is one reason I thought we could trust you. You seemed to have a sharp head on your shoulders."

The general gave a bleak smile. He gazed over at the white-paneled delivery truck loaded with gear for their overnight deliveries. Mack sensed how risky this business must be. "Why did you contact me?" asked Mack.

"Things were getting too hot for our last operative," answered Wells. "Now we can't find him. Could have just hightailed it off to the Middle Region. Lots of people are finding that a good place to become anonymous."

Mack imagined that someone could be on to their plans. Worse yet, there was a mole on the inside. Or the operative just got too scared to continue. *What the heck?* he thought. He still had some love for his country and especially for the dedicated band of professional soldiers he had fought with in the Desert Conflict from '24-33. It was no surprise that General Lu saw the advantage of becoming a leader on the world stage and grabbed for the ring. His kind could not resist the temptation of power. It would be almost impossible to stop him.

As Mack thought about this operation he had so hastily volunteered for, he suddenly was jolted into the realization that it could have an impact on Walt. "What if I get caught?" asked Mack. "Could they track Walt down for information? Hopefully, the Singletons could provide him with protection. No one would ever think that those straight shooters could be involved in espionage!" Yet there was an element of worry hanging over these questions. There was never any guarantee that the innocent were spared punishment when war broke out.

Mack climbed into the front seat for the return trip with the lieutenant colonel. They did not say a word as they switched up the return route. The general stayed behind. Mack was dropped off around the block from his house and stealthily entered through the back door. He knew that the last few hours had changed his life forever. What he did not know was whether he had made the wise decision. He did know that he had had no choice in the matter.

Chapter 13

Mercedes Singleton

2035

"Do not leave Jerusalem, but wait for the gift my Father promised,
which you have heard me talk about. For John baptized with water, but
in a few days you will be baptized with the Holy Spirit." Acts 1:4-5

The incumbent president, Santaya Woodring, was struggling with being able to follow up on her campaign promises. Violent protests occurred daily with arrests of repeat offenders, despite stricter sentencing and news blackouts by the primary news stations. The legislature had finally decided to suspend the writ of habeas corpus to protect the public from rebellious insurgents who were too dangerous to release with bail. They cited Abraham Lincoln's need to do the same thing during the American Civil War. But the general population was not so sure. They were beginning to have serious reservations that somehow their rights had been eroded to the point that they would never regain the freedoms they had relinquished. The country settled for the time being into a mood of depressed acceptance, but it was not without questions lurking in the back of its collective mind that the baby had been thrown out with the bath water.

The uneasy peace held except for small groups of radical trouble-makers and brooders who continued to interrupt wireless transmissions. The majority of these protesters were highly educated and tech savvy. They had managed to infiltrate the technical areas of broadcasting and were anonymous. Occasionally, sabotage transmissions would pop onto the TV screens spouting short, angry lectures on fascism, racism, or religion, particularly Christianity. There were also short videos and messages from the right defending the Bible and Christian tradition, as well as Western civilization. What bothered the regular populace the most were short video clips depicting brutal treatment of religious adherents or government overreach that trounced on the once taken-for-granted constitutional freedoms. Children being thrown out of their homes, churches burned to the ground, disgusting hospital wards for the terminally ill. These were sights that while banned from view, made their way into the hearts of the viewers who still held a modicum of compassion.

Yet, a portion of the civilian population began to see that there was a benefit to helping enforce anti-discrimination and non-tolerance laws, and often turned in friends and even relatives to the local law enforcement teams, now under the control of federal agencies. Sometimes they got an upgrade in housing, sometimes increased food coupons or even a government appointment. That was the prize so many wished to attain. It was their ticket to success in this centralized society. Every day, radical cells, religious bigots, and "subversives" were exposed and rounded up. The government had found the most socially acceptable way to deal with these factions was to send them to internment camps for their own protection and to help assimilate them back into mainstream thought through a cooperative program of re-education and physical labor.

The general population did not believe that this worked. They knew they were kidding themselves. Most of these anti-government perpetrators would never fold. They were radicalized in one way or the other. And they most often never returned. Prisoners were worked to death or simply disappeared. Concentration camps like those of WWII sprang up as their fellow citizens were incarcerated.

Most camps were in south-central USA where population centers were closed but where farming and manufacturing provided the backdrop for the work remediation required of the insurgents. The citizenry was not interested in what happened to the subversives. For ten years they, themselves, had been programmed to understand whom among their compatriots was the enemy. It had been an easy transition with schools, the occasional church group, and of course the heavy-handed government intrusion being in charge.

The camps were little more than sweatshops and enforced slavery. Each camp had a focus on customizing their work with similar subversives, so there were camps formulated around religious beliefs like Christianity, Islam, the Jewish faith and camps whose clientele were law breakers and government traitors. Those were the worst. Food was scant, medical care almost negligible, and they were run by contractors who tried to keep the insurgents delivering the goods and remediated while skimming off a sizeable profit for themselves. The public had little sympathy. Those carted off were the scapegoats for the tumult in the country. This continuous message disseminated by the media operatives was usually accepted by the public who then became willing accomplices to one of the worst human rights travesties in the history of the present United States. If they had been shown an accurate in-depth research investigation into the abuse of these camps, they would have had more compassion. It was a symptom of a populace turned against itself. Perhaps it was selfishness to survive.

***

Mercedes continued to work at Baltimore National Hospital, seeing fewer war veterans but more patients who suffered from depression, anxiety, and systemic fears. The family unit was often broken beyond repair and relationships were disposable. There was no underpinning for a moral society, so it was difficult to judge right from wrong. Often, patients physically hurt themselves or others in their sphere. In fact, most murders now occurred in these circumstances.

One day in the hospital cafeteria, Mercedes mentioned to Olivia that work was such a depressing environment with these clients. She wondered how Olivia could be so cheerful, especially after she had shared her narrative of her disturbing childhood. Olivia paused in her chewing, her sandwich poised in both hands, and looked Mercedes straight in the eyes.

"Well, I've been washed and changed on the inside. My world is not ruled by outside evil forces any longer, but by a Master who gives me hope and comfort. Do you know I hear from God at night, and He tells me things about myself … good things. I am blessed," intoned Olivia.

Then she lowered her eyes and took another bite of sandwich. Could she have been too bold in sharing the personal elements of her faith?

Mercedes paused. She wished she could feel like this. "Olivia, you sound like my brother Titus. He had an open channel to talk to God. I wish I could have that too. You are one of the lucky ones," said Mercedes.

"Where is your brother? Does he live with you?" queried Olivia.

"No." She hesitated on what to share. "He is on mission work in Asia. It is a very unsafe environment, and I don't have any details. We have not heard from him since he left. I know that is a bad sign, but I also know that contacting us would jeopardize his safety," stated Mercedes.

She got up with tears in her eyes, dumped her tray of recyclable containers into the receptacle and slowly walked back to Ward 7.

That night Mercedes struggled with Olivia's words. While she herself had come a long way in assimilating the faith beliefs of her brother, she still felt empty and overwhelmed with a sense of the unknown. *How can I get what she has?* she thought.

Her dreams that evening were ones that left her searching for something in the mist. She was wandering in their backyard in the dark at their home in Whitsville. In desperation, she kept looking for the lost object, but she just became increasingly frustrated as her search proved futile. She woke up with a start at six a.m. to the alarm on her watch, hardly rested and angry that she had not been able to control her turbulent nighttime thoughts.

"Well, that night of sleep got me nowhere!" she muttered. "I am so tired of these dreams of seeking and searching. I don't even know what I'm looking for." Frustration set in as she robotically put on her nurse's uniform and stuffed her protective supplies in her travel bag.

But her curiosity got the better of her and later that week, she asked Olivia if they could meet over the weekend on Saturday afternoon. Olivia paused. "I have somewhere I need to be later in the evening. Can we meet a bit earlier at one p.m.?"

"No problem," Mercedes replied with a smile.

Lunch was at Terril's Café. They both used their food coupons to buy the special of the day: vegetable soup and a cheese sandwich. Jeff ran the restaurant well, and they were thankful for the clean plates and fresh food.

Mercedes cut to the chase in their conversation. "I'm frustrated in my faith. I know it is private, but I don't know how to get God to talk to me. How do you do it?"

Olivia grinned. "I was baptized in the Holy Spirit a few years ago when I finally gave over control of my life to the Lord. You remember the first part of that story. And bam! He took over and filled me with the presence of His Spirit. I cannot help but feel an awareness of Him as I go about the activities I need to do each day. We talk at night too. I make sure I stay in touch mentally. Life is way too distracting and depressing."

Mercedes was a bit unsure. "I've always been a Christian. I just feel empty though. I want what you and my brother have. I'm envious."

"Will you sacrifice everything for God? He wants people who are all in. That is the hard part. It's not for the weak of heart," stated Olivia.

That was a troubling question for Mercedes. She mulled over the question in her mind like studying for a difficult exam. The answer was elusive. Was she willing to release herself to the God who only dwelled in her head? Was she desperate enough for the something else that Olivia seemed to have? Was she willing to accept the sacrifice and the persecution?

Mercedes replied, "I'm not sure. I think so. Help me in my weakness. I want to feel alive again."

Olivia placed her tender, worn hand on Mercedes and whispered a little prayer. "Lord Jesus, settle in Mercedes' heart with your presence through the Holy Spirit. Speak your truth to her this day. In your precious name, amen."

She accidentally let out a small sigh. Then on her intake of breath Olivia whispered, "Come back here at seven tonight. I have some place to take you."

Mercedes mulled over the afternoon conversation for the next several hours, but at seven, she was returning to Terril's with another food coupon. Instead of going in to sit down at the table, Olivia intercepted her at the door, grabbed her hand and led her along the dimly lit alley running along the food establishment. There was a back staircase littered with leaves and festering garbage. It was enough to keep the curious at bay. It led to the basement where a group of people were quietly lifting prayers, two or three in moans, a handful reading, others rocking, and some making unintelligible phrases. All were oblivious to the fact of their presence.

She sat down next to Olivia, who began to pray for her dear sister Mercedes. Mercedes listened in earnest and with an openness which surprised her. Somehow, she felt at peace with this little band of believers praying to God intentionally and openly. There was a passion in their voices and a pervading happiness about their persona. From then on, often on Saturday nights she would wander inconspicuously into their presence and begin to ask God to pour down His power upon her. When she was ready, when she at last had given the Holy Spirit permission to do His work, He finally did.

Mercedes lay on the cold floor feeling nothing but supernatural warmth. She was not sure how long she had been in this position. There were still whispers of the faithful to be heard in the background and she was aware of the single light on the ceiling. Then Olivia came into view.

"Oh, Olivia, it was beautiful. I was visited by God, the Holy Spirit. While we were praying, I finally decided to tell God that I was all in. I wanted to be made whole again and then I just remember the change. I know I was lying on the floor, but all I felt was His warmth. His voice told me how cherished I am. He said I had always been His, I just had not known that this belonging was real. It felt like amazing warmth invaded me and captured me in its presence. And the love I felt was so sincere. He held me and let me know that all my shortcomings and failings were forgiven. I was washed clean; totally. Did you see me cry? I have never cried like that. It just poured out, not from fear, or misery, or hurt. It was from belonging and beauty and joy. I know I cried. I could hear myself. Oh, Olivia, He is real!"

"Yes, He is, sweet sister. I could see that He had a hold of you finally and was working on the pain and the hurts of the past. He came to heal you this evening because you allowed Him to do the work. I am so thankful that our Lord loves us so much. His Holy Spirit is such a comfort. He brings Jesus so close to us. Now you know that He will never leave you. He is always in you and has claimed you as His own."

"It feels so good," said Mercedes. "I feel … well, free. Was I that bound by lies?"

"Satan always wants us to live in his false identity. The Holy Spirit tonight just broke that hold on you. Now you can see yourself the way Jesus sees you," shared Olivia.

"He truly thinks I am so precious that He loves me that much? I have never felt anything quite like it. Oh, I feel delicious!" said an elated Mercedes.

Olivia laughed. A serious young man walked over and asked her what was happening. Briefly she introduced Mercedes to her brother, Arun.

"Arun," said Olivia with pride, "this is the friend I was talking to you about last week. Mercedes Singleton, please meet my brother Arun David Polysoing."

Mercedes was stunned. "You mean this is the brother who was lost in Cambodia? When did you find each other? How did it happen?"

"It was such a miracle," Olivia replied. "It is a long story and right now you need to just center yourself in the presence of God. I need to see what my brother has been up to. He rarely makes it to our meetings anymore, but I am sure he is up to the Lord's work. He had such a dramatic calling; God is moving mountains for him to have an impact in the world for the fellowship of believers. Sit here and rest. I'll be back in a few minutes."

Olivia got up from her kneeling position on the floor and hugged her brother. They moved off to the corner where they had a lively conversation. Mercedes could see concern cascading down Olivia's face. She was not good at hiding her emotions either. But the warmth and Presence still was stirring in Mercedes, so she closed her eyes and talked to the Spirit. She was at peace finally.

Chapter 14

Mack Gersham

January 2035

"For I resolved to know nothing while I was with you except Jesus Christ and him crucified. I came to you in weakness with great fear and trembling. My message and my preaching were not with wise and persuasive words, but with a demonstration of the Spirit's power, so that your faith might not rest on human wisdom, but on God's power."
1 Corinthians 2:2-5

Steadily, Mack made progress in setting up a new distribution system for General Hamilton. He was amazed by how innocuous the computer technology seemed to be to the outsider. While millions of dollars of equipment and supplies were being funneled off into storage units around the country, Mack wondered about those in the organization itself. How could it maintain its anonymity without someone spilling the beans?

He did notice that an occasional employee within the Pentagon ranks suddenly died of unknown causes or by accident, but that was typical. He would need to be on his guard so that he did not become immersed in the world of conspiracy theory. But it made him smile when he realized he was entangled in one, one in which he found himself simply because he believed that one man was honorable.

Mack's work with requisitions or coding had its down times. One day he thought he would experiment and surf into hacked sites for people he had known in his past. The first one was himself. Not much new there. He was surprised though that there was an in-depth study into his father and brother. The government always was careful when it came to security clearance. He was glad that his father was no longer around to disparage his character. He pictured Walt's face that last morning they were together, and he realized he still seethed with anger toward his father.

Titus Singleton was the next search. Amazingly, there was a secret file on him and his work in Nepal. Titus had not only taken up residence there to foster a Christian rescue network, but he was also instrumental in rescuing persecuted Christians from China via the Himalayas. *Amazing guy,* thought Mack. *Never a selfish bone in his body.* The file ended with a statement that Titus had been arrested and was taken to a jail run by the Chinese military. It was presumed that he was likely deceased. There was also an encrypted message marked with an asterisk at the end. According to secret intelligence, someone had reported a sighting of Titus just months earlier. He had been identified in satellite imagery as a prisoner in a Chinese concentration camp near the Nepalese border.

It would not be hard to differentiate him from the locals, mused Mack. *I hope he can withstand their interrogation. They must be keeping him alive for a reason. Don't think that chap will break. He is made of steel when you dig down far enough. Eventually, the Chinese are going to realize that.*

Mack thought of Mercedes and how she would take the news. Wondering what she was up to, he typed her name into the network and found she was living in Baltimore's metro center, still working for Baltimore National Hospital. The next paragraph floored him. She had been flagged as part of a religious group that was fomenting revolt. The majority of the group were Cambodian refugees connected to an earlier church named The Overland Community Church of Baltimore. The code attached to the memo pointed to the possibility that this group would soon be rounded up and deported to a field camp for work remediation. Several insurgents connected to the fellowship were listed by name. None of the names rang a bell. Mack knew what those camps really were … slave labor, disease, abuse, and an attempt to destroy the spirit. Oftentimes they spelled death. He had seen the figures that were not readily available to the public. Out of sight, out of mind.

Mack's mind raced.

How in the hell could a smart girl … he smiled at his mistake … *woman like her take these chances? Yes, she was raised by good, faithful parents, but in this day and age, you have to be careful. There are scads of people out there who feel it's their duty to report anyone who dares to ignore the federal dictates barring communal public worship. I'm sick of people who try to take advantage of good people to benefit themselves. They are like packs of wolves, stalking their prey. She needs to be warned immediately.*

He rerouted the memos he had opened to cover his tracks, closed his computer, and grabbed his small duffle bag. Doing something illegal no longer bothered him. Heck, this was nothing compared to what he was involved with at the Pentagon. He was becoming the mole of moles and he loved it.

Stopping briefly in the restroom at the subway station, Mack shuffled slowly into a stall and donned his convincing disguise consisting of a worn hoodie, hat, sunglasses, and a small mustache for pizazz. He half smiled at himself in the dirty mirror. Mack took the subway from

D.C. to Baltimore. It was crowded and dirty, standing room only. It smelled of dirty clothes, unwashed bodies, and heavily seasoned food. A large group of international workers rode this route and brought their own meals with them. Something about the curry, red pepper, and garlic was appealing. It spoke of a meal that was prepared with care for someone who was loved.

In Baltimore, Mack walked the mile and a half to the neighborhood where Mercedes lived. He did not think much about his safety. The cities were relatively free from crime now that the drug lords and black marketers had divided the metropolitan sectors into territories. Stay in your own hood and all is well. Still, he touched his holster under his arm to make sure the Glock was secure.

He hung around down the street from the bus stop as dusk approached. Pretending to read the news on his cell phone, he glanced up at the passengers disembarking from the five-thirty bus. No one looked like Mercedes. They all had a dull look about their eyes except for a couple that shyly smiled at each other. Mack was not jealous. That kind of life was futile in a society where there was seemingly nothing to live for except existence itself. He stared fixedly at his phone for another twenty minutes until the next bus arrived. It was packed.

She stepped off in the first group of travelers. Clearly worn from her tiring work, she also had a glazed expression, yet there was a spark in her step that spoke of something positive … a hope, perhaps that this gray world would pass away and warm up.

Slipping through the crowd, Mack copied the pace of Mercedes and stayed back several yards. As the crowds thinned closer to her home, he noticed that occasionally she would glace around as though sensing that something was amiss. About a block from her destination, Mack picked up his pace and strode quickly to her side, cupping her elbow in his hand.

She stopped with alarm. "Please keep walking, Ms. Singleton," said the dark stranger. She slowly stepped forward. "I'm here to warn you that you are in extreme danger. Your gathering of Christian believers is targeted for a round-up by authorities any day. Stay away from this group and cease your entangling collusion. It is not worth the danger in which you are placing yourself. If the authorities question you, deny any involvement other than temporary curiosity. Reject your connection to them and they will give you a second chance. Do you understand?"

Mercedes was shaken. When she nodded yes, she turned, but already the stranger had released the pressure on her elbow, turned and was walking back down the street in the direction from which he had come. Mercedes was so stunned that for a moment she simply froze in the blustery wind on the sidewalk. Who was that stranger and why did his voice seem so familiar? She believed him. She would need to warn Olivia at work and the others on Saturday, particularly Olivia's brother who organized their small band and others like it. They could find a new and safer place to gather.

This group had become like family to her, and she had little fear at this point of being caught. Yet she was also flummoxed by the knowledge that the government seemed to be tracking all its citizens.

How can they know where I am and what I am doing? she questioned. *I've never been in trouble with law enforcement before. How did I get on their radar so quickly?* It irritated her and started to make fear wander in her mind.

Get a hold of yourself, Mercedes. You said you were all in with being a Christian. Keep your focus. Slowly, she picked up her pace and started to form a plan to help relocate the little group of the faithful. She felt purpose in doing so. Prayers started to pour off her lips for this band of followers in need of protection.

Chapter 15

Mercedes Singleton

January 2035

*"May the God of hope fill you with all joy and peace
as you trust in him, so that you may overflow with hope
by the power of the Holy Spirit." Romans 15:13*

Unfortunately, Mercedes' warning was too late. She had waited impatiently for Olivia's brother, Arun, to arrive so she could share the potential danger with him. He was one of the organizers of this small faith band and, like Olivia, had been rescued from the same orphanage in Cambodia. His rescue had come two years after Olivia's. Only recently had he reconnected with his sister because he had been adopted into a home in Canada. Years had been spent tracking her down and then he stayed distant to keep her identity secret. He finally trusted himself to make an appearance in her life. But he did not have the softness of Olivia. There were so many wounds from the past. It was evident he still carried this weight on his shoulders and was angry with the persecution of the followers of Christ. His soul rebelled at the injustice of losing their right to worship as they pleased. He felt like he could not breathe.

As the small group trickled in on Saturday, strangers, two larger men who seemed distant, came with them. The gathering was suspicious from the start. A handful of them turned around and headed up the steps. Before their prayers were lifted up, Mercedes stood to share the warning she was given. At once one of the men grabbed her and twisted her arm behind her. "Come, my lovely," he said with a snarl, "and the rest of you rubbish too."

Some of the band tried to break free, but there were reinforcements outside. Those who did not cooperate were tazed into submission and thrown into one of the police vans.

Outside, for Mercedes and Olivia who huddled together, a dilapidated green van was waiting, idling in its haze of ethanol fuel. "Get in," barked the leader. They were shoved inside and had to sit on the frosty floor. Immediately they were taken downtown to a processing center.

Mercedes was shocked. "Officer," she said as she climbed out of the van, "I have been in no trouble with the law. Please check my record. I can vouch for my friend here as well. Please run a check on our security cards."

He laughed, but not from anything funny. It had a wicked sound to it. "Don't try to get smart with me, lady. You are both participating in illegal faith gatherings. The new law is now in force, just passed a month ago with more stringent guidelines. We don't need to give you any slack. Guess you ladies didn't get the memo that you are public enemies. Go complain to your god." There was the laugh again.

In the detention center, they were strip searched, forced to turn in their government-issued ID's, and given a set of clothes worn by all convicted of being subversive elements in society ... whether you were a murderer or a follower of Jesus, it was one and the same. In the whirlwind of the processing, Mercedes saw that Olivia was not far behind her in line. Olivia gave Mercedes a thumbs up and pointed upward. One of the woman attendants smacked her hand.

"We will not be out of line in this facility. Keep your arms to your side," she growled. Mercedes gave her a slight smile.

Both were thinking with relief that half the faithful had either not arrived at the prayer meeting or had escaped when they realized something was amiss. The church would continue to exist and worship despite the persecution. Perhaps they would find the little letter she had crafted and placed in a tattered Bible in the front row. It had made suggestions of more private and safe venues for their gatherings. She had written it to the attention of one of the elders who had not been arrested with this night's raid. Hopefully, the police did not do a thorough search of the premises. She did not want to be responsible for implicating one of her brethren. Thankfully, she had just used his first name on the note.

By midnight, they were on a bus to who-knows-where with nothing to keep them warm in the frigid conditions of the northeast. They were headed west. The bus chugged on into the night, stopping for a bathroom break or two, or gas, or both. Two guards sat with guns on the front seats, and one was in the back, mostly dozing. There was little conversation among the passengers, the majority of whom Mercedes had not seen before.

This must have been a jackpot night for rounding up Christians, she thought wryly as she gazed at her fellow prisoners. She could not help comparing this sad-looking band to the stories of persecuted Christians in the Bible. She noticed that there was a sense of resignation in their faces, and the lips of those around her were moving and speaking in silence to a Presence unseen. There were passengers who seemed frightened about the unknown, but not confrontational.

At first, Mercedes felt like she was in a surreal motion picture as the events of this strange night unfolded with shocking alacrity. It took just moments to process the reality that she had lost her freedom and had no venue to turn to for help. She quickly became aware of the fact that she was now considered a felon and had been denied the basic right of defending oneself from accusation. Mercedes realized that her participation in the outlawed church and her confession that she was a Christian had sealed her fate. There would be no miraculous release and no different outcome.

She too moved into silent prayer along with her accused band of travelers. "Please Jesus, Lord and Master; protect me and this small band of faithful followers. We are just trying to honor you as our Lord and Savior. Keep our hearts strong for you and keep us from the harm intended by those who do not know of you. I love you." She cried tears of loss but tried to be strong. She saw Olivia two seats up. She turned for a moment back toward Mercedes with a faint smile on her face. "How that lady loves Jesus," she whispered. "Nothing seems to faze her."

Mercedes was surprised that she herself was not more nervous or scared. After the first few tears, she recollected that a while ago she had known that this was a possibility, and she had taken the arrest with little trepidation. She figured Titus would have done the same thing. But now the bus was getting extremely cold, and she yearned for her warm socks, her fuzzy mittens, and her woolen coat, all of which were confiscated at the detention center. It made her angry to think that they would give her things to a government hack, knowing that she would likely freeze to death. The thought warmed her up a bit. "Dear Jesus," she said as she bit her lip, "give us some heat!"

After two days, the stiff and wary passengers piled off the bus onto a farm with a sign posted at the crossroads, "Central Station Rehabilitation Center." There were rolls and rolls of barbed wire piled on top of a steep steel fence at the entrance to the rehabilitation center. This was a camp for the Christian subversives. As such, there was less military presence and less control. They had learned from experience that the Christian believers were most often accepting of their punishment and caused little dissention in their containment. They also rarely budged from their faith. As the bus rolled into camp, the current residents barely acknowledged their existence. Most were slowly moving in from the fields, their hands frozen from working the icy tundra. It was hard to read their minds as their faces seemed expressionless.

"Get moving," yelled one of the bus guards. "You ladies have a new home. It's just like church camp," he laughed with glee. He took the butt of his gun and shoved an older woman down the steps. Olivia was there to pick her up.

"Are you all right, ma'am?" she questioned. The elderly lady gave her a brief thumbs up and walked back into the line. "Don't worry about me. I know where this all ends up. It is just a part of the journey that gets a bit more difficult. God will help us through." Olivia nodded.

The new crop of detainees was prodded to hurry from the bus and taken directly to a tight, musty community room where an amateurly produced video was projected on the stained wall. In it, a montage of former "convicts" spoke of their life at the center and how it had helped to reformulate their mistaken beliefs. They were proud that they had seen the error of their ways and were now moving to a place of contentment and support for the socialized community in which they were repatriated. "One for all," they chanted in unison as they ended their propaganda speech. The last clip was of them boarding the rattling bus to freedom with wide smiles on their faces. Something seemed to be missing in the send-off. They were either actors or victims of Stockholm Syndrome.

Mercedes could see how people might succumb to the reconditioning barrage as the days on the farm began to take their toll. The elderly were forced on strenuous marches for miles into the fields to weed and cultivate the early spring crops which had just been planted. On their meager rations, they often collapsed, were carted back to the infirmary, and then shipped to the local "senior" center. Most of them went willingly. The smell of the crematorium at the senior center never completely left their village, even in a strong wind. It was a reminder of what happens when you fail the system.

Olivia and Mercedes found support in each other and the women who were in their barracks. In the dark of night, someone would often be whispering part of a Psalm for support and comfort. Often the ladies would be chanting silently along with the leader, "The Lord is my Shepherd, He makes me lie down in green pastures ..." They giggled at the irony. They willingly lay down at night from the never-ending exhaustion at the end of the day. It was a time to unwind from the relentless hassle of the field guards and the camp guards. These were well-paid positions from the Federated Government and offered employment with rewards. The metropolitan areas provided the workforce to patrol the camps. They came with big dreams of making big bucks. But the separation from society and the boredom of the repetitive assignments kept most from signing up for a second enlistment. The guards were given wide latitude and often abused their charges for the least infraction. Mercedes felt as though she had been spirited back in time into one of the old WWII films she had watched in high school of the Allied prisoners of war in Nazi Germany. Back then she could not imagine such cruelty. Now she was part of it.

Olivia was always the bright spot in the dreary and drab camp. Despite the mud and toil, the cracked fingernails, the disrespect, and mistreatment from the staff of thugs working off their time for society, she was steady and hopeful.

At night she would nurse the weary. "Let me help that sore back. I have a compress I made from moss and old cloth this morning. It will feel good on those aching muscles."

Then the next night she would be somewhere else. "Let me help you massage those shoulders. I know how they ache. I believe we all need a massaging of our soul too. Let me tell you a story about how God came and gave me peace in my time of distress." Then she would speak in her sweet voice telling of her freedom adventure. Sometimes she even shared part of her chaotic life in Cambodia. That always was accompanied with tears. It was the only time Mercedes saw her cry. She was so strong.

Often, Olivia would stealthily slip her bread up her sleeve to feed a starving friend while denying herself the needed calories. She was the reason more had not given up and given in. Sadly, there would be the occasional Christian who renounced their faith and again pledged allegiance to the Federated States. But this group of women in Cabin 7 refused to break. That could be attributed to the positive influence of Olivia and her care. Part of it was the ministering of the Holy Spirit who held them in His arms in their despair and grief.

One dreary, chilly evening after their meager meal, the warden, Mr. Bowling, stepped out of his office and motioned for Mercedes to enter. They had not had the opportunity for interaction with him as he kept himself holed up in his office. The newly arrived prisoners had heard his speech at orientation, but aside from that, he usually was on his computer making reports and filing requisitions. News in the camp spoke of avoiding him at all costs.

Mercedes did not think much about the request. People in charge around here were always giving orders. She had learned to be compliant and do what was asked. It usually kept you from getting a beating or a day in the lockdown unit. He closed the door with a bang of authority. She looked at the lumpy middle-aged man and got a whiff of his bad breath obviously caused by a set of mismatched and missing teeth. Plopping down his blubbery form in his dusty leather chair, he motioned Mercedes to move closer to him.

"Do you like it here?" he said sarcastically.

Mercedes did not answer.

He stood up and for his size he quickly rounded the desk. Screaming into her face, he yelled again, "Do you like it here?"

Before she could answer, he swung his huge fist into the side of her face, knocking her savagely to the floor. Holding her down with his right fist, he ripped at her camp issued flimsy pants which provided no resistance to his assault. With one jerk he pulled them down to her quivering knees as she struggled beneath his heaviness. He struck her again with the back of his hairy hand and almost knocked her senseless. Sucking on her lips she could taste the tinge of blood but could not stop her revulsion to the smell of his rotted teeth. His hand grasped to unzip his pants.

Pinned down under the hunk of weight, Mercedes realized that there was no chance of freedom. Yelling for help was fruitless. The guards in the cafeteria were long gone, instructed to leave the warden alone. Turning her head to the side, she let out a silent scream and cried for help. "Jesus, help me." Immediately there was a Presence that came over her. A tangible comfort and a voice, "I am here." She was startled not by the thrusting grunts of Warden Bowling, but that the words that came were clear as day.

He is here, she thought with startled amazement.

The obese rapist climbed slowly off the filthy floor covered by what once was a cheerful braided rug.

"Get up, you filthy bitch," he snarled.

He gave Mercedes a dig in the side with his steel-toed boots and sat down on the swiveling desk chair as he zipped his pants.

"Now," he said sarcastically, "do you like it here? Have an answer, you slut, next time I ask. Now get out."

Mercedes wiped the blood from the corner of her mouth and stumbled out of the room while putting on her pants and covering her swollen face. There was a long red line down her cheek and her whole face blazed with anger and embarrassment. She ran straight from the cafeteria across the street to the medical center and blurted out at the nurses' desk, "I need some morning-after medicine." The "doctor" stuck his head out of the peeling door of his office.

"Send her in," replied the camp physician.

Mercedes proceeded to tell him the events that had just unfolded. He seemed somewhat passive but engaged. He coolly responded, "It was your fault. Stay out of his way. We don't have any such medication here. Only the basics, and that stuff is practically nonexistent. This place is the end of the line as far as pharmaceutical requisitions go. And you know sexual intercourse of any kind is prohibited at this facility. Now get out before I write you up for subversive behavior."

Stumbling down to her barracks, she flung herself on her bed and sobbed hysterically. The women gathered around her and said nothing, but they lay their hands on her body and prayed for God to intervene with might and power. They knew that she was chosen to be the current sexual prize for the warden until his fantasies would eventually move on to the next enticing tidbit. It was known that the warden was a sexual predator. He picked his victims carefully, like a hawk inspecting the landscape for the smallest of moving creatures. There was no chance of escape. They had all heard rumors of his predatory behavior as well. No one wanted to get on his bad side.

Mercedes did not move for the rest of the evening. She cried on Olivia's shoulder.

"He is such a brute. I will stop him," Olivia stated quietly and courageously, giving ample thought to her pledge.

Mercedes knew that she meant it. "Oh, please don't," cried Mercedes. "If it's not me, he will victimize some other innocent girl. I will survive. I will hold onto Jesus each time I'm called into the lion's den. He will be there. The Holy Spirit let me see Him already, Olivia. He cares about what is happening." Mercedes dissolved into sobs that wracked her body. It exhausted her to the point of incoherence. A voice inside her mind chided her for her sinful behavior of the past.

When she fell into a fitful sleep, she dreamed of Whitsville and the safe, comfy warmth of her bed at home. She could see the crocheted coverlet her mother had made and her favorite soft pillows beckoning her to sleep. Then a bear, black, mangy, and menacing, tore a hole in her window screen and with one bound leaped into her bedroom, jumping on her in the bed before she could even utter a sound. As she silently screamed in agony, she woke with a start. Sweat was drenching her body, despite the ongoing chilly weather.

The room was bathed in a glistening moonlight. The magnificent beams spread over her friends and herself, providing a shimmery cloak of loveliness. As she admired the beauty of the light, a voice again spoke in the stillness, "I am with you." Gazing at the moonbeams, Mercedes could see a shape in the filtered light. It looked human in form, with outstretched hands. She sucked in her breath as she recognized the man, the Son of God. Then a cloud scuttled over the moon and returned the room to the dirty and dank darkness of reality. Mercedes lay awake, folded in a Presence that brought comfort and restoration. "Thank you," she whispered. "I suffer for you gladly. Help me to move on. And please keep my friends safe from the evil that is stalking this camp."

When the enemy voice again tried to intrude, Mercedes calmly whispered, "My God does not seek to punish me for my past sins. I have repented. I will not listen to you, Satan. In the Name of Jesus Christ of Nazareth, leave at once." The darkness lifted.

***

As spring moved on into summer, the camp simply became more livable for the fact that the daytime temperature rose to 75 or 80 degrees. The warmth was invigorating and brought out more smiles among Mercedes' friends. The snow pea crops had been harvested as well as asparagus and broccoli, and they were now weeding the green beans and potato crops. Onions were plentiful as well as carrots and the cooks in the kitchen seemed to take pride in the tasty stews they crafted for dinner. Surprisingly, the crops became more prolific with the soil enrichment provided by the spewed ash from the volcanic eruption. The ash had been worked into the soil for the last few years and was bringing bounty from former devastation. In the fields, they could occasionally snatch a secret snack from the plants they tended when their guard was distracted or dozing.

Cabin 7 always ate dinner together, nursing their cracked fingers and sunburned faces as best they could. The conversation was often muted, but they cared deeply for one another.

One of the older girls whispered, "Olivia, you have to eat more. Your clothes are going to be falling off you soon if you don't. That will give the guards something to hoot at tomorrow. They're always watching us squat when we go to the bathroom. You think they could find something more entertaining."

Olivia brushed it off. "I haven't lost that much weight. Look at the rest of you. I had some extra treats today in the carrot field." She smiled, knowing she had tricked the watchman and them as well. They had all lost around twenty pounds and their government-issued clothes hung on boney frames that had once been round and shapely. Yet they didn't complain. It was a way to silently protest. It built up their inner resolve to hold on while keeping their faith.

That night they were issued new clothes for the next season. "Look," said one of the women. In the cuff of her pants were the pages of a small testament rolled up and exquisitely hidden. As darkness invaded the cabin, she read verses from Romans. Each successive night, she would lift up the words of life from Galatians or Ephesians. One of her favorites was Ephesians 1:17-19. "I keep asking that the God of our Lord Jesus Christ, the glorious Father, may give you the Spirit of wisdom and revelation so that you may know him better. I pray also that the eyes of your heart may be enlightened in order that you may know the hope to which he has called you, the riches of his glorious inheritance in the saints and his incomparably great power for those of us who believe." Whoever sent those pages had chosen them well. These were Words of Life made Flesh, and they savored them like a king's feast as they drowsed off to sleep. The Holy Spirit guided their thoughts as the holy words were read. For these ladies, the meaning of the testimony became real. The suffering was for a reason. Their refining of the faith was a gift amidst the horror of imprisonment. The pages were passed inconspicuously to the other cabins of religious prisoners and provided the succor that came with the words of the Master.

The following morning, Olivia was all aflutter. It was so unlike her. When she sidled up to Mercedes on their field detail, she let go the torrent of anticipated sharing.

"Oh, Mercedes, I have the most wonderful message to share with you today. It was so difficult to not just blurt it out this morning. Last night your brother Titus visited me in a dream. It was him, really him, and he said he had a message for you."

The stunned look on Mercedes' face said it all. "Titus—he's alive? Oh, thank God."

"Yes. He was in a Chinese Communist concentration camp. They were in the process of moving him to a temporary camp near the coast in preparation for a transfer to a Chinese-controlled island in the Pacific. However, there was an immense explosion at the fuel depot next to their camp. Amidst all the chaos, screams, and smoke,

Titus found himself being guided by one of the guards of the camp to a doorway opened by the key the guard carried. The guard was a Christian. He whispered, 'I am a brother in Christ.'

"Along with Titus, there was a mother and her baby and two teenage boys. The guard hurried them down to the river where there was a Cambodian fishing trawler that had unloaded its catch and was preparing to disembark. Titus and the others were spirited down to the underbelly of the ship as fire engines screamed and smoke continued to cover the grounds. He told me that now he is in India, preparing other local Nepalese youth to climb the mountains safely and continue the rescue efforts for our brothers and sisters in Christ. Because of his looks, he was too conspicuous and endangered the operations. He is where he can be of the most help."

The tears pouring down Mercedes' cheeks revealed her feelings. "Thank you, precious Jesus, for your provision and care. I am so happy to hear that my brother Titus is alive. And thank you, Holy Spirit, for your revelation and inspiration for this miracle. You are wonderful." The news was a boon to Mercedes' flagging spirits.

For Mercedes, the abuse of the warden continued almost weekly. Depending on the day, he would stand at the office door.

"Get in here. We have business to address."

She went willingly.

The warden would waste no time getting to the point. "Hurry up and take off your clothes. We don't have all day." He would watch her undress. If she was too slow, he sped up the process with a hearty slap of his fat hand across her face.

A more wicked fiend would be hard to find. He found excitement in her revulsion. "Don't you like me on top of you like this? Don't you think I drive you mad with excitement?" he would drool as he rubbed his groin on her body. If she would not answer, he would make sure to slap her again. "You're a wonderful specimen to be sent to us. Usually, the crop of Christians is old and wizened. But you, sweetheart, are a lovely specimen. I can't resist you." When he was done, he would grunt and roll onto the floor, working laboriously to stand back up. He laughed at her stoicism. "I know you like this," he chided as he swatted her buttocks. "You know you do. Now get out of here, bitch, before I choose another pretty and send you off for good." Mercedes endured and her friends prayed, especially Olivia. "Dear Jesus, remove this sinful man from among us. Keep my lovely sister in Christ safe from this monster." Nothing seemed to happen.

As the summer crept in among them on invisible feet, Mercedes began to get sick several mornings in a row. Often, she would find herself vomiting in the fields while she was on her knees weeding. She hid it from the overseer, but the women on her team were aware of her actions.

"Are you all right, Mercedes?" asked one of her cabinmates.

"Yes, but I feel sick again. I don't know what they are changing with the mess hall, but something in the food is messing with my stomach. Seems like once I vomit, I'm all right."

Marcia, the bunkmate looked at her quizzically. "Are you sure there is not something else upsetting your stomach? It seems strange that you would be feeling sick all the time and we are all fine."

"Oh, I get like this sometimes. Guess my stomach has still not adjusted to this new life. Our diet here is lacking, that's for sure. I'm trying to think of what I ate differently from you guys. Maybe it is the water. Since we don't have a purifying system, maybe I picked up bacteria of some sort."

"Could be. But again, we would all be sick as well. Plus, for you, it's almost always a morning thing. Once you get the nausea out of your system, you are good for the day." They had come to the same sorry conclusion before Mercedes did herself. She was pregnant.

When the realization hit her later that week after another episode, she was hoeing a cabbage patch. The shock made her freeze in mid-motion. "Oh God, no! It can't be!"

Her friends huddled around and hugged her. There was nothing to say. Mercedes broke out in excruciating sobs. "God, no!"

The guard at the end of the row saw the commotion. He rushed over and butted Mercedes and the other women in the stomach. "Get back to work, scum," he growled. They looked at him with anger but broke apart and returned to their field tasks. Mercedes worked slowly and methodically. She had to figure out what to do. What were her options?

"Olivia, before dinner call, I'm going to sneak into the medical clinic and talk to the doctor. Pray for me that this goes well. My world is falling apart."

That evening before she headed over to the dining hall for a scanty supper, she paused to wash up in the water trough that stood in the camp yard. She tried to inconspicuously slip into the clinic to see the doctor.

"Nurse Snyder, get me a pregnancy kit pronto."

The nurse eyed Mercedes with disgust. What kind of a Christian did she think she was, meeting one of the men from their partner camp for sex? She must be a slut.

The nurse stood over her as she administered the kit. Although it was outdated, she recognized the model and felt confident that its results would be accurate. Mercedes sucked in her breathe when she saw the almost immediate results.

"Oh no. God help us." What she saw confirmed her worse fear. Then the doctor sauntered back into the room as Mercedes sat there in stunned silence. He had a smirk on his face.

"Yes, you are pregnant. You have intentionally broken the rules of conduct. Who did you hook up with? You will need to fill out these medical forms for further treatment." She understood he knew who the culprit was but that would not be an acceptable answer. In fact, it would earn her at least another year in the rehabilitation camp. She refused to answer.

"Your refusal to answer will most likely get you into solitary. Get back to supper and do not say anything about this to your friends. We don't want the detainees to think that sex is a way of life in this camp."

Mercedes pushed back the tears and the panic. She bit her lip and hurried back to the dining hall. All her friends looked at her with sympathy. They could read her face and the flush that crept from ear to ear.

While she sat at the table, Mercedes mused silently about the slight hope that they would now send her back to civilization, at least to give birth. That night she stole out of bed to talk in whispers to Olivia.

"I took a pregnancy test today at the clinic. It confirmed my worst fears. I'm pregnant with the child of that bastard warden." She could not control her anger for the moment. "What do you think the warden is going to do when he hears about my predicament? I'm so scared. The warden is a monster. I have no inkling of how he will react to both me and the baby if he finds out."

Olivia held out her hand and hugged Mercedes. "Let's hope that he doesn't learn about it from the doctor or the staff. Hopefully, they will keep it private."

"Fat chance that will happen. I know the doctor, if that's what he really is. From my training, I can tell he knows next to nothing about medicine. He's a lackey for the warden. He just tries to look good so the warden will give him a glowing recommendation when he leaves here. He probably figures if he plays his cards right, he might even get a ticket to leave early."

"Oh, Mercedes, let's pray for your little baby. He or she is such a gift from God. And let's pray that those in this camp who are in darkness would recognize that God not only loves them, but that He forgives them for the evil they have done to us. I pray that God will make a way for this little one to survive in such awful circumstances. God have mercy."

As Mercedes was leaving for the work detail the next morning in the drizzling rain, the nurse at the clinic called her in.

"You'll stay here today," demanded the doctor. He examined her and quickly administered a shot. "For the pain," he explained.

"What are you doing?" she questioned as she lay on her back squirming uncomfortably on the worn examining table.

"I'm not sick. I'm pregnant. Do you even know what that is or has your training omitted that course of study? Now let me get back to my work detail. I am perfectly able to continue." Her speech was becoming slurred.

She was having trouble focusing on the ceiling as things started to swirl in the room. She thought she was going to be sick.

"Well, we're performing an abortion, of course," he said with an emotionless tone of voice. "It's protocol."

"No!" yelled Mercedes. She was aghast that she had not thought of this possibility earlier. She could have tried to escape. But the only escape she had now was down an icy tunnel into semi-consciousness.

The nurse quickly cinched her arms down to the side of the bed and fastened cold metal clamps to her feet.

"This won't hurt you a bit," said the doctor as Mercedes gave way to the sedation. She could hear voices talk of hair and feet and felt a stabbing pain in her uterus. She felt sick and started to convulse in dry heaves, knowing enough to turn her head as she vomited bile.

Her abdomen was on fire, and she could feel blood flowing between her legs, but her mouth could not form words to cry out. Eventually she fell into a troubled sleep, waking in the middle of the night.

There was a young, shy nurse attendant sitting by the side of her bed, and when Mercedes stirred, she got up and asked how she felt.

"Awful. How could they?" she cried through clenched teeth.

The nurse gazed down at her hands. She seemed genuinely sorry for Mercedes.

"They don't know," she whispered. "Your little guy was so beautiful. He was big for his age. I'm sorry."

Mercedes would have answered, but a sharp stab caught her breath. The nurse took her temperature—104 degrees. Mercedes could not sit up without excruciating pain.

"I'd better get the doctor. He doesn't like to be disturbed, but this is pretty bad." Compassionately, she hurried out of the clinic. Mercedes could hear the door bang and then she dropped into a stupor.

For days she was in and out of consciousness. The infection that set in after the abortion was ravaging her internal organs, and she hung onto life by a slim thread. Her cabinmates came to the clinic door each day but left with no word of her progress. Each night they prayed for hours for her recovery. It came, but only with the heartbreaking news that her uterus had accidentally been cut by the excavating scalpel. The doctor told her he was sorry. Most likely she would not be able to have any more children.

"I was sent here to finish my residency," he stated. "I was only in my first year of medical training, but they offered these clinic opportunities at rehabilitation sites to shortcut our medical school and broaden our ability to work on patients in unconventional ways. It was an easy choice for me. I did not have any training in abortions, but I did the best I could. You should eventually be fine and be able to resume your regular duties. Now stay away from the warden. He is in an even fouler mood than usual. He knows what happened in here and he blames you. You'll be lucky if he doesn't transfer you to the camp down the road where the seniors usually end up."

Mercedes could not help but think how this event had shaped her life. While the doctor's life was made easier by his decision to come to the camp, hers was ruined by his botched medical malpractice. He was not fit to work on any breathing creature. Mercedes all but gave up on living, and she moved about each day in an almost dream-like state. Her depression settled in around her like a vise. Not surprisingly, she saw no more of the warden. He was smart enough to know that in a camp full of convicts who despised him, even he had to watch his step.

Time droned on for Mercedes. In the evenings, Olivia would spend time talking to Mercedes, trying to lift her spirits and give her hope.

"Mercedes, you are loved by all of us. The Lord has given your brother Titus new life. Remember the story I told you a few weeks ago? He's watching out for you too," said Olivia encouragingly.

"Yes, but Titus was saved. My baby was killed. Probably I'll go too," cried Mercedes.

"No, God has much more in store for you," Olivia replied.

"What do you hope for, Olivia?" asked Mercedes.

There was a look of dreaminess about her friend. "I can't wait to get back to talk to my brother Arun. Do you remember meeting him? I was angry the last time he visited our little band because he told me he had decided to join the CLF and fight for our Christian rights. I told him that Jesus did not condone violence. He would not buy my argument. He is strong willed like that. Anyway, I want to just tell him I love him and that he needs to listen more intently to what the Holy Spirit is leading him to do. Arun likes to go his own way and then check in with God as an afterthought. Never a good strategy," Olivia said matter of factly.

"A lot of us are like that," said Mercedes with a slight grin.

"In some ways you two are alike. You are strong and resilient. Mercedes, if I don't make it out of here, will you find him and tell him what happened?" pleaded Olivia.

"Don't say anything so awful, Olivia. We could not survive this place without you," said Mercedes.

"He has a secret mailbox in Baltimore near the train station. It is just a wooden box that hangs on the side of Mike's Bike Shop on Front Street. It is the fourth box down. He told me this was the best way to contact him in the future," Olivia shared.

"Yeah," Mercedes replied. "I would like to meet him again. You mean the world to me. I couldn't love you more as a sister."

They hugged and cried. Olivia cried the most.

***

"Mercedes, you've been reassigned to the kitchen for health reasons," shared the head cook on the way to dinner. "Stop by and let me find out what I need to know about your skills."

She stopped in after dinner and was interviewed for ten minutes. "Well, it is evident you can cook, but have only the basic skills. It is nice to know that you were raised by a family that prepared their own food. Hardly anyone does that anymore. Well, they are forced to do it more often now that food is being rationed. That is a good thing. Tell you what. You've been through tough times here. I need someone to help with food prep. Can you wield a knife and a potato peeler?" asked the head cook.

There was comfort in her motherly questioning. "Yes, I can do that."

"Good. You will come here each morning when the crews leave for the fields and help mostly with vegetables. We prepare as you know bulk food, large pots of it, usually soup, for the detainees. After you are finished with the cutting and slicing, I want you to manage this stove. Make sure that you keep the temperature low and don't burn anything. If dinner is ruined, there are no replacements. You and your friends will just have to eat whatever comes their way. Got it?"

"I think I can manage," said Mercedes with a touch of a smile. She recalled an old conversation with her mother.

"Mercedes, for the life of me, I don't know why cooking in the kitchen is so difficult for you. Just look around this place. What is going on with this supper you were supposedly preparing for us?" queried her mother.

"Well, Mom, it is a disaster. I'm sorry I set the smoke alarm off again. Somehow when I put things in the oven, I forgot to set the timer. That stuffed chicken with rice and mushrooms looked sumptuous. I figured if nothing else, I would smell it when it was ready to come out. So, I sat out on the porch reading that new novel from the series *Lost Loves* that I find fascinating. Just checked it out from the library today," said Mercedes.

"So that was a chicken? I was not sure what animal it was. I just know it's burnt to a crisp. This is the second time this month that you almost set the house on fire. We need to come up with a solution to your lack of culinary skills," replied her mother.

"I know. I'll check out some cooking DVDs and get inspired," said Mercedes.

"I don't think that inspiration is the problem. I think it is the follow through and the attention to detail. Maybe we will just have to make peace with the fact that you are not a cook," her mother countered with a smile.

"Can I rescue the chicken?" Mercedes said with a chuckle.

"Just tell it to not bother crossing the road. It's done in anyway," her mother answered as they both laughed.

Mercedes coached herself now at the camp. "I need to stay on top of my chores here. The team needs nutrition in the evening. They are slowly dying from lack of sustenance. Maybe I can help the cooks with some suggestions for an improved higher calorie menu." Her mom would like that. It would be redemption of sorts.

Working in the kitchen gave her time off between morning chores and afternoon food prep. This allowed her more flexibility to visit the sanctuary in the woods constructed by the believers. In a wooded grove near the end of the camp, a group of internees had crafted an altar out of packing crates. Nothing adorned the altar but a crude, hand-carved cross. Occasionally someone would leave flowers, a memento, or a stone with the name of a dear one or a camp acquaintance that had passed away. Death in this camp came all too often. Mercedes would kneel in the soft forest undergrowth and pray in a simple yet heartfelt conversation to her friend and comforter, Jesus.

At times, the Spirit would intervene and carry her thoughts to Jesus when the words would not come. Lying there, she would sob until her reservoir of tears ran dry. This kept her going and connected to reality as she struggled to recover from her brutal rapes and forced abortion. When she left the arbor one late autumn afternoon, she noticed an earthy patch of white mushrooms with something that resembled a frilly apron underneath. They were partially concealed under the falling leaves at the wood's edge. At once she recognized that they were a deadly variety called Destroying Angels. Appropriate she thought for such a place.

She recalled her mother's frequent walks into the woods during her childhood in Virginia which involved healthy lessons on what the forest provided and what was best to leave untouched.

"Now, Mercedes, these mushrooms must be left alone. They are absolutely deadly. One taste will shut down your liver and kidneys. Then it will be all over. Look at them carefully and never forget. Do you see what makes them different from the ones we eat?" cautioned her mother.

"Yes, Momma," she replied, understanding the severe results of this plant that looked so innocent.

As Mercedes came back to the present, she slowly walked past the mushrooms and then did a brusque turnaround, scooping up a handful with leaves and placing them in her pocket. She heard the words bouncing around in her head, "One bite will shut down your liver and kidneys and you will be dead." Over the next few weeks, she crumbled her supply and set them on the windowsill by her bed to dry. She knew the fast-acting effects if they were ingested–shut down of bodily functions, loss of consciousness, and death from just a mouthful or two. When they were dried, she always carried a small supply in a petite pouch tucked in her pocket, not knowing whether she might be driven to eat them someday in a bout of depression or if she would stick them in the warden's soup for revenge. She was not brave enough for either, at least not yet. They were her insurance policy.

One evening as early winter neared its zenith, there was a huge commotion in the dining room. Internees came running from the dining room to the kitchen.

"Mercedes, you need to come help Olivia. The warden is killing her," yelled her friends.

She ran out with the rest of the kitchen staff, tearing off her duty apron, and then hurriedly turned for just a second. Everyone rushed to witness the melee, even if it meant cruelty to an innocent prisoner. Here, their lack of stimulation often got the best of them. There was always guilt afterwards. As she came through the door, she could see her friend Olivia repeatedly being savagely kicked by the warden with his steel-toed boots. While she rushed in to rescue her friend, there was a sudden cry of "Fire," and the warden bolted from the building, watching the pack of angry eyes following him. The camp guards were already at the kitchen, throwing water from the well into the door and commanding the detainees to follow suit. They did so reluctantly, knowing that their scant rations would prove to be even worse if they did not cooperate.

Mercedes and her friends from Cabin 7 gathered around their fallen friend.

Mercedes wiped the blood from Olivia's face. The moans of agony were making her sick. She looked at her cabinmates. "Please carry her to the infirmary and I will meet you there. I have something I must deal with quickly," whispered Mercedes. They looked at her quizzically as she raced out of the building. Swiftly Mercedes moved into the side room of the cleared-out kitchen and cut through the smoky interior to find her prize. There was the dinner tray of the warden still sitting on the counter, the stew still steaming. No one thought it was unusual to see her coming around the corner carrying a dinner tray for the warden, and she was easily lost in the commotion. Stealthily, she placed the tray in its regular position, looking around to see that her friends had taken Olivia for help, and raced back to the team who were investigating how the fire started. It had easily been extinguished. The cause was simple; it was just a boiled over pot of soup unattended during the melee, and a kitchen towel that had burned and scorched the wall. The remaining soup was a loss. The blackened wall was behind Mercedes' stove.

The warden stomped back to his office and dumped his steaming dinner into the trash can. Then he logged onto his computer to report the incident with Olivia in case it would later cause repercussions: "Incident with client that resulted in punishment for insubordination. Client was a troublemaker at the camp and had been reprimanded before. She was prone to seizures which were getting progressively more difficult to control. Could eventually lead to death without proper medication. Patient had just finished eating when she had an extremely strong seizure which knocked her to the floor. She hit her head on the base of the table and blacked out. Unfortunately, the injury is most likely fatal. Next of kin will be notified by official correspondence," noted the warden.

One of the guards was called to bring him a flask of alcohol and within minutes, the warden was horridly drunk. During the night, the residents heard an awful commotion from the warden's office. The shouts, cursing, and crashing of furniture sounded as though a thunderstorm had taken up residence inside.

"Heaven help us," said one of the detainees. "We are all going to pay for this tomorrow."

Mercedes was too deeply invested in praying for her friend Olivia and her survival to hear the ruckus. Her roommates shared with Mercedes what had precipitated the attack. The warden had come out of his office during dinner and waved at a new detainee to come into the office to answer questions. The new girl could not have been older than thirteen, but she was a beauty in the making with long strawberry blond tresses and a delicate face. She was innocent and sweet and was sent to the center with her father and brother who were in the men's camp. Scared and timid, she was at the mercy of the warden.

Olivia, though, had taken the initiative. Standing up, Olivia shouted, "No, you are not going to rape another innocent girl in this camp, you filthy monster," and she moved in front of the shy teenager who began to scream in shrill, hacking sobs, understanding the motives of the warden. The warden had advanced on Olivia like a wildcat despite his blubbery appearance. He was so quick that she could not fend off the first heavy fist which knocked her to the ground. Then he proceeded to viciously kick her repeatedly with his boots in the face and torso while the blood squirted out of her nose and the gashes on her head. He was merciless and brutal. Through it all, Olivia lay unconscious on the floor.

"You disgusting creature," yelled the warden. "Don't you ever question my authority. You are worthless. Understand? Worthless," he repeated as he had kicked her viciously. "Jesus Lover, nothing but a crying baby. You can meet me in hell, you little bitch, and you are not going to tell me what I can and cannot do. Goddamn it. I hate all you people. You make me sick."

Leaving a vast puddle of blood behind during the fire alarm, Olivia's friends whisked her off to the clinic where the doctor took one look at her. Her eyes had rolled back in her head and her breathing was shallow.

"She is in a coma, and I don't have time for a revolutionary in this clinic. Her brain is most likely already swollen from the looks of her eyes. Get her out of here. If the warden sees her, he is likely to have my skin too," yelled the doctor.

"But what can we do for her?" asked the ladies of Cabin 7.

"Get her out of my sight. She is finished one way or the other. Go pray," spit out the doctor with a nasty smirk.

And so, the friends of Cabin 7 gathered around her bunk and began their entreaty to the King of Kings to spare the life of one so rare. All through the night could be heard the droning of spoken prayers added to the silent prayers that were lifted up for dear Olivia. The tongues of men and angels broke through the night sky. Mercedes was distraught and continued to wipe down Olivia's feverish brow with a cool cloth. Olivia moaned and struggled to catch her breath. It was obvious from her bluish skin that her ribs had been cracked and were restricting her breathing. Her face and head were swollen almost beyond recognition.

"God, dear Jesus, hear our prayers," wept Mercedes. She repeated this through the night until she was so hoarse that she was noiseless. The ladies all gathered around her cot on their knees. There was to be no sleep in that dwelling for petitions rang through the skies. Despite their cries, Olivia's breath continued to be increasingly shallow.

"Please, Jesus. She doesn't deserve this. She is good. So good. God have mercy on her soul," prayed Mercedes, deep in grief.

The morning dawned bright, but unusually quiet. The ladies of Cabin 7 carried Olivia's lifeless body down the old dirt road to the homemade chapel in the woods. Since it was their day off, this Sunday morning turned into a funeral service. The detainees stood in silence beside the road to honor their sister of the faith. Her closest friends dug her a shallow grave with their work shovels. Lovingly, they wrapped her in what remained of the cabin's curtains and covered her with an array of dried wildflowers that had been gathered by Olivia earlier in the fall. An angel had fallen to save another.

All work had stopped when the ladies returned to their cabin. The reason was whispered from guard to employee to prisoner. The previous evening, the warden had received a computer dispatch via Homeland Security Headquarters in Washington D.C. stating that he had been recalled immediately and was to catch the six a.m. bus leaving from the premises. There was a nagging voice in the back of his head that told him that he was destined to lose his job. God... "Christian swine" ...he spat as he waited for the bus, a shabby suitcase and boxes by his side.

"I wish I had put a few more of those self-righteous infidels under the ground. They spread like vermin, infecting brains, and behavior. We should have eliminated them all as soon as they were rooted out."

In the same communication, there was a request for the return of Mercedes Singleton to her hometown of Whitsville, Virginias. It read,

> Warden James R. Bowling. You are notified that Mercedes Singleton, a detainee at the Central Rehabilitation Facility, has been pardoned of all crimes charged against her. She is to be released upon receipt of this order. Please send her effects with her as she is to be transported home immediately at the government's expense to Whitsville, The Virginias.
>
> General Marcus P. Hamilton
> Commander – Cyber Security, Potomac Division

Mercedes got the message two days later when the new warden arrived and read the earlier correspondence. He seemed just as cruel as the earlier supervisor, but instead of having a weakness for young women, he had a proclivity to base his worth on results. This was just a steppingstone to better pay and advancement in the government pay scale.

Before breakfast, he called the camp to order that morning at six a.m. "You have had quite a vacation here of late. My theory of rehabilitation camps is to keep the inmates involved and out of trouble. The yield of our agricultural fields has been abysmal, given the weather and the recuperating soil. I expect the summer crop yield to increase fifty percent and an increase of twenty-five percent for the autumn and winter crops. There will be no more lunch breaks and Saturday will again be a workday. Sunday will be a day of rest. We need you strong for the fields, right team? Any questions?"

The camp faithful looked at each other in distress. He would kill half of them with exhaustion within the year if he conducted this decree. But then, he did not care. They were expendable. There always seemed to be an endless stream of believers in Jesus to fill the spots of those who could wage the battle no longer.

God help us, they thought. *We can only take so much.* Just then, the rain began to fall and the new warden, realizing he had no control over that, allowed everyone to return to their regular work detail for the day.

Looking back at the camp through the dusty back window of the bus, Mercedes allowed herself to say a prayer for her beloved, deceased friend Olivia as well as the remaining friends from Cabin 7. "Lord, protect them from the evil one." She couldn't say anything more for the cascade of tears that fell onto her tattered clothes. She was relieved and distressed all at the same time. Her mind raced with questions. *How was I pardoned?* wondered Mercedes. *Did it have to do with the warden? Did someone get word out that I was mistreated?* The only logical reason she could decipher was that it must have come from someone within the government who had influence. But who could this be? Who would speak up for a new believer? She racked her brain but came up empty. Perhaps it was a miracle. Finally, as she dozed off to sleep on the interminable, freezing ride, she briefly gave up questioning the sequence of events. All she could mouth was, "Thank you, Jesus."

Chapter 16

Mack Gersham

December 2035

"Now it is God who makes both us and you stand firm in Christ.
He anointed us, set his seal of ownership on us, and put his Spirit in
our hearts as a deposit, guaranteeing what is to come."
2 Corinthians 1:21-22

All Mack's days and nights seemed to be swallowed up in the never-ending work detail of General Hamilton. Mack had had to revise his computer's programming daily to prevent someone from tracking down his work because there was an upgraded computer system soon rolling out for use at the Pentagon. The Resistance was pressing in on the end of its ability to fool the new and improved tracking hardware for military requisitions, and Mack could feel an impending pressure to do more with less time.

One night when he had barely fallen into bed, his sleep was disturbed with a vivid word swirling on his lips, waking him with a start. "Mercedes." He frankly had not followed up with her since his warning, assuming all was well. He knew her to be cautious enough to heed the warning. She was a reasonable woman and would think through the consequences. She had never been overly religious, so he assumed she would find a safer venue to worship her God.

Sleep eluded him as he tried to clear his mind of this premonition. Finally, he got up, splashed water on his face, dressed in his work uniform and decided to head back to the Pentagon.

Guess you got a weak mind after all, buddy, he said to himself. He would have smirked, but he was too tired. He had a gut feeling that something was up. When he got there, he logged into his account after again scrambling the programming code to the parameters he had set prior to logging off. After forwarding the request through four different servers, what he read horrified him. Mercedes had indeed been arrested by a Fed team sweeping through the population centers searching for radical religious groups that posed a perceived threat of rebellion. She had been sent to a camp in Missouri twelve months earlier.

What he read next made him even angrier. Updated medical records stated that she had suffered a severe injury from a surgical procedure performed on site. She was suffering from complications and her health was compromised. Despite this, the reporting doctor had recommended that she stay at the camp to continue rehabilitation. It was noted that no next of kin had been contacted. The warden, Mr. Bowling, had signed off on the medical report stating that she had a good chance of recovering, but that he had put in a request for her to serve another five years of work for her continued rejection of retraining efforts. Her radical views had not changed since she became a ward of the state and she clung to the beliefs that had taken her to the camp in the first place.

Somehow, Mack knew there was more to the story between the warden and Mercedes than was communicated in the memo. "Damn stubborn Singletons," Mack muttered. "Once they set their mind to something, you can't shake them for anything." Mack thought of Mercedes' brother Titus. He was the same way. Warnings went no place with him either. *Why didn't I think of that when I talked to her earlier?* he thought. Yet he smiled at the Singleton trait of independence which he highly regarded.

It was not long before Mack had crafted a pardon letter for Mercedes and forged the general's signature. He transmitted it through the proper channels of the Pentagon. And for good measure, he recalled the warden, assigning him to a recycling garbage scow in the North Atlantic. He would now spend his days in the rotting filth, separating and recycling the waste of Baltimore and D.C. Out of sight, out of mind. It just got dumped into the Atlantic when no one was looking.

Mack also caught the note posted by the warden about Olivia's death and launched a government investigation for information. If Mack had known the true circumstances, he would have filed charges for incompetence and manslaughter. Perhaps Olivia had died of seizures. But seeing that she was assigned the same cabin as Mercedes, he guessed there was more to her story as well. He had firsthand knowledge of what those camps were like. He also had real government documents describing the violent offender camps. If the warden could be recommissioned to one of those places ... well, he would not last long.

Later that evening as Mack walked home from the bus stop, he noticed that the neighbor's welcome mat had been turned upside down. It was a simple signal using no form of telecommunication, to notify Mack that he should report to either Lt. Col. Wells or the general himself. He knew where the rendezvous time and place would be. He would have to hurry, change into civilian clothes, and grab his communication gear stashed down the street in an abandoned shed. He also took his gun. Within ten minutes he was organized and on the road. A government car had conveniently been left for him on the next street by the post office. Soon he was cruising below the speed limit to a secluded farm in the Virginias' eastern panhandle.

It was the old stomping ground of Lt. Col. Wells when he was a boy, and it held a thrill for Mack too. It reminded him of home. Nostalgia flooded over him for a moment, but he knew he must push it back in place. The ramshackle red barn once held a menagerie of sheep, old horses, and chickens. Mack was so familiar with the partially hidden driveway that he could almost drive it without lights or eyes. His military prowess had taught him to pay overt attention to details and distances. He was simply good at it. *Better not try it tonight,* he thought. *Messing up a government car that is not registered to me could have its consequences.*

Mack sidled up near the barn and the lieutenant colonel came out and motioned that all was well. Climbing out of the car, Mack could tell by the clenched lips of the lieutenant colonel that things were getting dicey. He was curious as to what to expect.

General Hamilton explained that the organization of the Resistance was about complete. He had used his personal contacts with officers coming back from the Middle East Desert War to craft a military unit that was committed to resisting the infringement of the military elite. They knew their intentions of taking away the powers of the United States and handing them over to the World Nations Alliance. They were committed to stop them at all costs.

These men were skilled fighters, but better yet, they were out-of-the-box thinkers, and they formed a fighting unit that prioritized allegiance and stealth. Each of the six or seven cells worked primarily in the Middle States. This was their current means of protest against the alignment of the military to General Lu's camp. They knew eventually the country's power and autonomy would be transferred into the clutches of the World Nations Alliance if Lu succeeded.

Thanks to Mack and other IT engineers, military hardware including nuclear rocket launchers, telecommunication devices, and survival supplies had been delivered to a network of depots in the Middle States. Their meeting revolved around the new task force that had been set up under General Lu's orders to find out what rogue group was siphoning off supplies and where they had been stashed. Using the new military reporting system, it would be impossible to continue the work that Mack had faithfully executed, and it was likely they would be tracked within hours of making any further requests. Mack could feel Lu breathing down his neck, and if caught, he knew the punishment would be death as a traitor to the country.

"It's just a matter of time," sighed the general. "I have a big decision to make. I either need to take General Lu's treasonous behavior to the president and convince her of what is happening behind her back or let her go down with the rest of the country, believing in a schemer who will destroy the nation. If we stop the madness of Lu before he ruins us all, wouldn't that be the better solution?"

The three of them talked long into the night about alternative plans, methods of escape, and whom to trust. On the last item, there was no assurance that they knew.

Before they left, the general asked Mack to gather all the codes for the requisition centers as well as inventory lists. "We need to have a copy placed in a safe location. Make one for yourself too. If I need it, I'll let you know." The lieutenant colonel looked uncomfortable with Mack keeping the information, but he didn't say anything. He had seen how men had failed them already in this operation, and he knew this was a life-or-death mission for the general. He would die for him rather than betray him.

They shook hands.

Mack could only feel a heaviness fall on them as they crept out over the crunching gravel onto the main road. He checked his mirror two or three times to make sure he was not being followed. He had known that eventually their actions would come to this. What was General Hamilton going to do?

Heck, Mack thought to himself, *what am I going to do!*

Chapter 17

Mercedes Singleton

December 2035

"I pray that out of his glorious riches he may strengthen you with power through his Spirit in your inmost being." Ephesians 3:16

She stumbled from the belching bus, her limbs atrophied from sitting huddled up as close to herself as possible to keep warm. Slowly she traipsed down the hill constantly maintaining eye contact on the small house she called home. As Mercedes began to enter the flagstone sidewalk, her father saw her and leapt from his porch seat to embrace her.

Emotion at finally being home and feeling safe washed over Mercedes. First, she clung to his frame, and then she began to wipe her silent tears on his shirt. He had known of her arrest but nothing more. It was a miracle that she was standing here in front of him. Occasionally people were released from work camp, but usually at the behest of a federal legislator who was receiving cold hard cash on the back side.

Virgil pulled out a well-used handkerchief, a perpetual habit, dried his daughter's tears and led her into the house. Walt had been watching the whole scene from the window. He had to refrain from lifting her up and swinging her around with joy. She had become his adopted sister. Mercedes had shown him, an orphan, that he would always hold a special place in her heart. No one could have loved a blood-born sister more than he loved Mercedes. He took her hand in his as she sat next to him on the sofa and kept patting the top of it.

"Mercedes is home now. Walt is so happy." When Walt was stimulated emotionally, he would often revert to baby talk. "Don't worry, Mercedes, I am your little brother, and I am going to make sure you are safe from now on. You are never going to leave Whitsville again. I am your protector," replied Walt in all seriousness.

For Mercedes, moving back to normal life was difficult. Her first month was mostly a fog. Days were long and frosty. Nights were full of nightmares. She shared her experiences with her father, but not the worst ones. They were too raw. Virgil knew there was more to her history, but he did not pry. He had heard through the faith network that life in rehabilitation camps was compared to hell on earth. They were forgotten zones by the regular public who viewed them as a necessary evil. Most ignored the atrocities that occurred every day to people who had simply declared that they placed their trust and their lives in the hands of their Savior, Jesus Christ. They suffered for Jesus.

What kept her sane were her evening devotions and the verbal conversations she had with God in which she poured out her heart's burdens and cares. "God, how could you allow evil to overtake the innocent? How will you avenge Olivia's blood? When will you return to rescue the innocent and judge the guilty? Cover my friends with your mercy," wept Mercedes. Almost all the conversations ended with the same repeated questions.

This repartee with God and the quiet time to think and breathe slowly brought her back to reality. She felt comfort in knowing that God shared with her that He had a plan. The Holy Spirit awakened her one night, reminding her that He knew His beloved children were being persecuted. He promised that the time would come when He would intervene to correct the rule of evil, returning the world to His love and His goodness. "Hold on to the hope that your faith brings. I will make all things new in its time."

"But we need it now, God," Mercedes begged. The Spirit did not reply. Mercedes knew that mankind itself would never be able to climb out of this mess. If anything came to the fore from her experience, it was that man is flawed and sinful. Humans had figured that they could get along without God and craft a higher quality life without Him. It had the familiar ring of political campaign slogans that promised a more perfect world. *We are making a lousy mess of the whole thing. We will never learn*, she thought with chagrin.

Yet the inky gloomy nights also held her most alive experiences with God. The Holy Spirit reminded her that this was a time when she leaned into Him out of necessity. She had seen the face of Jesus reflected in her friend Olivia, who had given her life for a friend. There was no greater love. Mercedes realized that to have a full and fulfilled life, she would need to make her relationship with God personal and primary. The world was out of control. But what she could do was be His emissary, sharing the more perfect love that she was being taught despite the enemy's evil plans. The curtain of depression was lifting.

By early spring, Mercedes asked if she could pitch in at the local hospital, which was desperate for help. Soon, she became the mainstay of their medical community, both with her medical care and her reliance on the Holy Spirit to guide her walk.

She was forced to confront her hatred of the warden and to seek forgiveness for her anger. While it made little sense, she realized that the anger held control over her soul, so one night she determined that with the Spirit's help, she would give it up. It was difficult, so difficult.

It cut against common sense and justice. "But justice is Mine," said the Spirit. Never did she forget the dream of Olivia's concerning Titus.

"Jesus, I know you called Titus into a place of service using his particular gifts. I also believe you have saved him to continue the work of mercy and rescue. Hear my prayers for his continued safety. And bless Olivia's brother Arun in his endeavors to protect the Christians here in the States. Place a hedge of protection around them both. Lord, touch them with your Spirit. Let them know that we have asked for favor and covering. Be with them as you bring the wisdom of the Spirit into their endeavors. Amen," prayed Mercedes.

Mercedes began to live again. As the months traipsed by on the calendar, she became more accustomed to her natural environment realizing that this little slice of the world was her call in life. Despite all the trials, and sickness, and unfairness of recent experiences, she found contentment in living in the broken world in which she had been placed.

Ignoring the federal mandate that all public religious expression be curtailed, her father Virgil would assemble the few who remained of his flock—those who were either still alive or brave enough to counter the law. Three elderly women each Sunday would whisk into the side door of the church while Walt and Virgil unlocked the front doors and propped them open for the Lord to know He was welcome there.

Originally Mercedes had attended these services, but they were slow and plodding, full of repetitive lessons and made her mind groggy. Her biggest issue was her inability to concentrate. Of late, she had instead taken this time to climb to the top of Bald Knob with her Bible, which as of yet was still not outlawed as a book of hate. After checking for silent copperheads sunning themselves on the heated slabs of limestone, she would lay back and read passages of The Psalms or the Gospels or, if she was daring, Revelation. What was best was just resting in the Lord and giving herself time to listen to Him. She heard a litany of truth during those morning times of worship. "Mercedes, you are chosen by Me," "You are perfect in all ways," "I chose you before you were born," "Love Me first, and then love those who surround you," whispered God.

As the weeks and then months went by, He told her where He was during certain parts of her life. "Mercedes, did you know that I was always with you? Did you understand that no matter your life experiences, I have already choreographed a way to use them to benefit your future? I have entered your pain as you have poured out the sorrow of your abortion, the brutal rapes, and Olivia's murder. I want to carry that pain for you. Will you release it to me?" asked God. She was able to do so, for she now trusted God in His promises. What came was something besides human comfort. It was the Presence … all around her … almost suffocating her. There could be no doubt that the words spoken in her ears and the pressure on her heart were none other than the Holy Spirit leading, affirming, guiding, and cherishing.

In the ensuing days, Mercedes continued to heal, not completely, but enough that she was able to move to a less fragmented center where her pain was addressed and covered with the salve of His Presence. On one such Sunday morning as she basked in the sun with the Bible resting on her chest, she caught a movement out of the corner of her eye down on the path at a place where the shrubs were sparse. Immediately she could tell from his gait who it was. Despite his expert efforts to camouflage his movements, she was able to track his progress to about thirty yards away from her. He was in the last thicket of vegetation before "Old Baldy" raised his silver head.

What can he be doing up here and why is he stalking me? she wondered. *Oh God, please let his motives be pure.* She gathered up her belongings around her and then said courageously, "Hello, Ricardo. Are you out for a Sunday hike too?"

He jumped up in chagrin but rapidly recovered. "Well, to be honest, I had nothing to do this morning, and when I saw you out for a stroll, I thought I would check out the local sights and see what you found so appealing up here. I had been attending your dad's services for a few weeks at his invitation, but they are just not for me."

He took his eyes off hers and gazed at the distant mountain chains that rose in rounded uneven ridges trimmed in different shades of indigo. They stood the test of time as tinged sentinels of purple, gray and charcoal, seeming to speak of strength and permanence.

"Beautiful, isn't it," he said, glad he could come up with a distraction. Hopefully, she had taken the bait. "Why aren't you down with your dad at service?"

Now she was surprised. He was glad he had her unbalanced. He knew he could cause trouble for the family. He continued, "I went to service last week when your dad said he was doing some history lessons on how people in this area love their neighbor. It was an interesting morning with good old-fashioned stories on being sacrificial in your love. But it was too much lecturing for me. The world is not really like that. I can tell your father does care for people and I appreciate him giving me a roof over my head. He is someone who practices what he preaches. Can't say that I've seen that very often in my life."

Truthfully, Ricardo had gone to services for only one reason. He was half convinced that there was a definite connection between the Blues Resistance and the church. Disappointingly, no one was there except Walt, the preacher, and the old ladies, none of which posed any threat. But his main target continued to be Walt. He was the twin brother of Mack Gersham, a former intelligence IT officer now working at the Pentagon. He was under suspicion of having connections to the Blues in an unknown capacity. The missives he had received the past few weeks offered information from his resume.

Ricardo had had communication that Mack might be the key to connecting the dots between the lost requisitions and the brave hit-and-run attacks by the subversives. Despite repeated interviews in the past couple of months by the federal agents who arrived with no invitation, the residents of Whitsville could be linked to no criminal activity. General Lu was unwilling to let up on the pressure of catching the big fish, whoever it was.

Chapter 18

Mack Gersham

June 2036

"The wind blows wherever it pleases. You hear its sound,
but you cannot tell where it comes from or where it is going.
So it is with everyone born of the Spirit." John 3:8

The plan had been laid out months ago and Mack was thoroughly familiar with the protocol. He bagged up private mementos and tossed them in an old army duffle bag which he put in the trunk of his car. Looking around his apartment, he checked to see that nothing was amiss. Everything looked as though he would be back in a minute. He would be unless everything went south.

Grabbing the cyber cylinder on which he had downloaded all the coded information, he walked out his back door and down the sidewalk to the next street where his car was again parked by the post office.

Silently he slid into the front driver's side and headed to the farm outside of D.C. in the Virginias' panhandle. His car's license plates were shielded from being observed by radar or camera, and he let his guard down enough to allow himself to think of what lay ahead for the Resistance. There never was a master list of soldiers who had thrown their hat in with General Hamilton, so he was not sure who to trust, but Mack was sure, at this critical juncture, that he was only one of a handful of soldiers who had knowledge of the events unfolding that evening.

His message from Lt. Col. Wells, which was sent to his car phone, explained that he would meet Mack at the end of the drive. If he was not there, move down the county road to see if someone flagged him down.

Slowing down on Old Route 7, Mack peered into the thickening darkness. No one was there with the appropriate light signal, so he slowed his speed and crept down the highway for a mile and a half. Pulling his car into an old junkyard, he opened the trunk and put on a requisitioned uniform belonging to Lu's elite security forces, complete with night vision goggles, a firearm, and a radio that only transmitted classified government channels. He was not willing to try the radio. It was too risky as there was already something amiss. Jogging silently up the highway, he turned into the woods just before the gravel driveway and barely missed a patrol that was paying attention to the road. Their conversation was quiet, and Mack could not catch anything except a couple of words, one being Hamilton.

Slowly making a large U around the guard, he continued quietly into the woods. He smiled at the thought of the old game he and his brother used to play in the dark–Catch Me If You Can. He was always better than Walt at sneaking up on his opponent in the woods. Occasionally he would let Walt win.

Walt was always Mack's soft spot. The last time they played Catch Me If You Can, they had been about fifteen years old. The summer sun had set over the treed hills, and Walt suggested that with all the fireflies, it would be a perfect night to pick the special hiding spot. They designated the area for hiding and defined its boundaries. Walt volunteered to hide first. Mack sat out on the rickety porch, giving Walt more than the required ten minutes to conceal himself. The point of the game was to find the person hiding, sneak up on them, and scare them before they were able to come out of hiding and return to home base.

Mack smiled at his brother's eager anticipation to play such a juvenile game. Since he got pure enjoyment from it, turning Walt down was next to impossible. That night however, Mack could not find Walt. He searched the garage, under the porch and the dilapidated chicken coop to no avail. And Walt did not even try to make a break for it to home base. Mack was getting frustrated at the thought that his brother had bested him. Tromping over the boundaries again, he spied a pile of brush that rustled a bit too sporadically in the wind.

I've got you now, thought Mack. With one leap he jumped on the brush pile, only to jump back about as fast. Out came a grizzled possum with six babies attached and hissing as she plodded down the path to the house.

Just then, Walt yelled, "Home free" from the front porch.

"Damn," yelled Mack. "How did you do that? Where were you?"

"Come on, brother. I don't give away my hiding places. But I was planning this all day, so I know of places you never dreamed of. I heard you walking around me two times. You need to learn to be stealthier."

"Good advice, bro." Mack tousled Walt's hair. "Hey, I snuck a few of Dad's cigarettes out of his pack. Want to have a smoke behind the garage?"

Walt looked shocked. "He'd kill you if he found out."

"He won't find out if you don't say anything," said Mack.

Walt was hesitant. "How 'bout I watch you to see how it's done?"

Mack laughed and raced off. *What a brother*, he mused. He would not trade him for anyone else.

Mack's thoughts snapped back to attention. Near the barn, it was obvious that something was wrong. There were guards with dogs who were beginning to get nervous and growl. Mack quickly moved behind the barn. He used his old game skills to stay secluded. Spying the aged red oak tree that had spread its arms over the barn after years of neglect, he shimmied up enough to throw his leg over the first branch and stealthily climbed up until he could peer into the weathered abyss once used to drag hay inside for storage.

Lt. Col. Wells sat strapped to a farmhouse chair, the paint mostly peeled off. His head flung back unnaturally, and a large swath of blood covered the back of his military shirt. There was no doubt he was dead. It was so foreign to this soldier who always had an air of standing at attention about him.

A duo of interrogators was pressing General Hamilton but getting nowhere. With each question, they would slap him on the face and spit on him. Mack thought he recognized one of them, but his suspicion was cut short by both a shot sounding from an interrogator and a pair of barking dogs coming around the barn. They were slobbering and pulling on their leads to the chagrin of their handlers. "Shut the hell up," one said. "You will freakin' wake the whole neighborhood."

"Shut those mutts up," yelled the person who was clearly in charge. "Get the team in here to clean up this nasty mess and bring those bodies back to the truck. Don't allow any blood to be on anything but the tarps. Got it?"

"Yes, sir."

The dogs continued to pull in the direction of Mack's scent while the handlers pulled to return to the barn entrance. Mack wished he had picked up the kit of miscellaneous tools from his truck. There was a scent desensitizer that drove dogs mad. He huddled in the thickest cluster of branches and froze as the handlers scanned the trees. The noise was enough to waken a slumbering creature from under the floorboards of the barn. He had claimed this old barn as his territory months before, and the dogs had awakened one grouchy skunk. He sauntered out and stood in front of the dogs with disdain and instantly let out his charge before the soldiers could yank the dogs out of range.

The smell was overpowering. "Shit," said the handlers.

The leader of the expedition came out of the barn and chastised the handlers. "Get those dogs out of here. Take them back in your own truck now. I'll take care of the hostages." He chuckled at the name hostages. There was something about the tenor of that voice that Mack found familiar. He wracked his brain to think of where he had heard it before.

They disappeared and Mack slid down the rough trunk. He half walked, half ran to his car. He smelled slightly of skunk, but his thoughts were on escape. He knew where he was to go. Stripping out of his camouflage clothes, he tossed them in the trunk and headed south. It would be sunrise by the time he arrived.

Chapter 19

President Santaya Woodring

June 2036

"If you then, though you are evil, know how to give good gifts
to your children, how much more will your Father in heaven give
the Holy Spirit to those who ask him!" Luke 11:13

The president was awakened from her sleep at five a.m. Her snoring husband did not move a muscle when her executive aide jostled her shoulder. "Emergency meeting of the chiefs of staff in an hour. General Hamilton has been assassinated," she whispered.

The president nodded her head. Inside, her stomach was churning. She turned deathly pale, but it went unnoticed in the dark pallor of the room. "I'll be ready shortly. Meet me here in half an hour," President Woodring ordered her executive assistant.

She arrived five minutes before the meeting, hair pulled back in a bun and dressed in a tailored navy jacket, black slacks, and comfortable pull-on shoes. General Lu took charge of the meeting, briefly explaining that his security forces had picked up chatter from the Christian Liberation Front that they were planning a big hit. They had been successful. General Hamilton and his aide, Lt. Col. Wells, were discovered shot execution style in their government car by a military patrol assigned to guard the general's weekend house. Details of how this could have happened were incomplete. An intensive investigation was already underway.

General Lu had given orders to round up the known leaders of the CLF and charge them with treason and first-degree murder. President Woodring sat quietly, and was composed as usual, yet her face was unusually pale. She listened as the general proposed a tightening of the expression of free speech for hate groups that continued to thrive in the new order. Their ability to share their subversive diatribes via pirated airwaves was wreaking havoc with the safety of regular citizens. They were having their rights challenged by their fears for safety. This restriction needed to start immediately. The country would understand after this horrific event. The president nodded.

President Santaya Woodring asked pointed questions about the general and Wells. "Was there any physical evidence as to who killed them? Did anything of value turn up in the search of the car? What proof did they have that it was CLF?"

"We're still sifting through the evidence," said General Lu bluntly. "I'm working now on a press release and funeral plans with full military honors for the families. We have contacted them both."

In somewhat of a daze, the president returned to her private office and flicked on the television. It was not long before the murders were headline news with pictures of Hamilton and Wells in their starched military uniforms looking attentively at the camera. Santaya looked away. She could not breathe. Two days earlier she had given an address to the graduates of the Army Academy and had been invited to a private luncheon with General Hamilton. Most often, she politely declined such invites, but unexpectedly she warmly accepted the invitation.

Near the end of the lunch the general asked her to step into his office for a moment to discuss something of a personal matter.

Hamilton had decided to take a chance on the president.

He cleared his throat and began. "Madam President, we have some very troubling news to share with you. Over this past year General Lu and his support team have systematically undermined the integrity and independence of the United States. He is currently embedded in a plot to overthrow our government and align our country with the World Nations Alliance. The intent is for America to abdicate her sovereignty in favor of being part of this international consortium of nations pressing for world peace and the sharing of economies and resources. He has been plotting this for several years now. We are aware of his intent to accept the position as vice chairman. Knowing Lu, he is not prepared to stop there."

Santaya looked at him in shock. "So, what proof do you have that something so preposterous is happening unbeknownst to our intelligence community? I find this hard to believe even though I know that General Lu is a self-serving man looking for status and power. Most generals are." She looked at General Hamilton and dared him to counter her assessment. He did not bother. Instead, his assistant Lt. Col. Wells spoke up.

Santaya had difficulty making eye contact with him. She turned stiffly and sat up straight. He had the almost exact likeness of someone who long ago meant the world to her. He was gone. It was like looking at someone who was resurrected from the dead. Wells produced a packet of transcripts of authorized documents that were secretly downloaded from the archives of the World Nations Alliance and scanned over the most condemning parts. "Our source is absolutely dependable," he shared with conviction. Santaya was glad that they at least had someone of integrity on the inside of the WNA. Spies were often outed by well-meaning employees who did not understand that the rules of engagement required such activities.

"So, what you are showing me in these dispatches are from General Lu himself? If I am to believe these, he has sold us all out for his selfish profit and a power grab. How far he has effectively moved forward to overthrow our government is frightening," said the president.

"We are still trying to figure out the nebulous network of his deeply embedded organization. We have an idea of the bare-bones organization, but we haven't been able to fill in all the players. They hold these things tight to the chest. I think there are even members of Congress who are on board with his plans. We have proof that part of the intelligence community has also enlisted in the plot, so it makes it more difficult to access the information we need. If you can give us sources to contact that you trust, we would appreciate it," replied General Hamilton.

The general then shared the basic plan to counter Lu's plot, beginning with the disruption of military supplies to a more broadened effort to flush out the enemies of the State. Hopefully, this would enable a resetting of the government to its call to be a republic. "We will not be a pawn on the world stage." He let her know of the unbelievable heist of military supplies that had already occurred under his command. "We have the weapons to start a small war. What we need that is crucial to our cause are people inside the government whom we can trust. If you can generate a list, either of us would be willing to retrieve it at your earliest convenience. I am also giving you names of people you can contact who are on our list as operatives who hold leadership within our organization. For your sake and ours, I am only giving you two of them," said the general.

As the general moved closer to her, Lt. Col. Wells pressed in. "Your life is in danger as well." He looked at the president with critical concern. Her gaze was locked with his. She could not look away. There was a bit of discomfort on her part. He showed no reaction.

Pausing to process this startling information she continued. "Thank you, Lieutenant Colonel, for your concern. You are an honorable man. I trust you and the general. I am disappointed in myself for not paying attention to the warning signs earlier. I gave Lu so much power to wield. It is difficult for me to realize that all the work our administration has done to keep the world stable has just been an opportunity for Lu to snuggle up to these fiends. There will never be peace this way. Man is too easily swayed by power. In the process of takeover, it is always the little people who suffer most."

She became more engaged in the conversation. "Now, how do you want me to help? It is time for me to get back to my roots," replied the president with great sadness. She realized in a moment that it would be almost impossible to head off this plot that had been years in the making. It was masterminded by the most powerful people in the armed forces and world governments. She wondered who else was involved. Who could she trust? Most of her staff had come in as party appointments. They would shrug this off as a conspiracy theory at best. At worst, they would pass the word on to Lu that the cat was out of the bag.

General Hamilton continued with purpose. "So, by the end of the week, we should be wrapping up our cyber hacking. We have enough arms stashed in depots to pose a threat to any government. But they are hot on our tail in tracing our internal operations. You will need to find a trusted confidant who would be a go between to carry the cylinder with our entire operational code from the rendezvous point to your office. We need a person who would have to be beyond reproach. Someone you know personally, if possible. Their covert actions must keep them beyond reproach in their loyalty to you."

Approaching the president, the general spoke almost inaudibly. "Can you find someone who is dependable and skilled in espionage? There would be danger and death if they were discovered. The worst would be having all our operational details falling into the wrong hands. Your trusted informant could then make the transfer of information personally to you at the White House," stated the general.

General Hamilton placed in her hand a crisp note with the address of the old farm in the Virginias. She alone would have access to all their inventories and the location of each counter-revolutionary base once all the details were consolidated and they had moved forward. Step one would be to hand over resources detailing their actions thus far in this espionage action.

"I think I know whom I can trust. I will talk to him today," she shared. "I need to give you his name and have you run a check on his past. From my interactions with him, he is beyond reproach. We worked in Army Counterintelligence together. He will make the necessary trip down to your farm. If he is compromised, I will let you know." There was a good chance Lu knew who she was going to pick, but she had to take a chance. She was on board, but this was a terribly distasteful business. She wanted the world to be a place where mankind worked for the betterment of each other, where kindness and caring were the nectar of community. Instead, it was back to the never-ending power grab and destruction for self-interest. "How can people be so evil?"

"Our country thanks you for your bravery," sighed the general. Santaya nodded at the gravity of his words.

"Lt. Col. Wells will personally hand deliver a packet of information encrypted with our plans for the future this weekend at your presidential retreat on the Potomac after meeting with your emissary in the Virginias in a few days. Please make sure your staff is alerted to the fact that he will be visiting on official business. We'll make up something that sounds logical as an explanation for his appointment," stated General Hamilton. She dared to glance at Wells again with an almost motherly look of endearment. It seemed odd, but there seemed to be a trust there that encouraged the general.

Out of protocol, she held out her hand to both officers. Surprised, they shook her hand, first the general and then Wells. She seemed to hold his hand just a bit longer than necessary. Inside the president was a heart breaking and crying with the pain of another separation from the son she loved. Yet she showed no emotion. She nodded and left the room to be joined outside by her aide.

"We have work to do," she whispered to her aide, Shirley Smythe. "I need to get some private help with a matter. It's critical."

***

The president sat in her oval office, frozen with the knowledge of the events swirling around her and the feelings of ineptitude. This assassination news shook her to her core. It was just days since she had talked to these two men. She felt like a large part of her soul had been trampled and she willed herself to breathe normally. Slowly she slid her top desk drawer open an inch or two and gazed at the face that had become ingrained in her heart. Lt. Col. Wells; Lt. Col. Shamir Wells. The TV was blasting information about his rise in the military system and his next of kin, Doctors Michael and Melissa Wells, originally from the Virginias who had served as missionary physicians in Africa and then Minneapolis, Minnesota. Now they were currently working in the Metro Center of Houston. A grieving couple was visible on the screen, holding hands and drying tears. He was their only child.

Chapter 20

Santaya Woodring

2006
30 Years Earlier

"And you also were included in Christ when you heard the message of truth, the gospel of your salvation. When you believed, you were marked in him with a seal, the promised Holy Spirit." Ephesians 1:13

After graduating from Wellington University with a degree in International Studies, Santaya had begun her career in an area near and dear to her heart, the African Assistance Association, headquartered in Washington D.C. She had protested the military involvement in the war of Afghanistan and thought the money spent on military expenditures could be applied instead to assist with the severe famine in Africa. Santaya felt that her gifts as an innovator could be useful in assisting the poor and starving.

Collaborating with companies that dealt in Asian commodities, she was able to entice them to begin a supply chain transporting foods from Asia to Africa. These companies realized the value of an almost untapped market. It did not hurt that there were annual grants worth hundreds of thousands of dollars from the UN to provide aid to this region. The companies used these monies to simplify the process by vacuum packaging the foodstuffs and providing saltwater purifiers on a mass scale.

Santaya took a leadership position with the African Assistance Association to ensure that the chain of command met the goals of those in dire need. So much money was wasted on poorly planned programs that had good intentions but failed to meet the explicit goal of assisting the suffering. Santaya knew that every dollar needed to be expended with success in mind.

Moving to the Republic of Congo, Santaya teamed up with a brilliant student from Kenyan University, and they began a training school for the use of the water purifiers which worked on both salt and fresh water. The school soon realized that it was hampered by the startling absence of technological training in this part of the world.

The duo formulated a plan to create a technical college focused on teaching information technology to promising students who had lived through thirty years of civil and religious unrest. Her efforts received notice by her supervisors, who went along with the plans as they began to get more public press and government grants in the hundreds of thousands for research. Her bosses were glad for the publicity. The recognition was a bonus and aided in enticing first-year recruits to sign up for enrollment.

It was a struggle to move this part of the world into the new century. Local leaders began to believe that their own could develop practical business skills. So many had been left behind in the globalization of economic growth. This could be part of the solution to encourage their impoverished people to look to the future. Santaya was an idealist, but it came from her altruism and sincere love for others.

The young man was Shamir Todoten, a native of the Republic of Congo, a bright, promising, and idealistic adult as well. Congo's future would rely on such sons and daughters. While raised Muslim, he was not a follower of any faith. His attendance at the university in Kenya showed him the potential to move his country forward. It did not take him long to not only be impressed by the passion of Santaya for his people, but to silently fall in love with her.

As they planned the layout of the modern technology college, they also enticed staff from around the world to come to the Congo for the enterprising adventure. Romance blossomed slowly and they became involved in a quiet, affectionate affair which evolved six months after her arrival. The locals did not frown upon this union. Her employer, the African Assistance Association, could care less. Rather, they were concerned about private deep-pocket donors who were hesitant to share advanced technology with developing nations. They had been fooled before when their philanthropic donations had been sold off to the highest bidder on the black market. Santaya knew the heart and soul of Shamir. "He is above reproach," she shared with her superiors. "You can trust my judgment." They had in the past. Her record was convincing. So was her pitch to the investors.

Several months into their relationship, as the college was rising brick by brick, Santaya realized she was pregnant. She told Shamir that she would go back to the States to get an abortion. "I just think it is a better option for me. While your medical facilities can do this here, I want to be sure that medically I do all I can to make sure I am safe and unscathed during surgery."

Shamir stared at her.

"What is it?" she asked.

"You can't take the life of my child," he cried. "I was brought up to believe that the lives of my people are precious. All life. It is a gift." He reached out and took her hand. While he did not hold to the foundations of his earlier faith, Shamir still believed in certain truths. He was pleased that he would have a son.

Santaya smiled at his audacity. "And how do you know it is a boy?" she joked.

"You will see. God has answered my prayers," smiled Shamir.

Something about the way Shamir looked forward to having this child spoke of love to Santaya. She thought about his zest for life and decided to accept his belief in the value of all human life. As she began to show, she took to wearing African kaftans to disguise her enlarged abdomen. She was elated with the joy Shamir got from celebrating the progress of their growing son.

"Santaya, I am headed over to the school early today. The electric team from the city will be coming to wire the school and install the computer systems for us. They have texted me with a heads up about guerilla insurgents in this area who are ripping out electric lines in the nearby villages. They are insistent on keeping any type of Western influence out of Africa. They're dangerous. News is that they killed the principal and one of the teachers at a school in Congala last week. We must be vigilant. I will warn the team today when we meet to stay on the alert. I wish we didn't have to deal with these types of problems," said Shamir.

"I just don't get it. Why are they so against progress for their own people? And why kill to gain power? Anyway, I have last-minute plans to address today as well. With President Omri and the cabinet coming for our Grand Opening in three weeks, we will need to get our food and refreshment reservations finalized. Some of the ladies in town are helping with the preparations, as I struggle with cooking," admitted Santaya.

Shamir laughed. "How did you survive in America? Fast food?"

Santaya threw a pillow at him. "I'm not good in the kitchen, but I make up for it in other areas," she retorted.

Shamir planted a kiss on her lips. It was warm and comfortable. "You are so right, my lady."

With a flourish, he opened the door and hurried off to the school.

Santaya plotted out the timeline for her day. Although she was exhausted, this project was bringing to fruition the lifelong dreams of the two of them as they encouraged their African neighbors to strive for a life that would bring economic success and personal fulfillment. The dream was becoming a reality as each successive portion of the center reached completion.

Two of the AAA execs, her bosses, were currently scheduled to attend and the publicity was poised to make this a world event. Their own newly installed satellite communication system would carry the news stream. People the world over were exhausted from the conflicts of the past decades and wanted to hear good news. There was a hunger for peace. This type of news story would appeal to those who sought hope.

Several nights later, Santaya woke up to a hand clasped tightly over her mouth while a soft, urgent whisper let her know it was just Shamir. He was fully dressed. His cook had just warned him that rebel troops were close to invading their town, intent on destroying progress, the westernization of their way of life and those who supported such change. These were the same groups of Congolese rebels that had gathered again for another deadly assault. Mostly, they were ruthless, roving bands of young men, even boys, who had lost any empathy for others and embraced an angry ideology.

Shamir knew the danger they were in. While there were three security personnel at the school, there would never be a force strong enough to stave off a full assault. Most likely they would be one of the first ones targeted. Throwing his black cloak over her head, he dragged her out the door and rapidly ran with her to the end of the street and into the bush. They heard gun shots and saw fires begin to rage where the school footprint stood. Santaya sucked in her breath. "How could they?" she cried. "They are killing their own future!"

"Quick, be quiet," whispered Shamir. They went deeper into the woods until Shamir was comfortable. He thrust his cellphone into her hand as he pushed her down on the warm, dry earth. Trees wrapped their soft tendrils around Santaya as she sank wearily to the ground. "I will call when it is safe. Stay here."

"Please, Shamir, don't do anything dangerous. I need you," whispered Santaya.

He waved at her quickly as he sprinted off in the direction of the school.

Santaya huddled in seclusion in the brush all night. She could smell smoke and hear sporadic gunfire for five or six hours after Shamir had disappeared. She pulled the black cape tightly around her. Even though the outside temperature was quite warm, she shook and cried tears of disillusionment. She thought perhaps she could say some kind of prayer to some kind of being asking for the love of her life to be spared any violence and the school to be miraculously left standing.

Before sunrise, she could hear heavy duty trucks rolling into town with loudspeakers calling for the townspeople to come out from hiding. Santaya understood the local dialect and recognized the presence of government troops attempting to reestablish control. She unfolded her cramped body and shook off the cape. Wandering down the street toward their house was a walk into a horror movie. Mangled corpses, their bodies splayed in all directions, dotted the landscape. She sucked in her breath when she saw the bodies of her gracious next-door neighbor Marlata and her small sons leaning against the front wall. They had been shot execution style.

Perhaps the rebels were trying to get information from them as to where Shamir and I had gone, she thought.

Burned buildings, still smoldering, scattered the landscape. The carnage was awful. Thankfully, the students were not already bunking in their dormitories, or the death toll would have been steeper.

Most of the dead were staff for the new IT college who had come from abroad. Santaya wandered around the smoldering wreckage asking about Shamir. The locals were in shock, and she got no response. She clutched her stomach and felt a stabbing pain. "Shamir, where are you?" she screamed.

That evening she was provided transport on a government military truck ferrying soldiers back and forth from the site that now seemed foreign to her. Everything was gone. She was reeling from the pains of labor. The transport dropped her off at a missionary hospital in the capital city, leaving her at the door, never stopping to confirm that help might indeed be inside.

Blinking away the dust from the convoy, Santaya pushed open the door weakly and all but fell in. "I am having a baby," she babbled to the receptionist in English. After that, most everything was a blur. She remembered the instructions of the female doctor to push, and she heard the cry of the child, but all she could think of was Shamir. Santaya could hear herself yelling, "Where is Shamir?" through the whole birth process. Nothing else mattered to her. He was the one who wanted to hear their baby cry for the first time. He would be so proud. "What is it?" asked Santaya. "A beautiful boy, miss."

Santaya cried and turned her face away from the baby. Her mind had returned to reality, and she was already formulating a plan for his future. When she looked at him finally, it was easy to see the serious face, so much like Shamir. His steely gray eyes gazed at her, and she knew she would love him for the rest of her life because of her love for his father. The next day, she wrote a note to the medical missionaries, doctors Michael and Melissa Wells, who were a wife and husband physician team from the States. During her first post birth check-up, they had shared a bit of their medical mission work in the Congo. Despite being childless, they were using their time and skills for God's glory, with the hopes that He would grace them with children in the years ahead. So far, they had not been able to conceive. That tidbit of information had completed her plan.

She boarded the military truck back to Aketi and received the news that upon finding Shamir, they had buried him in the twenty-four-hour period required by his Muslim faith. He was in the graveyard at the edge of town. Santaya slowly walked the path to the considerable number of new graves. There were men, women, and children mourning their loved ones, but she stood silently and whispered to Shamir that he was the proud father of a son.

"You would like him, dear Shamir," she told him while quietly weeping. "He has your face. He will have your world and mine wrapped up in his little body." The image of that gravesite would forever be etched in her memory.

The missionary couple read Santaya's note and decided to accept her request to adopt her baby as their own. She had asked that they name him Shamir, and they respected her wish. For them, he was a gift from heaven. Now they had a child of their own. God had answered their prayers. It was obvious that his mother was American, but they also knew that she wished to remain anonymous. Santaya did what she felt was right. This child would have a part of Africa in him always, yet he would also find a home with his American parents.

Santaya returned to the States, quit her job, and joined the Army Division of Counterintelligence. She would find a way to someday reconnect with Shamir back in the States. Her soul cried to see him again. And she finally had.

Chapter 21

President Santaya Woodring

2036

31 Years Later

"May these words of my mouth and this meditation of my heart be pleasing in your sight, Lord, my Rock and my Redeemer." Psalm 19:14

Slowly she closed the drawer to her desk. Her executive aide who had come unnoticed into the room startled her.

"General Lu is calling. Can you take his call?" the aide asked.

"Yes, go ahead," replied Santaya. She concentrated on trying to keep the moisture from her eyes.

Four weeks later, she along with millions of Americans watched the death by firing squad of the three Christian Liberation Front leaders.

The United News Reporter blared across the screen. "As we have all heard, after a very intensive military investigation, these three have confessed to their part in the murders of General Hamilton and Lt. Col. Wells. What a spectacle we have today. I can barely see the guilty insurrectionists down below under military escort. Oh, now they are closer. Can you see them marching up to the wall? It is hard to believe, but they seem to have slight smiles on their faces. It has been months since there has been a public execution here at Andrews Air Force Base. This time, the government has decided that this is open for public viewing to deter other insurgents from attempting similar executions of our honest citizens. I can see the sergeant in charge of protocol offering each of the offenders a blindfold. Yes, they have all rejected his offer. Good grief. One of the guilty is yelling something at the crowd. Let's listen in for a minute. Maybe they are confessing."

Before the shots rang out, one of the victims yelled for all to come to Jesus to find salvation. Another cried, "Forgive them, Lord," and the last one began the first line of a song in a melodious tenor voice. The firing squad in tandem cocked their guns and shot in unison. Three drooped heads were observed, followed by blotches of blood oozing from numerous wounds. Three more saints joined the chorus at the throne of God.

"It appears to be quiet now that the guilty have been dispatched," followed up the United News reporter. "But we are getting a host of incoming streams of scores of public celebrations, glad that the religious zealots have met their justice and are no longer a plague on our peaceful society." The coverage ran for twenty-four hours with continued recycled stories about the general and lieutenant colonel and their service to the country.

The government declared the CLF a terrorist organization and known members were rounded up and imprisoned as enemies of the state. President Woodring was quietly trying to discover what had gone wrong with her secret envoy scheduled to rendezvous with General Hamilton. She had chosen one of her most trusted contacts from her Army days at the Division of Counterintelligence who was still in the Pentagon. He trusted her and agreed to make the delivery. He had vaporized before the information could be transmitted. The tracking mechanism seemed to suddenly shut off. She wondered if he could have betrayed his country as well. Far from it. It is just not like him. Then her mind moved on to other serious scenarios. Was he captured? Would Lu find out that she knew what he was choreographing in his grand scheme to be the dictator of the world?

Santaya continued her presidential duties as if nothing had happened. In fact, she made it a point of ingratiating herself to General Lu whenever the situation arose. He wallowed in the attention. And he relished the thought of someday squashing her like a bug on a windshield.

She knew that when the time was right, he would spring the trap for her. She needed to be prepared.

Chapter 22

Ricardo Medina

2036

"But the Advocate, the Holy Spirit, whom the Father will send in my name, will teach you all things and will remind you of everything I have said to you." John 14:26

As the weeks on the job at Kingston Regional Hospital wore on, Ricardo became quite proficient at repairing or restoring different medical and mechanical devices. He was a whiz at retrofitting machinery with parts salvaged from discarded tools or outdated machines. The generator was humming when gas was available and was able to run for hours at a time on the rebuilt solar panels. He had assisted a team which tracked down the nearest electric-producing windmill sites. They stood aloft on a steep ridge seven or eight miles to the north. Tapping into the generating system using his former skills gleaned in the war, Ricardo accessed the power grid when the windmills were not producing power. They ran a small line all the way to Whitsville, and the town celebrated his prowess one windy day in the Appalachian peaks. He laughed at the devious nature of the expedition.

Just think. Here I am breaking all the national laws concerning electric power. These people have no entitlement to receive electricity from the power grid, and yet I've given them something more valuable than gold. I'm helping the rebels! he thought in amazement. In a way he was hesitant, but in a way, it made him feel good about himself. *I just don't get these people. They are so stubborn. They never give up. But doing this will get me into their confidences a lot quicker than living here for fifty years. This might just be the "in" I need to hunt down valuable Blues Resistance information,* thought Ricardo.

When it came time for Danny to leave the hospital, Mercedes was not sure what to do with him. He was too young to be on his own and she would not release him to those who were his next of kin. She had taken the time to borrow a car and drive out to their ramshackle home down by Cross Creek. The visit was quick. They certainly wanted ed nothing to do with him; he was just another mouth to feed.

She asked Ricardo if he could temporarily share his cramped residence with Danny until a solution to the problem was settled on. There was a small couch now in the shed he could sleep on, and Danny hung out with Ricardo most of the day in the hospital anyway, so they seemed quite compatible.

Ricardo did not especially like the idea of a kid hanging around, especially when he thought about the reason he was sent to Whitsville in the first place, but he grudgingly agreed to see how it worked out for a month or two. He would have to come up with a better excuse than to say, "It won't work because I am a spy for General Lu seeking information on the Blues Resistance." Since he had been the stranger who needed a place to stay when he arrived in Whitsville, it would be hard to argue that he could not extend the same kindness to someone else in need.

There was a set of checkers on the shelf in the shed and one day Danny asked Ricardo what they were used for. He pulled them down and dusted off the old cardboard box.

"You never played checkers before?" asked Ricardo in disbelief. "Well, sit down young man and let me show you the work of a master."

"Thanks, Ricardo," said Danny sheepishly. "Seems there's lots of things in my life that I should have done and just didn't."

"Now the object of the game is to capture the other guy's checkers. You do that by jumping over them going forward. You can only move one space at a time unless there are more opportunities to jump over additional enemy checkers. If that's the case, keep going. Moves must be diagonal. Do you know what that means?"

"Sorry," said Danny. "Not sure what that is."

The game moved slowly for the instructional part of an hour or so. Even though Danny did not have a chance against Ricardo's mastery, he enjoyed the challenge of surviving the onslaught of Ricardo's round men for as long as he could. After a few months, Danny had learned from the master and gave Ricardo a run for his money.

"I think we need to graduate to chess," sighed Ricardo. "I haven't played since high school, but I'll see if I can locate a set somewhere. Virgil might even have one."

"I'll ask Mercedes tomorrow at the hospital," said Danny. "These games and the strategy behind them remind me of the Blues and their ability to avoid trouble when it comes close. I wonder if those guys played these games. Must have because they sure are sneaking around these parts without getting caught."

Ricardo perked up. He wondered if Danny was privy to some channel of information he was missing.

"You know any Blues?" asked Ricardo nonchalantly.

"Naw, but the guys at the hardware store are always telling stories about them and what they are about to do in these here parts. Anyway, we wouldn't know if they was Blues even if we talked to them every day. They are sworn to secrecy on pain of death."

Danny laughed at that. "Dead men don't talk," he chuckled. "You want to be a Blue, Ricardo? I do. Can't wait till I get old enough to join up."

"Now what would they use you for?" chided Ricardo. "I don't think they can use your checkers skills. Now maybe if you could fix machines or stuff like that, you might be of use to them. Maybe I should join instead of you. What do you think of that?"

"Well," said Danny with a downcast face, "I don't like it. I'd miss you. You're like a brother to me. They could use a tough guy like you."

For Ricardo, those weeks together with Danny turned out to be the happiest in his life. He told Danny little snippets of his past, not enough to put anything together, but enough to show his hurt and humanity. Most of the adventures were about the war. Danny was enthralled with the action and the tension of military life. He shared often how he would like to join the Blues when he turned eighteen.

Ricardo laughed. "It really is not all that glamorous, kid. Getting shot at and killed is not all it is cracked up to be. Anyway, the boundaries of who is right and who is wrong are all messed up. I'm not sure what the objective of the Blues is other than causing commotion in this part of the country. And the government forces aren't much better."

"Are you kidding?" asked Danny. "They are cold-blooded killers and only work for blood money. I could tell you stories of the old days around here when they raided our houses and rounded up five guys as suspected spies. One of them was my pa. Never saw him again, and my ma was never the same. She died of a broken heart. That's why I had to move in with my aunt and uncle. Don't you ever say nothing good about those creeps again. I will hate them until the day I die."

He stormed off dragging the toes of his shoes in the dirt.

Despite this dust up, Danny and Ricardo formed a special bond finding worth and affirmation in each other. Danny was learning about engine mechanics at the hospital as well as a healthy dose of electrical engineering and IT skills as he hauled Ricardo's tools and supplies from one job to another. He was naturally curious, and Ricardo liked teaching him. They had private jokes and stories that made them laugh repeatedly. Mercedes loved hearing Danny's loud guffaws as the two of them sat under the linden tree at lunch and became immersed in a game of chess. There was something healing about the sound of laughter.

On a sunny day, they called Mercedes over to watch the end of their match.

"I got him on the ropes," said Ricardo. "Watch him squeal as I tighten the noose."

Danny just laughed. "You are just trying to impress Miss Mercedes at my expense."

Ricardo laughed yet didn't seem to enjoy the comment. "It takes more than this to impress our Miss Mercedes. Anyway, I don't think she has time for games. She probably thinks we are slacking on the job."

The game got into high gear very quickly. Ricardo was besting Danny, but Danny was absorbing another strategy in the process that would come back to haunt Ricardo in later matches.

Mercedes took a moment for self-reflection. "You know, what you two men are doing is a good diversion from our humdrum lives. I think you are right that I need to loosen up a bit and start to enjoy life and its pleasures more often. Sometimes I just am consumed with work. Thanks for pointing that out, Ricardo," she said, smiling at them as she walked back into the hospital.

"Wow, you really hit a nerve with her," shared Danny.

"Think so? Well, it was for her own good. She's a workaholic and needs to slow down before she kills herself. She's trying to save a world that is not worth saving," opined Ricardo.

"Speak for yourself," said Danny. "I'm worth saving and even you are worth saving." Then he moved his queen in an unconventional way.

"In honor of Miss Mercedes, my queen, I call 'check.'"

Ricardo, trying not to be angry, stated, "Next time I'll pay more attention to the game. I was distracted."

Danny never gave up. Ricardo admired him for that. He himself was headstrong, and insistent that tasks be completed on time and with diligence. He was no slacker. Ricardo realized that Danny shared a pride in his work as well.

One evening near the end of the summer Danny said, "Hey, Ricardo. Do you think we could fix up this little house of ours to be more livable? I'm not complaining or nothin', but you and I both have enough skill to make this place into something we could be proud of. And it would benefit Virgil and the guests he entertains in the future."

Permission was granted immediately by Virgil, and for several weeks after that, evenings were filled with the sound of hammers and saws and occasional arguments as Danny, Ricardo, and Walt teamed up to turn the shed into a cottage. They loved every minute of it. Walt was the "gopher" and helped hold or deliver the requested materials. Surprisingly, he had a knack for geometry, and could figure out proper wood cuts with the best of them.

"I don't know how you can do that in your brain," stated a surprised Ricardo one day when they were trying to figure out how they could bring the two rooflines into conjunction with each other.

"Well, I just imagine it in my head and how it looks finished. Then I look at that thing you have there with all the angles and I can see what needs to be done. Easy as that," replied Walt honestly.

Danny just shook his head. But they soon saw that Walt was correct in his head math, so they didn't argue about it anymore. Walt was pleased as punch.

During the construction period, Mercedes also realized that Danny could not read. One day when the men were out working, Ricardo had asked Danny to bring a reciprocating saw up to the roof.

"What's this?" yelled Ricardo. "It's right there on the case; can't you read? Look." He pointed to the case on the ground with the name boldly stated on the side: reciprocating saw. "You brought me a hack saw."

Danny sheepishly exchanged the saws, but Mercedes took note of the situation.

"Hey Danny, can you help me put some of these canned goods in the basement?" she asked. While they were carrying the jars down the steep steps, Mercedes broached the subject. "I noticed you were having trouble reading the name on the saw case. Do you have trouble with reading?"

"Not much. I just can't figure it out sometimes," said Danny.

"Well, I'll tell you what. I can help you figure things out better. Can you come over on Tuesday evenings and we'll practice the parts you have trouble with?" coaxed Mercedes with her best smile.

Danny paused for a moment to consider. He was embarrassed that his reading skills were so poor. Yet working with Mercedes would be a godsend. She was like a big sister to him, and he trusted her. He knew she would not make fun of his ignorance.

"Well, if you want to, Miss Mercedes," he smiled. "But mark my words; if you start teaching me, you are going to have a whole line at the door of good-lookin' fellers who want reading lessons too."

Mercedes couldn't help but smile. Did Danny have a crush on her?

She began lessons on the following Tuesday. Her method centered on using adventure stories that would capture Danny's imagination.

The exciting story line would hopefully hold his attention long enough to struggle along with sounding out words and memorizing vocabulary. She would read him a chapter. Then he would sit by her on the couch after previewing what he thought would happen next and start off in a rush into the next pages. Mercedes would often pause him to ask questions. Normally this would bother him to no end. But because it was Mercedes, he mustered all the patience he could find in his personal reservoir, while keeping his answers polite.

On Tuesday, Mercedes started the lesson by reading a Psalm from the Bible. Danny just listened. He didn't connect with them. "What do you get from those, Miss Mercedes?" he asked.

"Peace," she replied calmly. "They got me through some tough times."

"I don't think they say much. But I sure did like that story you told me from the Bible about that guy named Jonah. Now that was a good one. If I could find a fish that big in the Bluestone, well, I'd have the world record for sure," Danny stated. "Do you really think that could be true? I don't see why God gave him a second chance. You're supposed to listen to God the first time. He knows who he's talking to and he's not someone to mess with," shared Danny.

"Did God give you any second chances in your life, Danny? He did for me."

There was a look on Danny's face that said it all. "Just coming to live with you was the best second chance a man could have. I see your point. Thanks, Miss Mercedes, for helping me see it," Danny said.

Mercedes smiled that Danny had described himself as a "man."

During a particular lesson after she had read another Psalm, Danny asked her if she had an extra Bible he could have for his own. "You got so many books around here, Miss Mercedes; do you have an extra Bible? I would like to try to read me some of those Jesus stories myself," he said rather sheepishly.

She returned from her bedroom. "I was saving this for my son or daughter," she said matter of factly, "but that is most likely not to be. I want to pass it on to you. I got it when I joined the church when I was about your age. Can I pray for you? I want you to find truth in it like I finally did."

Danny nodded as Mercedes moved down to her knees and into the most touching God-talk Danny had ever heard. It was like she was talking to someone she knew. She asked that the Spirit bless Danny with insight and wisdom so that he could hear, see, and touch the real Jesus. When Danny opened his eyes, Mercedes was wiping tears from her face. He had felt, while she prayed, something come over him like a Presence that was peace. He could not feel his legs for a minute, and he seemed to float in another dimension. Then the feeling was gone.

"I've seen Him," she whispered. "My life has been changed. I pray that it will be the same for you."

Danny was moved. He could tell she had a special kind of love for him. He never had felt that before. He swallowed hard. "Thank you, Miss Mercedes. I will treasure this book forever because it came from you." Mercedes wrote Danny's name and the date in the Bible. Danny wanted to ask her about the funny feelings he had just had, but he did not know how to start the conversation. He would wait till later.

Many nights, Danny would lie in his new bed in the renovated cottage and read his Bible by candlelight into the wee hours of the morning. Ricardo would wake up. "Blow out that candle. You're going to burn this place down around our ears," grumbled Ricardo. Danny would comply, but he would lay in the dark and talk to Jesus the way he imagined Miss Mercedes did every night. Ricardo would listen in. He was amazed that it seemed like a two-way conversation. He was concerned that Danny was being trapped into the fake faith of the Singleton family. There was no such thing as God's truth or love. The world was cruel and evil, and a person had to take care of himself before some creep took advantage of him. He was going to need to teach Danny the truths of the world himself.

"Danny, religion is garbage. The quicker you pitch it out of your life, the better off you will be. There is no God. I know. I talked to him lots when I was a kid, and not once did he step in to help me or my mom. He is just a crutch for weaklings. You gotta be tough like me, Danny boy," Ricardo complained.

Chapter 23

Walt Gersham

2026-2036

"Now the Lord is the Spirit, and where the Spirit of the Lord is, there is freedom." 2 Corinthians 3:17

Walt had unobtrusively become a member of the Singleton family. He had found a home in Titus' old bedroom and had made it his own. On the wall he had an original family picture that had been given to him from the cleanup after the fire at his house. It was charred, but he loved to see his mother's smiling face. She had been a saint. He didn't much like his dad's frown. Mom had asked that they get this photograph taken for her birthday present and their father had grudgingly complied. They were young kids, but Walt remembered the incident and how happy his mother was at the musty photography studio.

What Walt treasured most was a photo Mack had sent from his graduation from the Army Academy. There was nothing he was prouder of than his twin brother. He smiled when he remembered the small role he had played in getting Mack into the service in the first place. Walt had given his blood at the Reserve Center because Mack was drunk as a skunk. It was easy enough to switch brothers' arms when the one taking the blood was not really paying attention. They looked so much alike if you did not stare at them. In the bathroom, they had changed shirts to seal the deal. Since then, Mack called them blood brothers.

Walt did not hear from Mack often, but when he did, Mack would tell him he was working on top secret projects that needed to stay top secret. Whether he was or not, this thrilled Walt. He reveled in the mystery that surrounded his brother and would often concoct stimulating scenarios in his mind about how his brother Mack would have to survive the imagined dangers. He was always the hero at the end of the story.

The void of not seeing Mack was partially filled by the busyness of the Singleton family. Virgil was not capable of yard work any longer, so Walt took over caring for the yards at both the house and the church. He would work on small repairs and upkeep for both properties and was a godsend for Mercedes in keeping a close eye on the pastor, who was progressively becoming more forgetful.

One of Walt's gifts was bartering and trading. Perhaps people in the town felt sorry for him, but most of the time he was just sly enough to turn a good deal. On a limited budget, he would purchase food for the school and the hospital cafeteria, keeping the children and patients fed with an amazing selection of plant life found in the woods. He occasionally worked the black market that came through in caravans headed south, yet it was his garden, and the food supplies he and Mercedes were always canning, that were most productive.

Each morning he was up at five a.m. to begin breakfast prep at the school/hospital cafeteria. Sometimes he left Mercedes a surprise; squirrel or quail he had field dressed, field mushrooms, government surplus peanut butter, army rations and canned fruit. He would never be coaxed into revealing his sources, especially the locations of the treasured morel mushrooms. People in those parts went to their graves with that kind of information. Everyone knew that for all his mental shortcomings, he was an amazing hunter, trapper, and gardener. When someone asked where he got a surprising amount of unusual food stuffs, he would just grin and say, "God provides."

Every Sunday Walt attended the pastor's service, sang the hymns, swept up afterwards and locked the doors. He always did his work with a crooked smile on his face. Mercedes wondered about the noticeable limp and questioned whether it could have been corrected when he was young. Most likely. In those days, medical care was accessible to most anyone and a young child from Appalachia would be a good bet for Medicaid. Those days had disappeared with the world experiencing tremors from volcanic explosions, toxic viruses, and grisly war. Now even the metropolitan centers were but a step away from survival mode. The past two decades had brought mostly misery. Though they were promised relief every four years due to leadership changes during elections, nothing changed.

With his pleasant smile and desire to please, Walt remained a favorite of the town. Somehow, he could solve problems or find resources where others were stymied. He had salvaged items from a sizable number of the abandoned homesteads and barns in the area looking for metal to recycle and mechanical supplies which were almost nonexistent. The most striking find was his ability to produce up-to-date government rations and tools. People were getting curious.

One day while he was leaving the hardware store, a few of the guys broached the subject. "Hey, Walt, where you finding all those government surplus supplies? We're athinkin' that you found some Blues storehouse up there in the hills and are raiding it for the hospital. What do you say to that?"

Walt paused to collect his thoughts. "You can think anything you want. Maybe the Blues is givin' me the stuff they don't want. You ever think of that?" asked Walt in reply.

They all chuckled at the silliness of his rationale. "All we know is that you are one wizard of a feller for rustling up all that food to feed our kids. We appreciate it. Yep, you are Walt the Wizard." The name stuck and he loved it! "But remember, the Blues won't be so happy seeing their supplies disappearing. Watch your backside. They don't tolerate spies." A worried frown returned to his face.

Ricardo was amazed with Walt's finds as well, especially the government rations.

"Hey, buddy," he called one day when Walt was passing by him at the hospital, "where did you find those pallets of canned fruit? That stuff is current. It had to be from some government depot. Are you hiding something from us? Are you a secret agent or something?" He knew that would get a laugh from Walt, but he was hoping that Walt's newfound notoriety would cause him to spill the beans.

"Almost as good as that!" chatted Walt. "I'm a wizard, don't you know? I can make this stuff appear by magic." Then he laughed at his own joke. "But I won't be a wizard forever. Even I can't keep pulling a rabbit from a hat." Walt's face became gloomy. He seemed to know that this season of miraculous appearances would soon be over.

It was nearing autumn and Walt was in overdrive harvesting his garden, putting up his canned goods of meat, fruit, and vegetables and hunting for things that the woods produced in abundance during the fall of the year.

"Hey, Mercedes, are you going to help me again on Saturday for another round of canning?" Walt asked at the hospital on Thursday.

"Sure, Walt. What is it this week? Did you tell Danny we'll need some more firewood to complete the canning?" she asked.

Saturday morning Mercedes woke to the smell of a wood fire. No matter where she lived, she would always love the smell coming from crackling kindling and precision hand-split logs. It was the smell of man and nature combined to provide for one another. She stumbled out of the house somewhat disheveled and saw Walt attending the fire.

"You're up early. Nice fire," she praised.

"Well, we got a passel of work to do today. I don't want to run out of food this winter," cautioned Walt.

"You mean your 'secret supply' is running short? I thought you were a wizard," she joked.

Walt's crestfallen face made Mercedes wish she had not said anything.

"Sorry, Miss Mercedes. Things is drying up. That's why we need to get lots of stuff done today. Look what I got for starters." They had bushels of green beans, squirrel meat, carrots, corn, and peaches. "We got to make hay with these peaches, or they will go bad soon. Let's start with them. And while all this stuff is sealing in our jars, we can start on these mushrooms and tomatoes for drying. You're going to have to get a bigger basement, and I need more jars, especially lids. I've scoured all the old homesteads for these," said Walt dejectedly.

The government still delivered a monthly shipment of flour, salt, and sugar. The food was donated to the hospital and school. It was their goodwill gesture. Yet many of the people in the outer regions suffered from severe malnutrition.

Walt would often take his canned goods to the sick and elderly. His only request was that they return the jars when they were empty.

In the evenings at home on the porch or in the living room, Walt would often be a silent companion. He listened to the conversations of Mercedes and Virgil but rarely contributed unless it was useful news he had heard on his journey around the neighborhood.

In some strange way, Walt became a mainstay in the family. While Mercedes loved and revered her father, she used Walt as her anchor for her weary days so that she did not need to burden Virgil. Walt was a good listener for her rantings about administering the school and hospital, and he provided support when she was downcast. He would listen to the emotional turbulence from her troubled soul and seemed to be able to answer her with simple words that lifted her spirit. The hole left by the absence of Titus' wisdom and the loss of her mother was slowly being filled by Walt. Mercedes smiled at the irony.

Another surprising friendship blossomed between Walt and Danny. Just yesterday, she had heard the two of them talking about plans to take another foray into the woods.

"Hey, Danny, you want to go hunting today? Perfect day for it." Walt had found a kindred spirit who loved to traipse the woods with him.

Danny peered out of the cottage door. "You bet. I'll be ready in a jiffy."

Ricardo was peeved. He was possessive of his young bunkmate. He also disliked the fact that his working partner would be gone for the day on a much more enjoyable excursion.

"You guys sure do take a lot of time off from helping around this place," grumbled Ricardo.

They ignored the comment.

"Now, Danny. The first thing we need to attend to while hunting is safety." Walt was an excellent instructor. His old rifle had seen better days, but it was accurate and not as temperamental as the more updated guns with laser beams, scopes, and satellite assistance. "This here slide is the safety. You make sure it's on while we're walking in the woods. You always keep it there until just before you shoot. The old timers in this town can tell you some crazy stories about accidentally shooting themselves. It ain't a pretty sight. That's why old Bill down at the hardware store only has three fingers."

The amazement on Danny's face would have made a sullen person laugh. "Now he told me a bear had bit them off while they were in a wrestling match!" exclaimed Danny.

Walt laughed.

The catch was typically squirrel, quail, or partridge. Walt knew when it was logical to hunt deer—in the late fall—and he promised Danny they soon would be able to bring venison home. It was the prize of the forest.

One early Saturday, Walt knocked quietly on Danny's door at the crack of dawn. "Hey, Danny," he whispered. "You want to go hunting for mushrooms?" Danny stumbled to the door with his tousled hair and bare feet but with a look of excitement and expectation.

"We won't need the gun today. Hurry," continued Walt. "I have a surprise for you. But we gotta hurry."

Something was different about Walt's voice. Danny moved extra fast to get ready for the expedition.

Chapter 24

Danny Howmeiser

Early Autumn 2036

*"He saved us through the washing of rebirth and renewal
by the Holy Spirit, whom he poured out on us generously
through Jesus Christ our Savior." Titus 3:5b-6*

Rousing out of a deep sleep, Ricardo vaguely heard the conversation between Walt and Danny. He thought to himself, *There go those two kids running off into the woods for adventure into the great unknown.*

Then another thought burst into his head. Walt must have discovered something if there was no need for his gun. He always took it with him, even if they were just doing something simple like picking berries. Something was up. Perhaps he would finally get the break he needed. His missives to Lu's team were quite dismal. It had been difficult communicating with the Pentagon team in D.C. without a decent cellular connection. If he were caught with a working phone, that would be the end of his mission. Therefore, he was forced to write central command using encrypted codes whenever possible. These were forwarded by regular mail delivery, addressed to a home in D.C.

which was the secret operation center for Lu's underhanded business dealings. If there was an emergency message, he did have a battery backed-up military phone hidden in his duffle bag. Failing to contribute much valuable information over the last five months was not going over well with Central Command, and his letters were progressively getting shorter and less specific. He knew General Lu would soon be running out of patience and would recall him.

In moments, Ricardo had on his camouflage uniform stashed in his bag, and he jogged up the path behind the sleeping house and into the hushed woods. He figured they would not take the trail that branched off to Baldface Mountain, but instead turn right, heading deeper into the woods. He headed that way hoping his hunch was correct. Keeping out of sight was easy. Walt and Danny were deep in conversation, and they both looked thrilled to be on the chase of something unseen. Ricardo could not dare to get close enough to hear what was being said. The look on Danny's face told him that this might just be the big break he needed gathering information for General Lu. The anticipation was evident in the youngsters as they quickened their pace.

The morning mist was still clinging to the landscape, but the sun was slowly penetrating through holes that appeared here and there. Near the top of the rise sat an abandoned farm field covered in dew-swept grasses and tree seedlings. Walt paused and carefully looked around. Seeing no one, he overturned a musty, old tarp. The treasures he had unearthed! The guy had been like a deep-sea diver stumbling onto a shipwreck. Rolled up in the tarp were three Blue's camouflage shirts, small firearms, ammunition and of course, government-issued food stuffs.

"How did you find this stuff?" exclaimed Danny as he pulled on the Kevlar shirt. Danny could not help but grin. "I'm a Blues Rebel now," he said with a chuckle.

"Hush," said Walt. "This stuff belongs to the Blues for sure. They aren't going to like me stumbling into their secret hideout. It's not one of their major depots, but the springhouse hidden over there in the weeds seems like a drop-off location for when they are on the move. I found that first while up here shooting rabbits. It's so close to the wood's trail, it's easy to come and go without overhead detection. Those drones are always flying around here in search of them."

The ramshackle springhouse in the clearing had belonged to a dirt farmer and his family years ago. They had moved north to find better work in the auto factories of the Rust Belt back in the '50s, so hardly anything remained. The Blues were smart enough not to leave evidence in the house. But down below in the tangle of weeds and multiflora, the old springhouse, covering a tiny artesian spring, was the perfect place to stash goods.

"Wait here for me," cautioned Walt. He looked around again with the feeling that someone was watching him. "Let me check the perimeter to make sure all is clear. I don't want any Blues to think we are Feds looking for trouble."

He briskly walked from the springhouse for about forty yards to the woods' edge.

Ricardo had silently moved as close to that spot as possible and had tucked himself under a fallen tree that was half rotted and crumbling into pulp. He heard a strange buzzing sound, barely perceptible. Something seemed eerily familiar about that sound. In that instant, someone was running past him breathless.

With no warning, a huge explosion rocked the clearing. The center of the target was the springhouse in the farm field. Ricardo watched the whole scene play out and saw the missile explode near Danny. It threw Walt in the air. The blast pushed dirt and debris all over Ricardo and practically buried him alive.

Within seconds, a phalanx of six blue-shirted soldiers had raced into the clearing. One checked what was left of Danny and let his limp hand drop onto his still form while shaking his head in a negative motion.

Another picked up Walt who was softly moaning and flung him over his shoulder. The third soldier managed to get an arm under the shoulder of the Blues figure who had attempted to run into the melee at the last moment. It was obvious that whoever it was had serious wounds as the blood poured over his face and clothes while his leg dragged as if useless.

In less than thirty seconds, they had silently retreated into the sheltering woods. Ricardo was completely in shock. The momentary paralysis probably saved his life. Now covered by an extra layer of soil and sprawled under the log, he heard a loud thump to his left. Just past his outstretched hand, a Federal soldier in special ops gear was standing and giving orders to his team of twelve.

"How many did we get?" he ordered.

"Not sure, sir," a soldier replied. "It looked like three from the camera angle, but we can only find one body. I don't think anyone could have moved in that quickly after the strike to remove a body. It only took us a minute to arrive."

"You don't know those freakin' Blues," spat the officer. "They're like ghosts. No one hears them. Occasionally someone sees them. Let's see what they were after."

They examined the carnage of the missile strike, searching Danny's body again for ID or clues. "Those g-damned Blues must be desperate, recruiting kids like this. Jeez, he's only fourteen or fifteen at the most. At least we're making headway with recruiting."

They took photos of the area and then rendezvoused again near Ricardo.

"We'll need to get to Whitsville tomorrow to do some interrogation of the locals. Maybe we can shake some info out of one of those hillbillies for a pint of whiskey. I can bet they all know who this kid is and what's going on with the rebel supply points. For now, we'll move back to the truck and contact headquarters. I wish they'd let us use the old interrogation rules. It was so much easier to get information. The sooner we get out of this godforsaken place, the better," the officer complained.

The troop wandered off in single file. Ricardo slowly untangled himself from the mound of soil and bark. He was in shock, but he knew Danny was in trouble. He stumbled over to his body and gazed down into a partial face that had one eye staring at him but seeing nothing. There were several fatal shrapnel wounds to his torso.

"Danny," yelled Ricardo. "Danny!" He picked up the hand of the young friend who had so often bested him lately in checkers and chess. Falling on his knees, Ricardo pulled the hand to his chest. "Danny," he whispered. And then for the first time in his adult life, Ricardo cried. His sobs echoed around the clearing. At that moment, he did not care. He felt. He felt grief and it could not be contained.

Just minutes later, several men from the village burst upon the scene. They pumped Ricardo with questions. Ricardo wiped the dampness off his face with his shirt and got up off his knees. Control was crucial.

"Well, I got here too late. Walt had asked Danny and me to go mushroom hunting this morning, but I slept in. When I woke up, I realized Danny had already gone, so I followed the path figuring out the most likely place they would be going."

"Did you see anyone up here?" asked one of the geezers. "Anyone in uniform?"

It was obvious that Ricardo was in shock. He was having trouble staying focused.

"Well, just as I got here, there seemed to be someone running up behind me, but I didn't have time to see them because the missile exploded in front of me at the same time. I was covered head to foot by the dirt over by that tree. When I clawed my way out, I went over to Danny boy, but I could tell he was gone." His voice trailed off, broken and miserable. "Why the heck was he wearing a Blues shirt?" cried Ricardo. No one offered an explanation.

"He was a good kid."

One of the men said, "Better get Mercedes. Don't think there is anything we can do for Danny boy. But where the heck is Walt? You seen anyone else up here, Ricardo?"

"No," answered Ricardo. "Got covered by the explosion with dirt and crap before I knew what was happening, like I said." His voice trailed off. He reached up to his ear and realized that blood was pouring out. He felt so woozy, that he half sat half fell to the ground. The men were sitting near Danny, conversing in quiet talk about what could have happened. Most likely they were right with their analysis.

"I'm thinking those Feds dropped a drone in here with a missile once they noticed activity on the hill. Must have known Blues had been through here recently. Guess they've been watching this area for a while," explained a grizzled old villager.

"Yeah, but where is Walt? Do you think they took him with them? Poor kid."

Ricardo recovered enough to grunt out a response. "I think the Blues got him first."

"You mean the Blues were here?" they said incredulously.

"I think I'm remembering right. Guess that was them. They were fast as lightning. From what I could see, they dragged him off in seconds and disappeared into the woods. Oh yeah, and the Feds are coming to town tomorrow. They're looking for connections to Whitsville."

He could have kicked himself for saying that. What was he doing helping these locals? He felt sick inside and out. *Well, at least it will throw them off if any of them think I'm working for the Feds.* He lay down on the ground and threw up just as Mercedes arrived. The look on her face when she saw Danny turned his stomach again. He tried to keep himself from crying, but he could not stop it. *Damn weakling,* he said to himself. And then he passed out for good.

A wet cloth was pressing against his head. He woke with a start. It was Mercedes. She had dampened a rag and drenched it in the cold spring water. "Do you think you can walk down the hill?" she asked in a monotone.

Her face was drawn but there were no tears. Death had come again to their little world. She hated the lack of humanity, the hate, the espionage, the cruelty. "For what?" she moaned.

Ricardo nodded in affirmation to the question. The Whitsville men gathered around him and lifted him off the ground. A few of them wrapped Danny up in the tarp pieces and carried him down at the head of the procession. They took him directly to the church as the rest all trooped in. Mercedes asked the men to lay Danny on the front pew, then she sat by Danny's body, took his wounded head in her lap and cradled him like a little child.

Ricardo watched her and thought, *Danny would have liked that. But he would have had some wisecrack to say about her cuddling that would have made me laugh.* Danny's voice was speaking in his head, and it made him angry.

Her eyes were still dry, but her face was covered with signs of grief. "My dad will be along shortly. We will see to it that Danny has a proper service and burial. I expect all of you to be here," she said in her grief.

She trudged up to Second Street where she found her father sitting on the porch in his chair. He was slumped over in his seat with his face in his hands. He had heard snippets about the events of the day. It was too much for his frail body to take. He was softly sobbing over the loss of the innocent Danny. Mercedes shared with him what the men of the town could surmise about the attack by the Feds.

"Oh God," he said. "Help these men against the oppression of those tyrants. And please, Jesus, place a special blessing on our beloved adopted son Walt. Keep him out of harm's way and bring him back. We need him." Virgil dried his tears. Mercedes covered his shoulders with an old sweater and held him tight until he drifted off into sleep.

When he awoke from his brief nap, the two of them slowly plodded down to the church where the local "undertaker" was already in the sanctuary figuring out what size coffin would be needed. Leaving her father there, she plodded on to the hospital followed by Ricardo. She was not sure where he came from, but it was a comfort to her to have him present in the grief they shared.

They walked to their work in silence. Both of their emotions were so raw that it was impossible to speak. Each of them was working through their memories of Danny and the joy and fulfillment he had brought into their lives. Danny … funny, mischievous, serious, full of life, curious, friend, child. Ricardo knew that Danny was the only person he would ever relate to as a surrogate kid brother. He was becoming angry at the thought of his senseless death at the hands of the Feds. Something inside him snapped and the result would not be good.

His mind was twisting back to the evil thoughts he had expressed when he arrived at Whitsville. Except this time the enemy had switched uniforms. If he had seen a Federal soldier at that moment, he would have killed him with no compunction.

Chapter 25

Virgil Singleton

Autumn 2036

"And we all, who with unveiled faces contemplate the Lord's glory, are being transformed into his image with ever-increasing glory, which comes from the Lord, who is the Spirit." 2 Corinthians 3:18

Just prior to Pastor Singleton's nine a.m. "outlawed" church service, the Fed Special Op convoy blew into town, spewing dust in every direction. They rustled the residents of Whitsville who were still sleeping out of their beds. Everyone was herded into the center of town.

The captain of the force explained that there had been enemy activity in their area, as they were all aware, and that they had been successful in the destruction of a rebel supply depot. One rebel had been killed, possibly more.

"We suspect that a few of the rebels have come this way looking for shelter after our aerial attack on the insurgents yesterday. We are seeking information as to whether anyone has come to you as individuals or to your medical facilities for care. We have good intelligence that there were several injured Blues who are unaccounted for in this raid. You can expect us to search your homes and property. Be honest with us as we question you on these matters. Things will go a lot more smoothly if you cooperate with us," ordered the captain.

All the townspeople were forced to stand in two lines on either side of the main street. Throughout the morning and afternoon, each citizen was grilled about their whereabouts the day before, their connection to Danny and their connections to the Blues revolutionary force. Did they have members in the military that had joined up with the rebel squad? Who had seen unusual activity in the woods when they were hunting? Who in town had connections to Blues members or were sympathetic to their cause? The Fed force knew this last question was a farce. All the residents were in some way supportive of the Blues, but few were willing to publicly step forward and defend them. They could be taken away and never heard from again.

Virgil Singleton stood out as a person of interest. The captain personally sat across from him in the blazing sun and asked a bevy of questions.

"You are the local preacher?"

"Yes," answered Virgil simply.

"And you still hold illegal services in your church, I understand?"

"Yes," he answered.

"And Danny Howmeiser has been living with you since his time in the hospital."

"Yes."

"Why was he living with you? When was he recruited by the Blues?"

Virgil could not help but smile. "He came to live with us because he didn't have anywhere else to go. He was a good kid who needed another chance at life. And he wasn't a Blue. He didn't even know much about them, I imagine, other than the fact that people sometimes talk about the way they help. Danny would love stories like that. He always liked heroes."

"The Blues are not heroes. They are traitors; get that right, old man." The captain slapped him on the side of the face. A trickle of blood rolled across his fattened lip.

Virgil was unmoved, but the townspeople who were present felt a simmering anger at the heavy-handedness of the questions. As the inquisition continued, Virgil seemed confused. The captain considered him evasive. He was kept for further interrogation along with two other younger men from town.

The Fed force moved on to the school and the hospital. Mercedes, as the medical official in charge, had not gone to the town center as summoned. She would be damned if she would leave her sick charges and answer questions from the brutes that killed Danny. But she knew she had to protect her father and the other residents. When the force called all personnel and patients to leave the building, she came out and pleaded with the captain to allow those who were sick as well as the children to remain in their rooms.

"You are more than welcome to interview the patients or inspect the premises," she stated with a hint of defiance, although inside she was shaking with both rage and fear.

He looked her over with an eye that covered her shapely form in more than a businesslike way. He wondered to himself why someone so pretty and intelligent would stay in this godforsaken hellhole.

"There are only five patients in the hospital. We have not had any new ones since Monday. Most are bedridden and living out their final days here with some degree of care and comfort. They are no threat to anyone. Come in and look anywhere you want. Ask anyone anything. But they are not coming out in the hot sun to be interrogated. Good God, what could they have to do with any of this?" she vehemently stated.

Mercedes struck a strange pose, firm and professional. She pulled her thin sweater tighter around her waist. The hem of her dress flapped in the wind and the captain glanced down at her dated cloth-ing and shapely legs. *We certainly are missing something,* he thought as he secretly wished more women would wear dresses again instead of gender-neutral clothing.

He took the semi-automatic rifle off his shoulder and set it down on the ground, holding the barrel in his hand to balance it. He said nothing but looked at her in disbelief. He was not used to being chal-lenged, especially by a woman, and that made him angry. But he was also aware that any type of negative PR still had ramifications that could find its way into the pages of the illegal press. He was not going to risk his career on this podunk town. There were already rumblings across the metropolitan areas that the heavy-handed approach of tam-ing the Blues and other rebellious factions was not well received by several sectors of the population. *Well, cry me a river,* he thought.

"Fine, miss," he said sarcastically. "And what is your name?"

"Mercedes Singleton."

"Any relation to the old man who is the minister here in town?" he asked.

"He's my father. He is a harmless senior citizen. He has nothing to hide," she replied, trying to tame her emotions.

"I beg to differ." His smile was mercenary.

He ordered his squad to search the hospital and the school for ille-gal substances and the missing wounded rebels. "I want to make sure that they were not here last night. Look for any sign that they had been here for treatment. Check the dumpsters and trash for blood and bandages. And where were you last evening, Ms. Singleton?"

Mercedes ignored his question, pretending to not hear the request as she turned to go back into the hospital.

He grabbed her arm and twisted her back to attention. "I asked you a question," he snarled.

"I was at home, as I am every night with my father. Now that Danny is gone, it is just the two of us," she replied with downcast eyes. She knew that she was intentionally leaving out Walt as a Singleton home resident, but any attempt to explain his absence would lead to a more tangled web of questions.

In the next half hour, the force had torn through the school and hospital, finding a few items of Army surplus food among the meager rations. "Where are these from?" asked the captain.

"They came with the last shipment of supplies from Baltimore along with the flour. It might have been a mistake, but we were not going to complain about getting canned fruit for the children. I wish they would make more mistakes," she wistfully answered.

Walt, she thought. *Where are you?*

The last one to be interviewed was Ricardo. The captain was amazed at how well he played his part as a drifter who was now the mechanic for the hospital. He had taken up helping the facility with his skills and did not seem happy to be answering the questions posed by the captain. Ricardo's eyes seemed to be made of steel.

As that interview concluded, Mercedes saw movement in the Fed ranks. *At last,* she thought. *I can stop the acting.*

Her thoughts were cut short by the sharp command of the captain to load up the old man and the other two for questioning.

She caught a glimpse of her father laboriously climbing into the back of the military vehicle.

"Dad," she screamed. Virgil raised a hand from the back of the flat bed, surrounded by Ops soldiers who were nameless and faceless, then pointed to the sky. "Dad," she cried as she chased the truck through the cloud of dust for several hundred yards.

She collapsed in the road, her tears running down through the dirt on her face. "Dear Jesus, dear Spirit," she cried, "help him."

Someone helped her up and half carried her to the house. It was Ricardo. He laid her in her bed, pulled the curtains and walked out of the house. Sitting on the steps, he thought through the events of the last few days and the options they presented. Now he doubted his intelligence work here. Yet he knew these people were insanely stupid to think they could change anything concerning the state of events. It was slow suicide. He hated them all. He hated the confusion and the lack of clarity. He knew he did not hate Mercedes. But right now, all he could think of was Danny.

Chapter 26

Mercedes Singleton

Autumn 2036

*"You, however, are not in the realm of the flesh
but are in the realm of the Spirit, if indeed the Spirit
of God lives in you. And if anyone does not have the
Spirit of Christ, they do not belong to Christ." Romans 8:9-10*

Mercedes had to officiate at the funeral service in the absence of her father. She had completed the arrangements to have Danny's body placed in a simple pine box. Death was common in Whitsville, with most of the population being elderly, or as they said, "seniors." Ricardo had dug a grave near the edge of the old church graveyard, but in a cheerier spot on the downslope where the light of the morning sun would dance on the grass above his head. In former times, this location would be prohibited by law, but no one cared anymore. Ricardo had also solemnly placed their set of checkers in the coffin. He smiled a faint twisted smile as he did so.

Danny, you'd like to take me to the cleaners again, wouldn't you? he thought, remembering their friendly competition and the times when

Danny relished his occasional victory. Ricardo recalled his last defeat, bowing to Danny the victor.

"You are now crowned King Clown of the Checker Kingdom," he had said with a flourish. Danny had let out a guffaw but smiled with pride.

"It's because you're the best teacher. I wish you were my brother," Danny said with some hesitation.

Ricardo had just smiled, but inside something warmed up.

However, Ricardo could not make himself go to the service. The townspeople poured into the small structure through the side door. Some of Danny's kin even made the effort to show up—the few who would claim they were related.

Mercedes had prepared the funeral as best she could. She found her dad's old worn book titled *Funeral Services and Prayers for the Deceased* among the disheveled books on his desk. There were notes tucked into the pages from past services he had recently officiated.

Mercedes thought long into the night about what she would say for Danny's eulogy and prepared her thoughts as best she could the next morning despite her nerves and feelings of inadequacy.

"Why am I doing this?" she said in a quiet whisper as she searched inside herself for bravery. "Please, God." She missed her father. His removal made her feel physically ill. She grasped for strength. "Please, God," she whispered again.

As she stood up and moved to the pulpit, the crowd hushed their quiet conversations.

"We've come together as the extended family of Danny Howmeiser to honor his short life," she began. "He was family because he wanted to be part of all our families. And many of us loved him as though he had been brought up as our own flesh and blood.

"I saw Danny transform from a shy, beaten-down kid in the hospital for an appendectomy, to a vibrant and life-loving young man just this past year. He seems to have fallen in love with life and savored every second of it. He also fell in love with those around him, his adopted family. We will miss him. For me, I became Danny's older … well, really older sister." The gathering chuckled.

"Most of you don't know that Danny couldn't read well when he moved into our shed, or as they now call it 'the cottage,' after his hospitalization. I would catch him looking at all my books and Dad's books. Somehow, I did not catch on that he knew he was missing something else from a very checkered childhood. One day I realized that he was struggling to read while the guys were remodeling their cottage. Privately I volunteered to help him learn the basics of phonics and reading strategies. Knowing he was a smart kid, I figured if he could just get hooked on adventurous stories, he would push ahead. He did not want my help but agreed more to make me feel good than anything else. It was slow going at first, but once he got a taste of success, he would devour some of Titus' childhood favorites in a weekend.

"It was a red-letter day when he asked me if he could have a Bible. I dug out the old Bible with my name on the inside cover. It was given to me when I was confirmed. Danny treated it like it was gold. Honestly, large sections he did not care for. But he loved the stories where Jesus took the time to talk to people who were hurting.

"On a chilly evening when we were studying difficult vocabulary, Danny looked at me and said, 'Mercedes, you know who the greatest person in the world is?'

"I thought he was going to say 'me,' or perhaps Virgil, my dad or Ricardo with whom he bunks. But he said, 'Jesus Christ. He is the only one who can really take your hurts away. You see, I asked Him to help me forget that my family by blood abandoned me and He said, "I gave you a new family." I asked Him, "Can you work on my friends who don't know you're real?" And He said, "I'm already doing that."

"Then Danny reminded me of the time in the hospital when I told him about the entrance to heaven and what I had seen in that vision.

"'Miss Mercedes,' he shared. 'I know it's going to be an even better place than that because all the darkness and all the sickness and heartache will be left behind. All you'll hear is laughter and happy thoughts and everyone will be singin' to Jesus. I have a song the Holy Spirit gave me when I couldn't sleep one night.'

"Excuse my bad memory and my pitiful attempt at singing, but here is the gist of it," whispered Mercedes, tears streaming down her face. "I found a copy of the words for it scribbled down in the Bible I gave him, so that's the accurate part."

Then Mercedes sang the sweet tune. It was a familiar mountain folk tune. There was not a dry eye in the church. All felt as though they had been visited by the Holy Spirit Himself.

> When it's time for me to wander off and meet God in the sky,
> I won't pack a thing except my soul and hum sweet by and by.
> For gettin' there's a journey sometimes tough and hard to bear,
> But arrivin' is the best part for my Savior will be there.
> He'll say, "Hi Danny, glad you made it; I've been hopin' you would come,
>
> I dropped some guides along the way with directions to the Son.
> You've become a keen wise man to know that I'm the prize,
> For the best place to live forever is with me in the skies."
> So now we meet, I'm singin' and I can't believe He's near,
> This is my forever home thanks to those who led me here.

Chapter 27

Mack Gersham

Autumn 2036

"For if you live according to the flesh, you will die; but if by the Spirit you put to death the misdeeds of the body, you will live. For those who are led by the Spirit of God are the children of God. The Spirit you received does not make you into slaves, so that you live in fear again; rather, the Spirit you received brought about your adoption to sonship."

Romans 8:13-15

Curses were flying silently from Mack's lips as he hobbled as quickly as possible along the narrow trail in the woods with his compatriot's help. His left leg was throbbing and the blood from his face wound had completely blackened the vision of his left eye. However, he was not as concerned for himself as for his twin brother Walt, who was slung over the shoulder of the strongest rebel on this tiny caravan.

When they reached Murphy's Creek, they briskly uncovered the canoes from the brush and pushed off for their headquarters fifty miles south of Kingston. It would be an arduous journey, mostly by night, but the nearly full moon assisted in their navigation. Paddling upstream was not easy, but instead of having the extra weight of the supplies they had hoped to ferry, they were carrying a gravely wounded man.

Ten miles up the creek, they pulled into a clearing, covered the canoes with brush and dragged Walt and Mack into a decrepit, abandoned farmer's home. Inside it was pleasantly still habitable. There was faded wallpaper on the living room walls decorated with pink and peach roses, and the kitchen still had useable pots and pans. The team had used it before as a comfortable layover for their travel up and down the Blues Trail.

Walt was placed in a bed and attended by former Army medic, Steve Halprin.

"How do you feel?" he asked Walt, while assessing his status. Experience told him that time was short for Walt. Without an immediate blood transfusion, he would not survive twenty-four hours. Even with one, his chances were slight. "Looks like you have a concussion and have taken some blows to the torso. Does it hurt here?" asked Halprin as he probed the large shrapnel wounds.

Walt grimaced.

"I'm going to give you a morphine drip for the pain. Sorry, there is nothing else I can do right now."

Mack pulled a chair up next to Walt's bed and stared at his brother. It had been years since they had seen each other, yet it only seemed like days. Once he had started to work for General Hamilton, he had had to stop almost all communication, not wanting to take the chance that Walt would someday be implicated in the web of the Blue's operation.

He had almost screamed when he saw his brother snooping around the storage facility they had targeted for their supply run. It was Mack who had suggested that the abandoned farm in Whitsville be a munitions drop. The Blues had set off at dawn to retrieve the small cache and take it back to Kingston when they were surprised by the Special

Op raid. The Blues had just a minute's warning that something was up when their radar detection system recorded a drone launch in the vicinity.

When Mack saw that it was Walt that was targeted, he tried to rescue him in the last seconds. He was disappointed in himself for breaking protocol for the Blues, but he was caught so off guard by the situation that he simply reacted without thinking.

The lids on Walt's eyes fluttered, then opened. He turned his face enough to see his brother giving him a lopsided familiar grin.

"Hey bro, you look like me." He semi-laughed through the pain as he saw Mack's beaten-up face.

A smile crossed Mack's mouth. "I walk like you too, you buzzard. Both of us barely made it out alive. What the heck were you doing on the ridge anyway?"

Walt whispered that he had discovered the supply cache on a hunting trip for rabbits. After he shot a rabbit close to the farmer's spring house, he decided to explore to see if he could find anything useful for the school or the hospital, so he broke in. "I knew that stuff belonged to the Blues once I saw what was in there. But no one had seen Blues for so long, I thought you guys had moved on to another location and wouldn't need this stuff any longer. We're desperate for food and supplies in town. It's rough. I spend lots of my time scouring the countryside for anything we can eat or use to make our lives a little easier."

Walt coughed up blood and took a deep breath. It was obvious he was in acute pain and was beginning to fade away while retelling the events of the day. Opening his eyes, he continued, "Well, I brought Danny up there this morning to help me bring the stuff back to town. I was thinking we could sell the military stuff to the black-market peddlers who stop by occasionally and use the money to get some stuff for the hospital or the school. Hey, where's Danny?" he asked with a quizzical look. "I left him by the spring house. Did you bring him with us too?"

Mack paused. "Danny took a direct hit from the drone rocket launched at you by the Special Ops troops. There was nothing we could do for him. Steve checked him. He's the best medic we've got."

Turning his face away from Mack, it was obvious that Walt was trying to process the events of the day, especially the death of Danny. He felt that he was responsible for the whole thing.

"I'm so stupid," he mumbled. "Pulling that poor kid into a world of people killing each other. How could I be so dumb? I knew it was off limits to get into the Blue's stuff. Knew it would mean nothing but trouble. But I did it anyway."

Mack touched his shoulder. "Don't you go beating yourself up. You know he's in a better place."

Walt stared at him blankly. "Yeah, but that better place was to come when he was an old man. He's just a kid. Just learned to read and wanted to be a mechanic like Ricardo. Did you know Mercedes taught him to read? It wasn't easy but the kid stuck with it and so did Miss Mercedes." A dry cough rattled through Walt's lungs as he tried to keep his composure.

"How is the Singleton family?" asked Mack, trying to question nonchalantly.

"Just great. Mercedes finally got home from her time spent in the government reprogramming camp. She is different. She was really messed up when she got back, but I cheered her up. I live in Titus' room now. I'm like part of the family. Titus is way far away in some place called Nepal, Asia and Virgil is busy with the few people who still come to his church. Virgil sleeps a lot. I do most of the cooking for the family. I love to cook, just like Mom did."

He winced at the pain that was now causing his body to quiver and shake. Taking Mack's hand, he said, "Mack, I ain't goin' to make it, am

I? Do me a favor. Bury me next to Mom. She would like that. Promise me. And get my two pictures off the wall in my bedroom, Titus' old room, and keep them for yourself. I don't have anything else to leave you, but I know where I'm going, and I'll be making my rounds past the pearly gates soon enough."

Despite his emotional state, Mack knew he must push for information helpful to the Blues, so he plied Walt with questions, knowing that Walt was in and out of consciousness.

Taking a break, the medic looked more carefully at Mack's wound and was not pleased by what he saw. "You got some serious issues with the left knee. Part of the kneecap is most likely cracked and the tendons that hold that together are partially blown away. Hate to say this, but you might never get the full use of that leg again."

"I thought the same thing." He knew he might be of no further use to the Blues in his current capacity, but he was an invaluable resource when it came to the integral information of supplies and distribution. And he still had the hard drive stowed away.

"You need to move on. Leave me here with Walt. Joe and Marcus can stay and guard. I will need them." Mack was thinking of a burial. At midnight, Mack sent orders with the next in command and they paddled away under gloomy skies, hoping to reach Kingston before dawn.

Sitting beside Walt's bed all night, Mack ruminated over the plan of what to do next. Occasionally Walt would stir, open his eyes, and give the sheepish grin when he saw Mack. Despite his pain, there was a joy in their proximity. Through tight lips he said, "I love you, Mack. See you in the next world. Make sure you get there." Then he slipped into a restless unconscious state. Mack started to prepare to give Walt some more morphine, but it was not necessary. He had already moved to his Father's house.

Mack's promise was kept. The following evening, the small expeditionary team floated their canoes back to the outskirts of Whitsville. Mack found the keys to Miss Lilly's mustang and coaxed it alive. There was no way he could walk any significant distance. The car was almost out of gas, but it still purred between the coughing. They put Walt in the front seat with Mack and drove with no headlights on up the hill to the old Gersham farm. Nothing was left but the garage, singed on the side from the house fire years before.

With their high-powered flashlights, Mack located his mother's simple grave, forgotten and overgrown for years. Mack was angry with himself for forgetting her. The small marble marker was there where Mack and Walt had placed it. Their dad had chastised them for spending so much money on something so useless. Mack pulled out grass and weeds from the surface and then let the other soldiers dig a deep hole next to his mother's grave. Slowly they lowered Walt into the hole holding the sides of the tarp.

Mack covered him over with another scrap of an old, shredded tarp they had once used for chores. Then he leaned down into the hole, whispering his final communication to his beloved brother. When he sat up, his eyes were glistening, but the other rebels ignored it. He stood up and took the shovel to cover Walt's body with the mix of sandstone chunks and poor soil. Working quickly, as though possessed, he whispered to his team, "Let's get out of here. Take the car back down to Miss Lilly's. I'll meet you there."

Despite his leg being almost useless, Mack hobbled off into the dark. He knew where he was going. Second Street. The lock was not fastened. "Figures," he said. "Some things never change." Once inside, he removed the two pictures from Walt's room, putting them in his canvas sack. Noticing a few items on the nightstand, he slid them in too. With the stealth of an old tom cat, he was out and back to the rendezvous site quicker than he thought possible. "Leave me at the old farmstead down by the creek and go report to headquarters," ordered Mack.

The two soldiers looked at him questioningly. He was in no shape to be on his own, but they did not question his orders. Mack had plans to make.

Chapter 28

Mercedes Singleton

October 2036

"The Spirit himself testifies with our spirit that we are God's children. Now, if we are children, then we are heirs – heirs of God and co-heirs with Christ, if indeed we share in his sufferings in order that we may also share in his glory." Romans 8:16-17

She did not know if she could go on. A deep exhaustion overtook Mercedes when Virgil was brusquely spirited from town for questioning. He was the only member of her family left to her, not knowing Titus' fate, and with his departure, the fight in her seemed to vanish. The evil of this world enveloped her like a relentless tidal wave.

Each day she willed herself to walk to the hospital. With Walt and Danny gone, both she and Ricardo were left with twice the work. Ricardo tried to help more in the food prep area, but he struggled with the cooking. Despite her weariness, Mercedes had to laugh at his attempts to be creative with what was available.

"Can you tell me what this is supposed to be?" queried Mercedes one day while looking at a brown pile of goop on the plates.

"I call it afternoon delight. It is made of whatever remained from breakfast and lunch. I thought it didn't look too bad when I added a few green beans on the plate for color," laughed Ricardo.

"What does it taste like?" questioned Mercedes.

"Leftovers. I would eat it if I were hungry. We had worse during the war out on patrol," shared Ricardo.

"Well, I'm no help either; maybe if you didn't mix it up so much. I will see if I can convince old Granny Smith to come in and help with meals. She always could make something out of nothing for those ten kids she raised. People would starve to death before they would eat my cooking. For now, we will just stick to peanut butter and jelly for supper," she said with the faintest of smiles.

When she returned home late every evening, a large glass of clear well water was on the table with a plate of food wrapped up in a dish towel or covered by another plate. She was thankful for Ricardo, but too tired to have an appetite. She nibbled at the simple meals and prepared for bed. Life was like walking through a bad dream that just kept repeating itself.

Yet Mercedes was not one to give up easily. She knew how difficult it was to fight through the fog of depression. She and her friends had begged on their knees for Olivia to survive after the heinous attack by the warden, and she was going to continue to press against the darkness for the return of her father. Somehow through all this, rather than being separated from God, she had grown closer to the presence of the Spirit, who seemed almost palpable.

Each evening she would kneel on her old, braided rug and cry out.

"Dear Jesus," she would sob, "I am so alone. I want my daddy back. Dear Jesus, keep him safe and away from the dangers of the world. Help me to know that you are always doing what is best for me. I know you love me and you love my father and brother. But I am lost and alone right now. I am sinking into the darkness and am so exhausted. I need your help. Oh God, please help me." Then she would sink onto the floor wailing aloud until words would form on her lips, unfamiliar to her. The Spirit would talk and intercede, impressing on her His Presence and a peace that often lulled her into sleep, as she lay slumped on the floor.

Sometimes her prayers converged on the topic of the enemy who came to steal and kill, deceive, and destroy. She would enter the fray with the power she declared in the Holy Name of Jesus Christ of Nazareth who came in the flesh. She had come to understand that the enemy was the one who was behind all the breakdown, carnage, and destruction of the world. It was either resist him and his conquests or allow herself to be caught and defeated by his schemes. While her father had never taught her much about this battle, it was so obvious now that she had to do something.

She drew on the enlightened discussions she had had with Olivia. She had taught Mercedes to allow Jesus to use her to display His authority in the world. Despite her reservations on entering the spiritual battle, she was now in such distress that she finally stepped forth into the power given her through Jesus. Each night she was stronger and bolder in taking the fight to the enemy. A new determination energized her. She wanted to believe it would come true.

Every evening Ricardo would see her oil lamp flicker and dim. He would grab Danny's Bible and tiptoe to the front steps near Mercedes bedroom window. Eavesdropping embarrassed him, but her prayers gave him hope and an awareness that the God she talked to could be real. He remembered Danny's nightly conversations with God. Could He be as powerful as she gave him credit? Anyway, he rationalized, he was protecting her now that all the menfolk were gone. He also knew how vulnerable she could be in such a situation.

Ricardo did not open Danny's Bible. He brought it as a testimony to the presence of Danny whom he knew would have lifted prayers for

Virgil, Walt, and Titus as well. He just listened and bowed his head in his hands.

"Jesus, if you're there, I'm broken too. I miss Danny, my friend and my brother, more than I ever thought I could miss someone. Help me," beseeched Ricardo.

He stood up and retreated to the cottage. Instead of putting Danny's Bible back on his former neatly made bed, Ricardo laid it by his own bed on the wobbly nightstand. He could not figure out why Danny loved that book so much or why he read it far into the night, all the while declaring much of it boring.

Maybe sometime, he thought to himself. *Mostly fiction, I think.* Then he would drift into sleep, hearing Danny softly read the passages that Ricardo now knew by heart.

Two weeks later, the government bus arrived carrying an old and disheveled passenger. Virgil Singleton sauntered off the bus and walked down the hill to Second Street. A neighbor saw him slowly climb the stairs and sit down wearily on the porch glider. She ran to the hospital to get Mercedes.

"Your dad came back today. I just saw him trudge up the sidewalk onto the porch. He's lookin' mighty tired."

Mercedes tore up the street towards home. Nothing mattered except that she had him home again. She was not orphaned. He was back and life would reset. Her prayers were answered.

Chapter 29

Ricardo Medina

October 2036

"And do not grieve the Holy Spirit, with whom you were sealed for the day of redemption." Ephesians 4:30

The joy in Mercedes' heart could not be measured. While she had feared that her father, Virgil, would be mistreated in the interrogation center, she was relieved that he had returned much as he had left.

"It could have been worse, Mercedes," explained her dad. "Most of the questioning they had me go through for those weeks was about the Blues rebel force and whether I knew anything about the organization. They figured I must know something of what was going on with the Blues in the area. You know, you would think I would know something, but I don't. Anyway, they kept thinking that Danny was a rebel and our connection to the Blues. They had me laughing at times about that. I told them about how he came to live with us and why he was up in the hills that day looking for mushrooms. I could not explain the shirt he had on, but I figured he had stumbled upon a stash belonging to the Blues. They asked me the same questions every day. I don't think they ever thought I knew anything."

"Did you mention anything about Walt? Did they ask you about him?" questioned Mercedes.

"Well," answered Virgil, "they did press me about him a few times, but the Spirit kept telling me to say I was not sure where he'd gone. I kinda told a small fib, saying he had been gone for some time. In some ways his mind was gone, so I felt there was an element of truth there. I bet you miss him. How have you been getting everything done with both him and Danny gone? You look mighty exhausted."

"Well, at least you're home again, Pops. Ricardo has been helping as best he can," replied a very tired Mercedes.

"Glad he proved trustworthy while I was gone. I was not so sure about that feller. There is something about him that still bothers me. I think his past is messing with his mind. Do you think we could bring him into the family like Walt and Danny?" asked Virgil.

"To tell you the truth, I'd prefer that he keep his distance. I think he is more comfortable in his own space, and I frankly don't want him to get the wrong idea. What happened to the Baney boys, by the way?" questioned Mercedes.

Virgil was not sure what happened to the two young men who were taken with him. They had been separated from the beginning. Since there was no communication about their whereabouts, the townspeople were beginning to worry about their well-being. The government Op forces had little pity on the people living in the Middle Region. Yet Virgil was able to offer hope. While incarcerated, he met a young man working in the cafeteria who was secretly a Christian. He had been able to slip Virgil a small, battered scripture one day when they worked together in food prep.

"I got something for you," he mumbled as he slid a large napkin toward Virgil. "Stick this down your shirt before anyone looks over here." Then he carved a fish shape in the mashed potatoes and made it disappear with a flourish of stirring. Virgil imagined that there were other people of faith on the inside when he would see glimmers of humanity and compassion. It was not often, though.

When Sunday morning rolled around, Mercedes grabbed her Bible and headed up the path to her worship spot on Baldface Mountain. She was alert enough to see that Ricardo had been watching for her and even though she was walking at a quick pace, he caught up and matched her stride. He did not say anything and neither did she. No longer was she uncomfortable in his company. Yet underneath, she could detect that something was amiss.

After the recent interplay between the Blues and the Special Ops, he could not deny that there might be a connection to the Singleton family. Walt was the one who had taken Danny to see something, and Danny had on a Blues combat shirt when they found him. Probably Walt had told Mercedes about what he had found on the abandoned farm, or perhaps Mercedes had shared information with Walt, who could easily be an informant. What did Mercedes have to do with this?

Pacing themselves up the steep incline, Ricardo started to nonchalantly ask questions.

"Mercedes, do you have any idea where Walt could be?" asked Ricardo.

She did not reply.

"I was thinking maybe he got hit in the explosion too, but they never found any part of him. That doesn't make sense. Maybe he was taken hostage by the Blues or worse yet, he's an informant for the Special Ops and left with them. His brother was in the military. I remember the picture on the wall of Mack's graduation from the Academy. Walt was awful proud of that picture."

Mercedes stopped in mid-step. She wondered when Ricardo had been in their house and entered Walt's bedroom.

"I'm really not at all concerned about any rebels or Ops forces. They have caused nothing but disruption and destruction in our lives. As you can see, they have done nothing to improve the conditions around here, despite all their promises. I detest them both," she said bitterly. "For now, I'm just trying to step back and care for the people left behind because I know God genuinely loves them. I mean, I know God loves me. He always has and he always will. He cares for all of us. I will share a story with you when we reach the top. Right now, I am too out of breath to talk anymore," panted Mercedes.

Ricardo was dismayed that his interviewing skills had gotten him no place. Somehow the conversation had veered off onto God again and he continued his walk up the steep slope while mulling questions over in his mind that would get them back on the right track. The scowl on his face was obvious as they sat on the craggy rock warmed by the morning sun.

"Have you ever been hurt?" asked Mercedes as she turned slightly toward Ricardo. "I mean deep down, at the place where you can't feel like anything will heal it?"

There was no reply and she stared straight ahead. Ricardo had no desire to go there. Then she turned to face him again. "You've been hurt since you were a child. You are angry and disillusioned with the world because of it," stated Mercedes.

Not only was Ricardo shocked, but he also had a momentary flash-back to a time when he was about seven and the general was telling his mother to "…send the bastard out to play." His mother had tried to soothe his feelings as he was pushed out the door, but he hated her for choosing the general over him.

It was at that moment of his life that he acknowledged the fact that he was not first in anyone's life. His own mother had betrayed him and given her deepest love to a cruel tyrant who was nothing but a self-serving, prideful, and despicable human being.

"Yeah, I hated my parents. Most people do. What of it?" he replied with surprised emotion.

"You have lost the identity you were supposed to have. We were all meant to be loved. You're not alone," Mercedes softly replied.

"Guess you're right," he said insidiously as he touched her hand.

She pulled her hand back uncomfortably, then managed a faint smile. Somehow, she knew that he knew where this conversation was going, and he was trying to change direction.

"I wanted to explain to you about what changed my identity, actually. Part of it I have found up here. Part of it I found in the deepest, darkest place I ever went. That would be Central Station Rehabilitation Center," said Mercedes.

As she told her story, Ricardo noticed that there was no bitterness, no malice, only a sense of resignation and could it be … a touch of hope? She shared how she had met the Spirit as she called for help when the warden held her down and raped her; how the presence of God was so strong as she prayed for and buried Olivia.

"It is a new journey for me. I have seen the ugliness of Satan manifested in mankind. But the Spirit has also taught me that there is good in people—God's goodness, not human goodness. I know that it is that type of goodness in people that finally conquers evil. I am sure of it. I am an example of a life that has been changed. Don't get me wrong. I'm not perfect but I am different," Mercedes confidently stated.

Ricardo could feel an anger rising in him. If he had been there, he would have killed the warden. He was a user just like General Lu. Both did not care who they hurt if they got what they wanted.

"That makes no sense," he said quietly but with an inward seething. "I think it's weak to forgive evil people. The warden was never sorry for his actions. He is an animal. He should be shot. I have done it before. It would be easy for me to do again," said Ricardo angrily.

Mercedes paused. "I can't change him. I can only change myself. It has taken months for me to get to where I am today and finally finding healing up here talking to God. He said, 'Forgive those who sin against you.' I did not want to do it," said Mercedes, "but out of desperation I did. I cried out over these hills, 'I forgive the warden.' I am surprised you didn't hear me down in Whitsville. I screamed it at the top of my lungs until I meant it. All the hurt came up to the top. I had to let it go. When I did, the healing rushed in. I was covered with a peace I cannot describe, and the hurt was gone, but not the memory. I won't let that hurt crawl back in even though it tries to occasionally," she replied with honest conviction.

She closed her eyes momentarily and then opened them while thumbing through her worn Bible.

"Do you mind if I read aloud some of the words that have brought me comfort?" She didn't wait for an answer as she began to speak the words boldly, "I lift up my eyes to the hills, from where does my help come? My help comes from the Lord who made the heaven and the earth."

Mercedes raised her head, gazing into the vast sky, as though she was looking at the Presence. She was at peace.

"As you can see," said Mercedes, "I am not going to get involved in a petty skirmish about man hating man, rebels hating Ops forces and Ops forces hating Blues. Is that why you are here, Ricardo?"

Momentarily Ricardo was caught off guard. It was enough that Mercedes noticed the hitch in attention. How had she managed to catch him? He blurted out, "What do you mean?"

She did not respond. His response was all she needed to know. She stood up and smiled at the hawks soaring in the warm updrafts of the morning breeze. "I have to get back to church," she said quickly. "I promised Dad that I would help with the clean-up after church since Walt is no longer around. You know it's strange…"

She paused. She was going to share about the things missing in Walt's room. But something kept her from going on. Something told her to not go there. The sentence just got dropped.

Chapter 30

Mercedes Singleton

Late Autumn 2036

"After they prayed, the place where they were meeting was shaken.
And they were all filled with the Holy Spirit and spoke
the words of God boldly." Acts 4:31

As fall deepened, Mercedes spent more of her time with her father. The simple things needed attention—mending his pants, gathering his requested source books for sermons, making sure he ate something while she was at the hospital. She had taken on most of Walt's duties, including the upkeep of the church and the janitorial services with help from Ricardo. He was slowly becoming the new handyman around the house.

"Mercedes, are you walking with me to church this morning?" asked her father.

"Of course, Pops. I would not miss your fine sermons now for the world. Sorry I took a short break earlier. I hear the Spirit talking to me when you're delivering the message," replied his daughter.

"What? I'm getting interrupted and critiqued?" he asked mischievously.

"Oh, Dad, He loves your messages."

"That makes me feel better. Your mom always liked them too. She was the best at giving me a deeper insight into the Word. I miss her more than you know," he said sadly.

"I know. Are you going to ask me to do the closing prayer again?" asked Mercedes.

"Always," Virgil replied.

It was a time when she could just forget about herself and others and simply talk to God. When she was finished, the little old ladies would get up and leave, giving her a squeeze of the hand or a hug. Sometimes they had tears in their eyes. *They are there with me,* she realized.

Hospital supplies were notoriously low. With the insurgents increasingly causing issues in the area, the Feds had finally withdrawn all supplies from communities that remained in the Middle States region. Their failure to sign the allegiance pact with the Federated States had ramifications. The latest government edict stated, "All covert operations must be reported to governmental authorities. Failing to do so can lead to immediate imprisonment." Even the secret sources for meds from her friends back at Baltimore National Hospital had slowed to a trickle. No one was willing to get caught and suffer the consequences.

She understood.

On a warm Friday evening, while washing the church windows up on the ladder, she heard a voice below say, "You shouldn't be up on that ladder by yourself. Why are you doing my job?"

Mercedes looked down, almost losing her balance in her shock. She had turned with a start to see Walt standing at the bottom holding the ladder in place. For a moment she could not move, thinking that she was imagining his reappearance. There he stood after months thinking that he was either dead or had been enticed to join the Blues. Somehow, he had just materialized like a genie out of a bottle.

She scrambled down the ladder and hugged him as hard as she could.

"Walt, where have you been? I cannot believe you are real! What happened to you?" she exclaimed joyfully. Then she grabbed his hand, and they ran as fast as his injured leg would allow.

"Virgil needs to see you. You are an answered prayer. Thank you, Jesus," she yelled repeatedly, gaining the attention of the neighbors as she passed. She was almost breathless and sobbing by the time they reached the house.

The word traveled fast, and although no one wanted to appear nosy, Walt and Mercedes looked like the Pied Piper the next morning as they headed to the hospital. The townspeople pelted them with questions, shook Walt's hand, and badgered him with more questions. Even the old ladies from church joined in the parade, rejoicing, and raising their hands in Hallelujahs. They almost seemed young and girlish.

What shocked Mercedes the most were the questions they asked about the Blues. "Did you meet anyone you knew, Walt?" "Do the Blues have a camp nearby?" "Are the Blues looking for new recruits?"

Walt deftly answered simply. "I don't know much," he said with his silly grin. The grin seemed to have diminished since he had been gone. He had explained the night before about the big scar on his face and his reason for his long absence, but something was gnawing at Mercedes. Things were not stacking up. She could not put her finger on it, but Walt had changed. He had changed a lot. Something was not right. Virgil, Ricardo, and more than one town citizen felt the same way. Yet there were few conversations on the subject. It was better to leave things as they were than stirring up unnecessary problems.

In his conversation the previous evening, he had told Virgil, "I got hit with some shrapnel from the drone missile. When I came to, I was in an old farmhouse down by the river. How I got there I don't know. An old farmer was there and nursed me back to health. He said that he found me in his barn the morning after I left here with Danny, and he had a feeling I might be a Blue, but no matter, he just decided I was worth saving. I am glad he did. I asked him if he knew anything about the Fed Special Op strike in Whitsville. He said he heard about it, heard that a kid had been killed. I cried for days because I was the one who led Danny to his death."

Walt's face became downcast, but there were no signs of tears or distress. "The old farmer, Jess Smyth, decided he was finished with trying to scratch out a living here in the Middle Region, so he left last week to stay with his sister in Atlanta. He told me I could have the farm if I wanted it, but I told him 'Thanks but no thanks. I am headed back to my family in Whitsville.'"

Mercedes had listened to the adventure and smiled softly. Virgil nodded in encouragement when Walt paused to get his thoughts together. But Mercedes could tell that there were holes in the story. Perhaps it was from the concussion Walt received or just Walt. She would wait. She assumed time would fill in the missing puzzle pieces. She would be patient. Her father was on to something with the look he often gave Walt. She would follow his lead and watch.

What was even more difficult to explain was the change in Walt's personality. The person he had been was a simple man and easy to read. Now he somehow seemed more complex, moody, and terribly forgetful. On Saturday morning, she got out everything to continue canning the late fall produce from Walt's garden.

"What are you doing?" asked Walt.

Mercedes put her hands on her hips. "Stop joking, Walt."

He looked at her and grinned that silly grin. "Am I forgetting something again?" asked Walt nonchalantly.

"Yes, we're canning this morning like we do every Saturday morning. You were always the one who did most of the work. You've got this down to a science," said Mercedes, trying to hide her exasperation.

Walt looked genuinely downcast. "I'm sorry," he whispered. "I can't remember. I'll help if you show me what to do."

It was a miserable morning.

"Are these the jars we're using, Mercedes?" Walt asked.

He held up two Ball jars of differing sizes.

"Just use the quart size, Walt," answered Mercedes.

Walt struggled to do anything right.

"I'm so sorry," he had to say twice as he broke two of the jars while shoving tomatoes forcefully into their narrow mouths.

"Why don't you go back to the tomato patch and get the last of the tomatoes that are still hanging on the vines?" she said in frustration, pointing to the oversized garden with withered plants.

Sitting down on an overturned crate by the fire, Mercedes wiped the sweat from her face. She spoke to herself. "I can't keep this up. I'm so tired." Then she dropped her head into her hands and cried, "Dear Jesus, help me. Now I've lost Walt." Immediately, she felt the presence of peace despite the turmoil in her soul. "I need help." She knew that the Spirit was listening. She raised her head to see Ricardo coming down the path.

"Need help?" he asked. She was relieved that someone with their wits about them could step in and help.

Mercedes grumbled, "I hardly know Walt. He has changed so much since his accident. I guess the shrapnel injury to his head has that effect. I want the old Walt back."

"Yeah, he's changed. His silliness used to bug the heck out of me. Now he is sullen and seems to have lost a portion of his memory," said Ricardo. "Was his brother serious?"

Mercedes stepped back. "Why would you ask about his brother?"

"Walt used to talk about him lots. Now he doesn't seem to want to share anything about him. He is really proud of his military background," stated Ricardo.

Walt looked up at them as they conversed. His face was hard to read. He seemed lost in thought and did not pay attention to what kind of tomatoes were being harvested.

Mercedes looked at his bucket as he moved next to her. "Some of these are way too ripe. They're practically rotten," said Mercedes, tossing some of the fruit into a trash bin. Walt slunk away sulking.

I've lost him too, she thought to herself. *Oh, how I wish it wasn't too late for the old Walt to come back.*

Chapter 31

Mercedes Singleton

November 2036

"Whoever believes in me, as Scripture has said, rivers of living water will flow from within them. By this he meant the Spirit, whom those who believed in him were later to receive." John 7:38-39a

Autumn stuck around that year, content as a cat napping by the fire. It was a welcome reprieve from the customary freezing temperatures that had set in over the past decade this time of year. The late summer had brought a type of quiet trance to the remote town of Whitsville after the maelstrom caused by the aerial attack of the Special Ops forces. Everyone felt that there was something just not right. Currently they were comfortable, but they waited, anticipating a jolt to their tranquility, which they were sure would return. In these times, there was no escaping it.

With the return of the two Baney boys, who had months ago been carted off for questioning, things began to feel steady again.

It was common knowledge that Jeff Baney, their older brother, had resigned from the government Special Forces of Africa but had disappeared before returning home. Most people supposed that he was part of the Blues Militia. But there was no proof. The Baney boys shared that the whereabouts of their brother was the most consistent question asked, although there had also been questions about Virgil, Danny, Mercedes, Mack, Walt, and Ricardo as well as other townspeople who had been former government officials.

Virgil slowly slipped into a state of decline that the elderly would call "going downhill." He slept for hours during the day and seemed to be losing interest in day-to-day activities as well as his church responsibilities. Often, he would spend his time reminiscing about days gone by, especially the early years of his marriage to Abigail, yet most evenings, the conversation turned to Mercedes' brother Titus and his whereabouts. This always moved Virgil to agitation and tears. These releases became common, and Mercedes bore up under the emotional barrage as best she could.

While her work at the hospital was time consuming, the number of patients had rapidly decreased with the corresponding deaths of several elderly patients. She had assisted her father with the funerals and was discovering to her surprise that she enjoyed ministering to the families who sought peace and assurance amidst their grief. She now felt that she had something of substance to offer instead of the repetitive and meaningless words used previously. The Holy Spirit prompted her each time to touch the hearts of the heartbroken and lonely with just the right words, for now she was willing to listen to His voice.

In addition, Virgil was struggling with his current leadership of the church. Time had taken its toll.

"Mercedes," he said one early mid-week morning while putting his arm over her shoulders. "I know you are not trained to preach, but I'm just tuckered out and need some help giving the message this Sunday morning. Can you step in and help?"

Without thinking, Mercedes said, "Sure, Pops."

On Saturday afternoon, Mercedes walked down to the church and moved quietly into her father's office. It had the same musty smell she always remembered from her childhood. A sound startled her, and she whirled around. There was Walt, dusting the pews and sweeping the floor.

"Just tidying up for tomorrow, Miss Mercedes. The other day I heard your father at the house asking you to give the message tomorrow and I want to make sure everything is exactly right. I hope you don't mind, but I invited friends from the school and my buddies at the hardware store. You might just have a crowd!" Walt exclaimed.

Mercedes tried not to show her displeasure with Walt. Ever since he had come back, it seemed that he was always interfering with things rather than helping. *Good grief,* she thought.

"Well, I was thinking that I only had to speak to the ladies and you and Ricardo. Now I am going to have to face a crowd who knows I know nothing about preaching. I better get to work."

Walt did not miss her subtle chastisement. He lowered his head.

"I'm sorry, Miss Mercedes. I thought you would like to share the Lord's Word with more people. I always thought that was what Christians were supposed to do—share the Good News, as Virgil always says," said Walt with sadness.

Now it was time for Mercedes to feel shame, and her face changed to a light pink. She turned and slid into the office closing the door. Then she plopped down in the ancient worn desk chair that should have been repaired decades ago.

Laying her head in her hands, she muttered, "God, help me think what I am to say. I want to honor you. I am sorry I must continue for my father, as I don't feel worthy. Give me patience and the love you have for your people that I may step in to properly bring the truth of your Word to your children as my father has for so many years."

She sat up and unfolded her tired hands, then got out a pad of yellowed paper and a pencil from her father's desk drawer. She remembered when she used to scribble on this same kind of paper years ago. She would come down to the church as a little girl and tell her father she was there to help him figure out the right words for his Sunday sermon. Then in her best kindergarten handwriting, she would put her pencil on the paper writing, "By Mercedes Grace Singleton. God Loves You. God Loves Me. God Loves All of Us." Then she asked Virgil, "How do you spell Amen?" When he told her, she asked, "Why isn't it A-women?"

Virgil had chuckled and pulled her up into his lap. "It's not about a man or a woman. It's like putting a big period at the end of a sentence that says, 'Yep, this is true!'"

Mercedes liked Amen even better from then on. Often when she saw it coming, she would raise her voice in a hearty AMEN. Virgil would fawn displeasure, but she knew he was only putting on an act for the church people.

She made highlighted notes on one side of the paper, pulled over her father's Bible and leafed through it until she found the verse she was looking for. Suddenly she thought of her brother again. Pulling the folded notes out of her pocket, she jotted down more thoughts, refolded the paper and headed out of the office, closing the door quietly behind her.

Walt was still dusting and sweeping.

"See you tonight, Miss Mercedes. I caught a few fresh bass this morning and I'll fry them for supper," he told her.

He put away his broom and duster and followed her up the hill to the Singleton house. Mercedes paused a bit to let him catch up when she realized he was coming. The injury to his twisted leg was causing him pain, but he did not complain.

"Should I take a look at that wound, Walt?" she inquired as he got closer.

"Naw, it's coming along. I have meds given to me by the old farmer. Left there by the fellas that dropped me off. Antibiotics for infection. I got too many to use. Could you use them at the hospital?"

Mercedes stopped in her tracks.

"You have antibiotics, Walt? Where could those people have gotten them? Of course I need them. They might be the difference between life and death!" Mercedes exclaimed.

Then she gave him a quick hug and kept walking. Walt stopped and let her go ahead, shaking his head.

Mercedes mulled over Walt's return after his amazing rescue and recovery at the hands of what was most likely the Blues militia. She half entertained the idea of trying to contact the Blues to obtain a permanent supply of antibiotics for the hospital. If they were flush with such contraband, it might be worth the risk in establishing a connection. Maybe. But it would have to be through Walt, and she wasn't willing to jeopardize his safety.

Sunday morning dawned brisk and clear. Mercedes got her father up and cooked him a hearty breakfast of eggs and sausage. Walt's homemade biscuits, prepared the night before, were decent.

Maybe he is getting back to his old self, thought Mercedes.

She put on an attractive long-sleeved mid-calf dress of pale pink, which was belted at the waist. The dress had been her mother's.

As she examined herself in the mirror, she exclaimed, "I look like a teenager from a generation ago." Somehow, the effect gave her a lift. Placing a white crocheted sweater made by her mother over her shoulders, she felt confident walking down the hill to the church with her father when she stepped inside.

As they walked in, they could see that Walt had already lit the small nubs of waxy candles on the altar. He had cracked windows for air.

The shutters were all open, at least the ones that worked, and the sunlight poured in through the side windows. The quiet was tantalizing. So was the peace.

Virgil sat in the front row reviewing the order of his typical service, and Mercedes glanced at her notes. Before she knew it, the three little ladies were tottering in and moving to the traditional pew where they had taken their seat for thirty, forty, or even fifty years. Ricardo strolled in looking unusually trim and clean-shaven. He gave her a thumbs up. To her surprise, a smattering of men from the gaggle that gathered at the hardware store came in hesitantly. They were followed by two of her nurse assistants and the primary teacher from the school complex. Of course, Walt assumed his usual seat near the back, and Mercedes gave him her best smile, acknowledging the extra guests.

Uncomfortably, she stepped up to the pulpit. Then realizing its constriction, she sidestepped to the right and spoke.

"My father, Reverend Singleton, has asked me to help him with the service today," she began meekly. "I appreciate the opportunity to spend some time in God's house with you. Let's begin with some hymns."

Then Mercedes trudged down to the old piano and tried as best she could to play the ancient hymn, "The Old Rugged Cross," as well as a more upbeat modern praise song from the early 2020s, "Hear Me Jesus," which few seemed to know. The songs continued with a winner, "Amazing Grace." *Funny*, thought Mercedes, *but even the non-churched visitors enjoy the lyrics.* And in her spirit, she was lifted up by the grace she knew enabled her to sing praises to a God and King she knew so well.

Instead of returning to the pulpit and her organized notes, she simply stood in front of the small crowd and began telling her story.

"It took me a long time to know true love." With that line, she already saw Ricardo and Walt sit straighter in their pews. "You all know that I grew up in this church. I've heard a thousand sermons by this wonderful man … most of them good." She glanced at her father who was already beginning to doze off in the sunny room. "But they really didn't stick. It was my fault. I was not ready for them to stick. You all know how tough it has been in the past fifteen years. The nation's turmoil from the volcanic eruption with its ensuing change in climate and population shifts; the Desert War bringing nothing but frustration and death and a truce that changed nothing. Even more pernicious, close to home, was the forced evacuation from our homes and the removal of services if we disobeyed. There has been a change in social norms, and we all know how the government now interferes with all parts of our lives. Our losses of freedom and services like electricity, education, and medicine have been devastating. I do not need to tell you these things. You have all felt the heartbreak of family and friends who have moved to the metropolitan centers. You dream of the loved ones who died from influenza or virus or on the battlefield. I miss my mom and my brother.

"Anyway, in all the craziness and brokenness, I got lost too. I filled the empty holes with my nursing profession and a live-in boyfriend who showed me the good life. While I seemed to have it all, my loneliness just increased, and life became more somber.

"Then I met Olivia. She was also a nurse at Baltimore National Hospital. We worked a lot of the same shifts and she seemed as dedicated as I was, but she was different. She was somehow happy. I was entranced with her view on life and wanted that happiness for myself. Often, we would have lunch in the hospital cafeteria. As I got to know her better, she became more trusting of me and eventually when I asked her how she was internally so good with the world, she told me she was a Christian. She had had a tough life. She escaped being sold into the Chinese sex trade market by a mother who sacrificed everything for her daughter. To save her and keep her anonymity, her mother gave her up to a Christian mission. Already Olivia had lost her father and oldest brother, or so she thought, to the Cambodian military's strong-arm tactics of intimidation and bribery. She came to America through a rescue adoption, became a born-again Christian, and when public worship was banned, she sought out the underground church. Eventually she took a chance on me and invited me to attend.

"'What's the big deal?' I thought. "Then I remembered my mom and dad and the faith foundation they had given me. My record was squeaky clean; even if I did get picked up, I could get out of it with a look at my history and connections. I had broken up with my boyfriend, my mom had died, and I was empty. I could not take it anymore. I wanted filled. Her church was so strange and different from this one. We prayed for a long time at the beginning of each gathering, bent over, faces touching the ground. People became immersed in the Holy Spirit and began speaking enriching words of prophecy about others and God. There were tears of repentance. I found myself on my knees crying out to God to forgive my rebellion and with that came the touch of the Spirit along with hope. What was best was that I could sense something else I had never experienced—a happiness in knowing a real live Jesus Christ. No, it was not happiness; it was joy. I began to know Him one on one. I loved it; it was like perfection, a place where the Holy Spirit started to show me who I am. He did not let me wallow in my false self any longer. He was honest with me. And He let me know whose I am as well. Not only did it make sense up here,"—she pointed to her head—"but more so here ..."—she touched her heart with both hands and paused.

"During this time, a strange incident occurred one evening. A dark stranger came up behind me after I got off the bus and shared with me that my participation in their worship activities was putting me in danger of arrest. I felt like it was an angel from the Bible, warning me before it was too late. But I was confident that nothing like that could happen to me. These people I worshiped with were far from being dangerous or harmful. They moved in love. But within days, Olivia and I, as well as some of the others at the gathering, were arrested, processed, and found guilty. We were sent to the Central Station Rehabilitation Center for years of hard labor and reeducation.

"It should have been hell on earth. It was in most ways. We were barely treated as humans. Our living conditions were pitiful. If it had not been for my godly sisters, especially Olivia, I think I would have killed the warden or myself. The warden was a monster. Out of the fresh group of recruits, he chose me to be his sex toy. I was repeatedly raped under the most cruel and vile of circumstances. In those moments, however, I also learned something. The Holy Spirit came and told me He was there with me. I knew it was true. He kept me focused on Him. There was such light in the darkness, that even the warden could not extinguish it. It was in me.

"I got pregnant, had a forced abortion by a so-called doctor and almost bled to death. But my sisters in Christ prayed me back to health. I cannot have children, but someday I hope to help give birth spiritually to many children as they come to know the Lord as I have come to know Him.

"While I was decommissioned, the warden took a fancy to a pretty, innocent teenage girl who was clearly frightened and lost in her new surroundings. When the warden made his first advance, Olivia stepped in and told him he would not take another victim from the women's camp. He beat Olivia to death in front of our eyes. While my sister screamed for mercy, he clobbered her with his fists and crushed her with his boots. I was, at that time, working in the kitchen. We carried our bloodied sister back to the dorm, but she never came out of her coma that night, succumbing to unrelenting cranial bleeding.

"I was angry with God. It was one thing for me to be a victim. I thought I deserved it for my lifestyle choices of the past. But Olivia was wholesome, good, and pure. Yet I knew, we all knew, that Olivia was in the heaven we all hoped to attain eventually. She was the one who had told me, 'I am with you.' She, the one, so filled with love and joy; the only person I have ever known who truly lived a life in Christ to the fullest, was gone.

"Anyway, that's what I wanted to share with you today. No religion or tradition or denomination or any of that stuff. Rather, I wanted to share with you the fact that there is a living presence of God who long ago redeemed us. That Presence is Jesus. And there is the living presence of God who hovers over us now, teaching and aiding us in our trials. He is the Holy Spirit. I call Him H.S. To find Him, you must invite Him in. But you must want Him. While the world around us is dark and destroying itself, inside I have found a Spirit who gives me peace with His presence. He speaks to me by name, giving me knowledge, truth, and comfort. He has come to let you know that God is in the business of claiming us for Himself. He is looking for an invitation from you."

Mercedes stopped and looked around. The room swirled a bit as she felt dizzy, but it was so quiet, you could hear only the squeak of the ancient wooden pews. All eyes were still on her. She moved to the prayer rail and kneeled. Around her there was a rustling, but she was lost in her tears and could not look up. She tried to choke back her sobs but was not remarkably successful. Finally, she looked up to see that the three old ladies were to her left at the rail, silently praying, but lips aquiver. Her father was to her right with his arm around Walt for support. She stood up. The men in their pews had remained in silence, with heads bowed. One was leafing through the tattered Bible in front of him. Ricardo was just gazing ahead, seemingly unscathed. He had heard the story. Yet something seemed new about this rendition. And there was something tangible in the room he could not put his finger on. It was a fog, a mist. He felt a Presence weighing on his heart. It troubled him, and he got up and quickly left the fellowship to clear his mind.

Mercedes wiped her eyes and spoke a quiet prayer. "Holy Spirit, bless each of these friends of yours. Gift them with the knowledge of your remarkable presence in their lives so that they will know that You, our God, truly reigns. Let them know how available you are. Thank you for walking into our lives today." She paused and added, "Amen and Amen."

Chapter 32

Walt Gersham

February 2037
The Day of the Lord

"And afterward, I will pour out my Spirit on all people. Your sons and daughters will prophesy, your old men will dream dreams, your young men will see visions. Even on my servants, both men and women, I will pour out my Spirit in those days." Joel 2:28-29

Later that evening as Walt was finishing the dishes created by a simple dinner of biscuits and ham with gravy and stewed tomatoes, he asked Mercedes if he could talk to her about things that were moving around in his head.

"Sure," she said, smiling at him as one would at a small child who asks a childish but thought-provoking question. "Now is a good time to talk."

Walt stood in the living room by an ancient chair and Mercedes motioned him to sit on the shabby sofa. He rubbed his leg a bit and stumbled into the beginning of his query.

"I was wondering if what I felt this morning in the church service was the touch of God," he asked quietly. "I felt like He was right there. It was like He had surrounded me, and He made me feel like I was so special to Him. It was like I was in His focus."

"Well, Walt, that is the amazing thing about God. The Holy Spirit is God, the God who is here with us right now. I never knew how close He was either, until I started to feel the same thing you did today while at the secret house church in Baltimore. Once Olivia's brother came up to me while we were praying in the Spirit, and he said he had a message from God for me.

"'God wants you to know that He is pleased with what you will be doing for Him. He has ordained your path. He is with you and will guide you through the darkest nights,' relayed Arun.

"I looked at him and wondered if he thought he was giving me good news. It certainly sounded pleasing at the beginning, but then quite ominous. Of course, this came to me the week before we were arrested. I began to understand that God was telling me about these things in advance so that I would know He would never leave me."

Mercedes gazed at Walt. She did not want to make this about herself. She leaned over and took his hand in hers.

"May I pray that God, the Spirit, will speak to you again and clear up some of your questions? The Spirit really is forever present. Most of the reason we don't hear Him is that we put up barriers of communication with Him."

As she looked into Walt's eyes, the comical aura that always seemed to pervade his visage seemed to vanish. Seriousness seemed to have replaced it.

"Sure thing, Miss Mercedes." With the reply, the old Walt seemed to reappear.

"God is really working inside of you this very minute, Walt. Open the door for Him. He won't disappoint," encouraged Mercedes.

And then they prayed.

Walt rose after the prayer without looking at Mercedes and mumbled that he was tired and needed to hit the sack back in Titus' former bedroom. He closed the door softly and knelt beside the bed. Trouble and indecision raged inside of him.

"God, I am in trouble—in my spirit, in my actions. Help me to do what you want. I know it is the only way forward. Nothing can succeed without your help. I need you now," prayed Walt.

He laid his head on the soft bed and waited. Perhaps he had fallen asleep, he was not sure, but he was startled to hear a voice … someone talking … not outside or in the room, but in his inner mind. It was a conversation including him. What followed was not overly spectacular or even specific in details, but Walt knew that the Spirit was giving him a framework for a new direction. He realized that he was now part of a plan that before this revelation was completely beyond his capacity to even imagine. He was getting a realignment of allegiances, new marching orders that did not deviate completely from what he had done in the past. He was told that his new commander had changed, and His name was the triune God.

When Walt looked at the clock, it said 1:45 a.m. Quietly pulling on his warm coat and heavy boots, Walt tiptoed out into the darkened living room. He knew contact must be made tonight. Time was of the essence. Up on the hill near the site of Danny's death, there was a government-issue emergency cell phone transponder. He figured he could get off a couple of sixty-second calls without being picked up by the roving Special Ops scanners. There were people that needed to be informed of his next step.

***

Mercedes woke with a start. She sensed that something was amiss. There was a presence in the house that she could not explain. Perhaps her father was up and confused about what time it was. Throwing her chenille bathrobe over her gown and reflexively sliding into her worn slippers, she headed out her bedroom door just in time to hear the latch on the front door softly click. Peering out of the front window, it was easy to distinguish Walt's profile in the moonlight.

Most likely he is struggling with his new awareness of the God with us, she mused. But she also noticed as he moved away quickly towards the shaded path behind the house that his posture was straighter and that he walked with less of a limp or could it be no limp. *Was he healed today as well?* she wondered in amazement. "Thank you, Jesus, for the work you are doing in Walt, for showing up with your Spirit this morning. You have brought comfort and presence into our bleak world. What a relief it is to know you are here and that you care. Thank you for providing your Spirit to inform others that you are real. They can now share you as I do."

She could not fall back to sleep. Thoughts were rushing through her mind, questions, and events. She heard the screen door of Ricardo's cottage faintly close with the wooden thud muffled by a hand that grabbed it at the last minute. As she peered into the dark, she could detect him, bundled up in very dark clothes as he headed along the same path Walt had just traveled. They were going up into the woods and the dark night mystery of the mountains. Mercedes' mind raced.

Would Ricardo be following Walt? Why? What was going on to which she was oblivious? Were they up to something together? Was she being played for a fool?

Thoughts raced through her mind as she tried to put together the long series of events that had occurred since her return to Whitsville. Ricardo's strange appearance and his unusually extended stay for a drifter. Her work in the hospital with Danny and his untimely death on the hunting trip with Walt at the hands of the Special Ops forces. The attack that led to the town's interrogation and her father's arrest. The coming of the Spirit to the church the day before, and the change wrought on Walt. The world seemed to be turned upside down, yet she knew there was a still peace that centered in her soul despite the uproar.

She plopped down on her father's favorite chair and fell into a troubled sleep. Olivia came to her in her dream, holding out her hand to Mercedes. She told of the wonderful place where she was now residing, a heavenly house with Jesus. Mercedes could hear her sweet voice. "You need to be brave and continue the work God has sent you to do. Be strong. You are strong. Do not doubt yourself. Just listen to the Spirit," Olivia's sweet voice intoned.

Immediately she felt the Spirit come in and lift her to her safe place up on the mountain, Old Baldface. It was cool, but very sunny. He sat next to her, but she was afraid to look at more than the hand that held hers, the hand she had felt the year before at the Rehabilitation Center. She could not resist looking up into His face. When she did, she saw His glory. She could not stop staring at the beauty.

"Yes, you are called to do my work," He simply stated. "Do not fear. I will see you through to the end. You will know whom to trust and who will speak in deceit. Are you willing to walk with me?"

Mercedes felt the answer rise in her throat. She was convicted. "Yes, oh yes!"

They stood up in the gentle breeze and He led her to the edge of the mountain. She could not feel her legs or her feet, but somehow, she moved under the power of His presence. She trusted Him.

"Always watch for me. I will never leave you or forsake you," He reminded her.

And then she was standing on the edge of the precipice alone, with the wind swirling her hair into her warm face. Her feet and legs were reclaimed, as she became aware of her surroundings, rather than Him.

"Oh glory," she breathed. And behind the veil she could hear an echo, "Glory and Amen." It startled her, waking her up.

The living room had turned quite chilly, so she rose to pile more logs into the wood burner. The crackle and pop of the burning gave her a sense of comfort as she again curled up in the chair, recalling the vision in her mind.

When she heard the door softly squeak open, she was not surprised to see Walt, but her presence startled him.

"I couldn't sleep. There was so much running around in my head," he recounted.

"Please sit down, Walt," she said breathlessly. "I want to tell you what just happened to me. God the Spirit just showed up. I need to tell someone. I need to know what He meant. I want to remember it all and I think that if I share it now, I can do a better job of remembering. Do you mind spending a few minutes with me, the crazy Spirit lady?"

Mercedes was embarrassed that she had put Walt on the spot, but he seemed to be relieved to just be a bystander as she shared her latest encounter. She was thankful that she did not have to do any explaining as Walt was always so accepting of whatever she told him. He was a comforting presence because he did not have any ulterior motives.

"Sure thing, Miss Mercedes." He sat down on the couch again and Mercedes launched into the account of her vision/dream as the moon cast more light into the room.

When she was finished, she said to Walt, "What in the world does He want me to do? It sounds important, earth shattering, something that is necessary for His Kingdom! And what about the part of whom to trust and who is deceiving. Can I know that? I'm human and I surely haven't been particularly good about that my whole life up to this point!"

Unexpectedly, Walt leaned over and picked up her hand. He held it between his two worn hands. It was surprisingly warm after his jaunt outside. He looked at her intently. It startled Mercedes and she wanted to pull back, but she did not. His goofy look was gone.

"Mercedes," he said. "I heard God today. He told me to get back to His work, only this time it was to be under His supervision, not my own perverted idea of what is right and wrong. I wasn't sure what He meant, but I prayed tonight for clarification, and He came to me and explained the basics of what I needed to do next. And"—he paused, wondering whether to go on—"and, He told me to trust you and tell you the truth. He would watch out for you Himself."

Walt looked intently at Mercedes for a reaction. She seemed a bit uncomfortable, not so much with his message but with something that seemed different in him. Walt was different. Quite different. *Well, of course,* she thought. *He met God today.* But that did not solve her unsettledness. She looked intently into his face. The moonlight highlighted his hair and eyebrows and hazel eyes. She sucked in her breath. That was it. She saw it now. The dark dot in his right eye. She knew.

"Mack," she whispered. "You're Mack, not Walt." And she pulled her hand out of his.

Her mind swirled. *What is happening? What happened?* The realization of this fact left her speechless. How could she have been so ignorant? There were so many signs. She should have been more observant. Maybe God had protected his identity. Did anyone else catch on?

"Why are you pretending to be Walt? Where is he?"

Mack gazed down at the floor. "Walt's dead. I buried him next to Mom this past summer after he died. We tried to keep him alive after the attack by the Special Ops drone strike, but he was seriously injured, and we could not risk sending him to a hospital and endangering others. In some ways, acting like him made me appreciate him for the special person he really was. I loved him. I just could not save him. Most folks around here figured out who I was, but they kept tight-lipped knowing that I could put the town in danger. They know I'm working with the Blues."

"But why come back pretending to be him?" quizzed Mercedes, now full of questions and still shocked with the revelation.

"Listen, Mercedes, I am deep into a movement that is trying to survive by a thread. God has told me to trust you, but I am hesitant to share specific details with you because anything you know can be used against you and put you in grave danger. The enemy we are fighting has no sympathy for traitors," Mack explained.

Mercedes could hear the voice of the Spirit speaking in her head. *He is one to be trusted. Believe him.*

She said, "Walt, I mean Mack, the Spirit has told me to trust you. He must believe that I am to be a part of whatever you are involved in. Somehow you must be doing God's work. What in the world is going on that is so life and death?"

Then Mack began an abridged version of his service time, his work for General Hamilton, the treasonous espionage of General Lu, the mission of the Blues.

Mercedes wondered to herself if God was really working to preserve His saints through all this bloody business. It seemed that both sides were striving for the annihilation of the other with no mercy. How could God use this battle to complete His plan? It was beyond her comprehension.

Mack moved on.

"I know what I need to do, and time is of the essence. There are people I need to personally contact to help protect what remains of the church and our counter-government forces. I need to reconnect with three people and work those angles doing what I can to help. I believe God will help us find a way to be successful and, in the end, honor Him. Never had I even considered that He might have any desire to be involved in current events. But tonight, I found out differently. It has taken some adjusting to get past my idea of what is good for mankind and our country.

"First of all, I need to reestablish my Pentagon contact and move to Plan B. Then I need to coordinate the Blues and the CLF, the Christian Liberation Front. That will involve you trying to contact Olivia's brother. And finally, I need to contact the president and give her what I have. It is a long shot, but tonight God told me to trust her. General Hamilton gave her my name as a trusted source for Blue's information. God's been working on her too, and she is just as much at risk as we are," shared Mack.

Mercedes sank back into the chair. She closed her eyes. It was almost too much to take in. Her quiet, simple, broken world now was to become an underground chaotic world of cloaked secrecy and uncertainty. She was startled to feel the warm lips of Mack pressed against hers. She opened her eyes in surprise but did not move.

He stood up. "Keep safe until I come back. I have made contacts with the Blues tonight to keep a close eye on Whitsville and you in particular. I will let you know somehow what is happening. My contact will know I'm returning to D.C."

He moved stealthily, even with his slight limp, into his bedroom, returning wearing a hoodie, cap, glasses, moustache and carrying a small duffle bag. She had seen that disguise before. It took her breath away.

"On my, you were the stranger who warned me about getting involved with the underground church. I could not place your voice, but I knew it sounded familiar. Thank you for trying," said Mercedes sincerely.

Mack turned at the door and smiled. "You will be getting some intelligence from me in the next few weeks. Can you find a way in that time to free yourself up from the hospital to seek out Olivia's brother? And someone needs to watch Virgil while you're gone."

"I know where to contact her brother if the mailbox is still operative. Olivia gave me the information. Finding help for Dad is going to be difficult, but I have an idea or two. I am sure the widows in the church will help. One really seems to connect with Dad. Ricardo can take care of things for us as well."

Mack looked at Mercedes intently. "He's a spy. He works for the Feds in a government capacity tied to General Lu. I caught his transmissions when I turned on my transponder a couple of times. He does not know I have been a step ahead of him as a cyber spy for years now and know how to intercept his transmissions. He has been relaying messages lately in the middle of the night. Two weeks ago, he passed on information that I might be Mack and not Walt. He thought this might be the case from your observations of how Walt had changed so much. The bedroom photo sent him on the search for answers."

Mack continued to share more details with Mercedes. She was shocked with the revelation and her complete lack of awareness of the espionage swirling around her. "He's been snooping around big time. According to one call, he found Walt's grave and dug him up. He even sent a sample of his DNA to Washington. Last night they relayed information concerning the sample: 'It belongs to Mack Gersham. He is dead. Take him off the suspect list.'

"Walt saved my life again. I will share the story of how this happened later, but for now, you must be careful with Ricardo. I questioned who he was from the start."

Mercedes was speechless. She had been living with two spies and was oblivious to reality.

"Oh Mack, he followed you up into the woods tonight about an hour ago," said Mercedes with concern.

"Yeah, I caught wind of the fact that he was following me. I used the 'Catch Me If You Can' tactics Walt and I used to excel in to shake him off. I bet he knows something is up. Tell him tomorrow I am on an overnight hunting trip back to the Snyder farm. Keep your eye on what he is doing without being obvious. He's got connections to the top and that's dangerous," warned Mack.

Mack stepped toward the door. He turned for a moment to take in the scene as though his brain wanted to sear this memory forever. "Keep yourself safe. You mean the world to me." He stared at her, giving her a momentary smile, then turned and closed the door. His figure blended into the faint mist of the night slivered with slices of moonlight.

She could not sleep anymore, so busied herself getting ready to go to the hospital, knowing that once again she was on her own in the morning breakfast preparations. It would be biscuits and gravy again.

But breakfast did not go smoothly at all. With "Walt" not there to help, she struggled to juggle all the demands at the same time. And where was Ricardo? He never missed work and he had always shown up to help with the dishes and kitchen duties after he checked on the furnace and electricity. Had he noticed that "Walt" was missing at breakfast? *Be calm,* Mercedes told herself. *Panicking will only endanger Mack.*

At noon she hurried home for a short break and knocked on the cottage door. With no answer, she stepped in. The cottage was neat and empty. A note was on the table.

To Virgil and Mercedes,
It's time to move on. My work is finished here.
Thank you, Ricardo.

Mercedes sat down on the step of the cottage.

"Walt, I mean Mack is gone and now Ricardo is most likely tailing him. Mack is in trouble. I shouldn't have accused Walt of being connected to the Blues. I got this whole thing started with my reckless thoughts!"

"Dear Jesus," she whispered. "Cover him with your protection. Oh dear Jesus, we need wisdom. We trust in you for all things. Help us. Amen." Then she yelled at the top of her lungs, "Amen" and crumpled down onto the cold flagstones. There was a surety in her heart that God would prevail.

A whisper of chilling wind blew across her shoulders and caused her to shiver. All she could think of was the breath of the enemy seeking to destroy.

Her mind shot back. "Our Lord will prevail. To Him comes all glory, honor, and praise. O Lord, show us your mercy."

The Spirit responded, "I am. Stay close and follow me."

CPSIA information can be obtained
at www.ICGtesting.com
Printed in the USA
LVHW051446110722
723006LV00006B/11